It

Finally

Happened

It Finally Happened

Craig Glatky

ARPress
45 Dan Road Suite 5
Canton MA 02021

Hotline: 1(888) 821-0229
Fax: 1(508) 545-7580

Ordering Information:

Quantity sales. Special discounts are available on quantity purchases by corporations, associations, and others. For details, contact the publisher at the address above.

Printed in the United States of America.

ISBN-13:   Paperback   979-8-89356-463-1
                eBook   979-8-89356-462-4

Library of Congress Control Number: 2024904722

TABLE OF CONTENTS

I would like to recognize J.K Rowling in making Harry Potter books and movies and I would like to recognize, George Lucas, and the Doctor Who show that I love and other shows I mention in my book, I also would like to make a special thank you to a hall a famer Walter Ray Williams JR for putting him in my book and other famous people that I don't mention sorry.

I would like to mention on this new revised addition of my book. In the memory of my Grandmother Rose Lerman, Grandfather Israel "Izzy" and my four great uncles Philp "Peter", Paul, Harry, Victor Lerman and my aunt Fay Lerma. I would also like to mention in the memory of my dad Arthur Glatky and my great uncle Morris Stone.

And I would like to give a special thanks to the person or persons at Bethesda for making the "Elder Scrolls IV and Skyrim. The Elder Scrolls V."

The most important thing that I must do is. I dedicates this book to a girl who I hurt so badly the girl who means so much to me as a friend that I really did not have. Not going to mention her name so I don't put a strain on her marriage. A. M. I'm so, so, so, so sorry.

The Beginning and End
IT FINALLY HAPPENED
Science Fiction, Non-Fiction,
Fantasy, Romance and Humor

Chapter 1

Beautiful Angel, Love of his Heart

In three thousand nine hundred and ten when it all began, the past came to the future, the future to the past. Until the man named Craig Galuta, Doctor Craig Galuta, found the cause and destroyed it, but it was not all. In the room where they have the brain scanner, lying on the bed is Doctor Galuta, where wires are attached all over his head.

The nurse, Sakra, was wearing a white mini skirt nurse's uniform and the very sexy white un collant en laine and spoke with a French accent, "Doctor Framharr, how far back are we going to go? "

"Well, let's go back to first grade. I think that should be a good start," replied Doctor Framharr, a man in his mid-fifties with black hair and six feet tall.

Sakra said, "Ok, turning the brain scanner to the first grade."

The loud humming sound started to form a picture on the screen. Craig's face appeared on the akrascreen, screaming in pain and it stopped, and a picture appeared.

"Doctor, that's not the first grade," yelled Sakra.

"I know, Sakra. It's kindergarten. That is weird, let's proceed. We will watch all of the past of Craig's mind on this monitor." the doctor instructed.

"Ok, Craig, now what is your mother's name?"

"Hanna."

"Please spell it."

"H-A -N-N-A."

"That is good. Now I want you to say your alphabet."

'Mrs Rayson is the kidergarn teacher.'

"Ok Ms. Rayson. A-B-C-D-E-F-G-H-I-J-K-L-M-N-O-…Q –R-S-T-U-V-W-X-Y-Z. "

"Craig, please think, did you forget a letter?" said Ms. Rayson.

"No," said Craig." "Ms. Rayson, the P it's running down my leg."

Ms. Rayson runs to her bathroom. All the kids could hear her laughing so hard then the kids heard a funny sound that they hear in their houses. She flushed the toilet. Ms. Rayson entered the room.

"Craig. Go and get out your crayons now and color."

"Yes, Ms. Rayson."

'The nurse Sakra being a very young nurse not having the experience and being very excited.'

"Doctor. Why is this important?"

"I don't know. He failed kindergarten on purpose. This was his second time."

First grade appeared. "Doctor. Look at his brain waves coming from his brain."

Doctor Framharr looked quite astounded by Craig's brain waves; they were very strong and so remarkable.

"I don't think he is human," said Sakra.

"He is human. Let's see what happens, shall we?" Doctor Framharr said.

"Good morning class, my name is Ms. Uniason, your first-grade teacher. And here are your first books. Take good care of them." The screen shows that Ms. Uniason is about five feet and eight inches tall with short brown hair. She was a pretty hot teacher, even for a six-year-old boy to see. The teacher tells the class about vowels and the students start to write them in the book.

Sitting just in front of Craig, with long brown hair, was the most beautiful princess named Alice Matterson. She was an angel sitting up so straight. Craig's heartbeat very fast. He goes into a trance. He is hypnotized by this beautiful woman's face. His hands turn clammy, very sweaty, and he felt something he had never felt before. Craig sneaked up behind her and gave her a kiss. The kiss had special powers. Invisible to the naked eye, a stream of bright, bright atoms was transferring from Craig's head to Alice's and vice versa. Craig had transferred some important information to her, and he does not even know it.

"Doctor! Doctor! Look at his brain waves. The signals are off the charts. Look at her brain. She is getting something out of it too! But I can't read the brain waves."

"Yes, I know Sakra. Now look at his brain signals now. They are changing. It does not make any sense. He is starting to forget her, but why? The memory in his brain is becoming fuzzy, the information is being push back, way back into the brain somehow. The brain, it settles down now and we can finally read out the signals, It says here, To Craig, people he does not see for a long time would not be recognizable, people who he sees not in 10, to 20 ,35, to 40 plus years, they will all look different to him, mostly all of them. "

"So, he doesn't see a classmate for 30 years or more, and they could look different? Even family members too?" said Sakra.

With a sad voice the doctor says. "And yes. The girl he kisses, only the first name will remain in his head, and he will forget what she looks like and her last name. The last part of the name will be fuzzy until someone reminds him of the last name. It will haunt him for the rest of his life. He will remember her, though, in the back of his mind. His heart belongs to her. The first name, however, will never be forgotten, and the smile that he sees in his head." laughs the doctor not understanding what is about to come.

Ms. Uniason looked up from her desk. She yells out as all the classmates saw Craig.

"Mr. Galuta, what you are doing!"

Craig could not say anything.

"I saw you kissing this young girl," she said.

All the classmates were in an uproar and laughed. Alice just smiled.

"Mr. Galuta. I want you to stand on the black square outside of my room."

As Craig opened the door, he stands on the black square. A song popped into his head. An old song. By a man name Glen Miller. He heard this song on an old station that's played very old music. Craig loves it. "Chattanooga Choo, Choo."

As Craig was dancing on the black square, he did not see Ms. Uniason popping out her head.

She yells out to Craig, "Stop dancing on that black square."

Craig looked up and smiled. As she goes back into the classroom, Craig started dancing again. It was noon, when they had lunch, that Craig came back into the classroom. And he opened his book to finish the vowels.

The machine jumped to his birthday when he was seven years old. Craig has a bowling party, there was this girl again. She came in late with her mother. Craig's mother called him over.

"Craig, you got another guest."

The girl had a tear coming from her eye. The girl's mother says, "we can't stay we have to leave."

Craig became deaf for that moment; he did not hear the girl's mother saying, "this gift that Alice gives you, it's her first modeling shot."

Craig says, "Thank you."

Craig tears open the wrapping paper and she had put the word 'me' over the girl's head so "Craig would know who she was." Somehow, she knew that Craig was going to forget her.

The girl turned away. Inside Craig's heart he felt pain. It felt like someone had punched him right in the heart. He wanted to cry, but his classmates were having fun bowling. Craig felt sick. His stomach ached and he did not know why.

The brain waves become great as she leaves. The brain waves reveal that she was going to be a famous model in the future, but not yet to be seen here. As the birthday party had ended, she disappeared. Not returning to class. Disappears from the eyes of Craig. Craig does not see the face, as the girl's face begins to disappear, deeper and deeper into his head. Craig moves on with his life. On the second week of May, on a Saturday, Craig is on stage tap dancing. Making all kinds of funny faces, having a great time. The people in the audience are laughing and give him a standing ovation.

"Hey, Doctor. I didn't know Craig was a tap dancer. I know we just saw that on the black square, but I thought he was just fooling around."

"Craig is a funny one," said the Doctor.

"We saw him in kindergarten, maybe he is a comedian, dancer, and a scientist. A jack of all trades?" Sakra observed.

"Craig has so many talents, that is why he is so strong. He will wander off the path, but he will always find the right path. He might seem like he got pushed so hard off that path, and he will feel sick, but I think this girl means so much to him, as she is a part of his heart," the doctor said.

CHAPTER 2

Summertime, the Journey Starts

June, Monday of the first week Craig's father calls him to get ready.

"We are taking your sister to the hospital right now."

"I'm ready," Craig yells.

Sara, his sister, was getting major heart surgery and she was going to be in the hospital for a few months. Craig's father looked at him seriously.

"When your sister comes out, be good to her. She is going to be in a lot of pain."

"Yes dad," Craig says, adding to himself, "a pain in the neck." But deep inside, Craig knows not to tease his little sister, so he stayed away from her when she got back from the hospital.

The second week in June, Craig went to Summer School. Somewhere in his head, something was missing, he couldn't figure out what.

Chapter 3

Brain Develops

The computer that is reading Craig's mind is speaking of what is Craig is thinking. Time flew. In July, after the third week of summer school, it was finished.

Craig ran home from the bus stop, and he saw that he was getting a swimming pool. It was all ready. Craig's oldest sister was in the water with the neighbor, Jack Mustang. Jack was Portuguese. Craig ran to his room to put on his swim trunks and into the water he goes. Craig kept saying a word over and over, it sounded like "ditty da, da didda da da."

Jack says to Lee, Craig's sister "What is he saying?"

Lee says, "Some song that Craig heard in his dance class."

"But Jack was smarter than that; it was too close to the Spanish word for welcome, 'de nada'. Jack knows that he never spoke Portuguese in front of Lee, and he never yelled out this word to his wife while Lee and Craig were around. They taught Spanish in high school; but they don't have any Spanish kids in Craig's class. They are all in other schools."

Jack says, "Very interesting."

So, Jack does an experiment, but fails. Craig did not know how to swim. Jack pulled Craig under the water and he was taking in water in his mouth and choking. Craig got scared, but Jack was not truly harming him. Craig gets fear and his brain. He loses 85 percent of his brain cells. That night, after having a good steak dinner, Craig took his bath and went to bed.

Eyes closed, he pictured total darkness. He saw all kinds of colors, colors that he had never seen before, and the brain started to heal itself. Stronger and more powerful than before.

The computer stops talking.

"Doctor. Do you think Jack knows about Craig?"

"No Sakra, Jack is an automobile mechanic for Great Machines of America and a weightlifter, too. Yet, he is a very smart man. How did Craig know Spanish that young? I wonder if it was the kiss."

CHAPTER 4

The first stage of Bullies

In the second grade, Craig started learning math. He whizzed through the two's and three's addition. Craig always loved math, but something was holding him back. Craig was lucky this year. No summer school.

During the summer of the second grade, a few of so-called friends came over to the house. The two older sisters hung out with Craig's sisters, and their two brothers and their neighbor took Craig to a wooded area to pick wild raspberries. Across from their houses was a small, run-down office building, and to the right was a path. All along the side of the building was a wooded area where wild raspberries grew. Big ones, like you buy in the store. At this time, Craig was still learning. He put a lot of trust in older people. If they said the ice cream man was giving away free ice cream, he would believe it.

As Craig was deep in concentration, picking raspberries, the boys took off to their houses across the street. They were yelling for Craig. Craig stopped picking and looked about. Craig started to cross the highway, and they said stop. There were no cars coming, but Craig stopped.

Craig did not know to look both ways. As a police car approached faster than usual, they told Craig to run across. As the police car hits Craig, he goes straight up fifty feet in the air. Craig landed right on the hood of the police cruiser and dented the hood and his feet smash the lights on top. He got the wind knocked out of him. Craig could hear laughter in the background and then it stopped.

The police officer got a story from the so-call friend; he said he was chasing a ball. Where was that ball? The police thought Craig was hungry and he might have eaten the ball. The police never asked where the ball was.

Being under, Craig seems to be wide awake, looking into his past. As if he was dying.

Craig goes back looking at all the things that have happen to him in the past.

"I will keep on going until I return to the present. I will see who I really am."

As Craig said this, the voice changes through the machine. The voice now seemed a little scarier than before. The black screen was turning red.

Craig was sedated, but fully awake, and could hear the two people in the room talking. The nurse speaks to the Doctor.

"Hey Doctor. Something does not feel right. Do you think he really is from a different place?"

"The words are not heard. The computer using a different frequency, He just might be."

The Doctor knows all too well where Craig came from.

"He is a human, Sakra"

The computer speaks one more time.

With a different kind of tone, and only Craig hearing that change, the screen turned to a deeper red color. As Craig is getting upset for some reason. But what?

A millisecond later and the screen turned back again to its normal color, and it stayed that way for the rest of the reading.

Chapter 5

Dreaming of becoming a Jedi Master

Craig goes to bed one night and is lying in bed with his eyes shut. Craig sees total darkness. As the eyes are closed, yet he feels that his eyes are wide open, looking deep into total darkness.

Craig sees himself moving objects with his mind like the mutant of the X-Men and like a Jedi in Star Wars.

Craig thought of his race, a thousand years ago.

"The people back then were very primitive. They would see something and, with no explanation, would say it was magic.

"The computer stops talking as Craig's starts to talk while under the machines scanning probes."

But before the beginning of our race, we were different. Who is to say that my people had special powers? Some were stronger than others, some were weaker, and some did not have it at all, and there were ones more gifted than the others.

"Being a part of a Levite. I often wonder if I had any special gifts. And I believe I had tapped into a part of my brain to give me such power but, I was afraid that, with such power, I could have used it in ways that I shouldn't. I was lucky to have great parents to be kind and mindful of others. Like in Star Wars, the dark side is about revenge, I often think of getting my revenge on a few. But as I grew, the feeling was not as strong.

"To see the future. Seeing one person getting hurt, or even die, is something. The best part of my brain. I can go to a place, and I can become the darker side of myself. Scary how the person looks so real. And without any warning, something would fall without any reason. Something that just won't fall by itself. Like a book lying flat on my desk.

By closing my eyes, I can picture myself going back to the past. I try to picture what really happened. I can see history being made. Going back in time. Thousand years, I can see what really happened. The thing that is foggy is, did the Levites' help to make some history what we know today?

"My feelings that a group of a higher rank told the Levites we can't use such power. And we became mortals. Maybe I am a "Jedi"; a true powerful man."

A picture forms on the screen. Craig is sitting on a seat at a kitchen table. A pencil laying on the kitchen table and he moves it.

The doctor who is a bit far out, in a voice that was not normal says

"I can't believe Craig even thought about this. There was no evidence left. A group of people change the information so the truth would have been lost. I think Craig has special powers himself. But what?" said the doctor.

The nurse speaks but it very soft. "I think the doctor has lost his mind."

CHAPTER 6

The Computer Starts to Read another Memory.

Third grade. Craig learns how to write and from now on all the students in the class must write. Craig writes like a doctor and the teacher, Ms. Gone, does not like it. Craig gets a C in his writing. During third grade, and remembering other years too, the teachers lied. Craig can't believe they lied. They would give them a crazy test, and the teachers would say, "don't worry, this test does not count."

"Well assholes it did. I never took tests seriously. The teachers said that the tests do not count so I am going to bullshit. Maybe that's why I end up in Summer School more than I should."

During that Summer, Craig went to the park. The park charged five dollars to go to the Museum of Science; Craig's father gave him the five dollars for the bus ticket plus twenty dollars for lunch and other little things to buy. Twenty dollars was a whole lot of money to Craig. He had never seen that kind of money before.

The park director says, "Stay in your group. Please don't get lost. Thank you."

Then they left their small town and headed to the city.

Craig remembered the city, every time his family visited the cemetery. They go the same way.

But Craig had something on his mind. A faint smile, a ghost, a pretty face of a girl long since been lost. Craig turned his head and sees a girl sitting near him. A pretty young little girl that reminds Craig of

Alice, Craig smiles. She was sleeping and her head was on his shoulder. She was maybe a year or two younger. Craig never got her name.

A dream, of a stranger, a girl with long brown hair and the face of an angel. A dream, a girl in his dream that watches over him and he does not know who it is. But the face, Craig thinks he has seen it before, but where?

That night, when Craig was going to sleep, his eyes close. Looking at complete darkness he sees a face. He can barely make it out; an angel perhaps. He called out to her, 'Hello, who are you?' She looked at him and smiled and then she drifted away.

Craigs oldest sister, "the boss", Lee, is controlling, but teaches him to be clean and other stuff. His second oldest sister, Sue, is a piece of work; he tries to keep out of her way. Lynn, his third oldest sister, plays cards like war and gin rummy with him. His little sister, Sara, is very smart. She always gets an A in class, but stay out of her way if she got a B. The world had just ended.

His fourth-grade teacher, Mrs. Wiseman, has the same religion as Craig. He did not know that Mrs. Wiseman had taught three of his sisters before. She said:

"I know you were out of the class the other day; I hope you studied for your math test."

Craig said, "Yes." It was easy addition.

In the fourth grade, a young girl passed away while she was on a camping trip. Debby Blue, she came down with something. Craig only remembered that she was a pretty girl. Craig was sitting in his chair. He stopped and thought and wondered if he had looked at Debby the wrong way and someone got jealous. Craig thought of the girl who he had kissed, wondering if she had special powers and she was watching his every move and she was jealous. Every time Craig looks at another woman, he feels like he is cheating on someone, and he sees the face of the most beautiful woman with the billion-dollar smile. But at that moment he forgets the name, but the name is in there, in the brain, but he just can't say it, yet.

CHAPTER 7

Knowing who I am but love is stronger

Craig's mind starts to play tricks on him. Being Jewish, he knows he must keep his religion and he must marry within it. Being a Levi is very important, but the girl who Craig kissed many years ago it did not matter to him, as his love is strong towards the beautiful woman. Love is harder than any material that is manmade or even mined from the earth.

"The computer stops for a brief moment. It starts to talk. Reading deep in Craig thoughts. Craig's farther wanted him to get married. Craig's farther did not care what religion who he married, Craig's father wanted to be a grandfather and have grandchildren from Craig."

Craig looked at the classmates and then he looked at the girls. He stops and thinks. He thinks harder, saying all kinds of names. "Alley, Alice" and then he remembers a name. Then he says the last name, "Madderson! Yes Alice Madderson."

The girl who I had kissed.

The computer stops talking and the brain waves of speech kicks in.

"Doctor. Why are these girls that he sees important? I just don't see it."

"Nurse Sakra. I hired you because you were the highest ranking in brains scanning in your class for being observant. Was that all lie!?"

"No, Doctor. I am very good at what I do."

The doctor said loudly, "Look at her! You don't see the girl faces?"

"No, not really why?"

The doctor spoke with a loud voice and sounded quite disgusted.

"They have no faces! Every girl that Craig thought about had no face. It is all a blur. He is thinking of Alice from first grade. She was and still is very special to him. He feels like he grabbed her heart and whipped it through a brick wall. Craig, he has tears coming from his eyes. His heart got ripped out as well, and he will never see this woman ever again. And if she did survive, would she still remember him?"

The computer kicks in.

During the month of September, it was Passover. Craig and his father went to services and when it was over, they stop at the Big B supermarket to buy some last-minute stuff like ice cream. Of course it was not for Passover. Craig's dad always made a good excuse.

"Craig we are buying ice cream. This ice cream has no bread in it and no you in it."

Craig said, "No you in it?"

"Yes," his father said. "No nuts." The father laughed, ha, ha, ha. Craig said in his mind, "Now I see where I get my bad of sense of humor. And we pick up some Egg Matzo, soup nuts; Passover Coke Zero."

When Craig said 'coke zero' a picture on the screen showed his face with a big smile.

"After the cedar and we do the very quick version. I could still smell the hot chicken soup. Roasted chicken, I always got the dark meat. I just love legs."

When Craig said this on the screen, the Doctor and Sakra, watching the screen, did not see Craig with a huge smile on his face that lasted for a minute while he laid in the bed.

As the day continued, Craig's four sisters and he go into what they called the TV room. With their nice size TV. It was a sixty-five-inch television with a DSP screen. They waited for dad to hide the matzo. Craig liked to cheat, and he tried to peak through the door, and the four sisters hold him back as they knew him like a book.

CHAPTER 8

The dawn of the bullies

Fifth grade, and Craig is having a tough time reading a ruler. It was so easy; Craig was too bored to study, so he just forgot how to do it. He did not care. Mrs. Jinkson took Craig to her desk and was going to show him how to read a ruler.

"It is very simple," she said in a very nice calm voice.

"Craig, do you know how to divide? I hope you can."

Craig said, "Yes. I know how to divide."

Mrs. Jinkson pulled out the ruler and she said, "All even numbers you divide, and all the odds ones you leave alone. You can count to sixteen, yes?"

"Yes, I can," said Craig.

Mrs. Jinkson said, "You know how to read a ruler."

Craig whizzed through that like it was saying ABC's.

Going home that day, Craig needed to practice his drums. It was early release day. Craig two sisters the oldest Lee was working. Sue and Lynn were watching their favorite TV Show. This show had been going since the beginning of time, over thousand years old. It is called the Young and the Restless.

Craig started his drumming and irritating his second oldest sister Sue. Feet banged on the floor and then came banging up the stairs very fast. Sue slammed Craig's door open; the door goes over the door stop and the doorknob hit the wall putting a huge hole through it. Like a crazy mad woman, Sue grabbed the drumsticks out of Craig's hands and she stormed out, slamming the door behind her, and Craig was shaking terribly.

Craig then remembered something funny, but not really. During Saturday services, he had to use the men's room. He entered the men's room and he locks the door to the bathroom. It smelled like some person just pissed all over the floor and walls. When Craig turned the lock, the lock mechanism broke. Craig does his thing while holding his breath. Craig was holding his breath for as long as he could, but he could not open the lock. The lock looked like it could have been a hundred years old and did not work properly. Craig panicked and the smell in the bathroom was so great. A few people heard Craig trying to open the door. They managed to open the door. An ass wipe said to Craig's father "don't let Craig have a lock on his bedroom door. He will panic if he can't get out." Craig, being a quite person, said to himself, "That's totally bullshit. The old F must like the smell of piss."

April came and they got a new student. Craig knew him, but did not say anything; the classmates, for one reason or another, did not like him. They were very convincing, and they wanted Craig to fight him, so Craig did, and he felt bad and regrets it. Craig's mind takes a 180. Craig had blood on his hands. Feeling bad that a few people could talk Craig into hurting another person was wrong. In Craig's brain he was tearing up. Someone is over him, a beautiful tender girl. Alice told Craig that this was wrong. It was that gentle face, and she was so disgusted with Craig, but Craig he was still learning. As the brain was still developing and not fully formed. Craig remembered something. He said, "I can't put my hands on it." He sees the color brown. He sees Alice, the beautiful girl in the whole universe in his mind.

Chapter 9

The Rise of the bullies

The computer kicks in again reading Craig's thoughts

Sixth grade was a very interesting year; this year was the beginning of the bullies and Craig started developing the brain.

With the help of the oldest sister, he prepares for a spelling test. When the spelling test was being complete, one words that Craig gets right and the other classmates did not know, was a word 'long'. When Mrs. Riley spoke to the class she said, "Class, I just want to say, only one student here got the word right "Congratulations". Congratulations, to Craig Galuta for getting the word 'long' right." Craig smiled and the rest of the class made a face. October came and Craig had his birthday party again, it was a bowling party. How his classmates liked the bowling party. Craig got this one gift from Doc McGoson. He gave Craig a small box and it was very heavy. Doc's mother said, "Doc saved this for many years." Craig unwrapped the gift. It was twenty-five dollars in pennies. Craig thanked him. Craig sits down and starts to remembered a story that he heard in service, years ago. A story that has some kind of morels . Not sure how the story went, as the brain started to remember, it was something and not too sure how it went, but it was about an old man very wealthy. When it was time to give to charity, he did not give a dime. And people knew this, and they hated this man dearly. He was good to his workers but a rotten person for not giving to charity. Yet this old man gave ninety percent of his earnings and never asks to be recognized. And on that day, when he died, the entire town's people were happy. The entire town's people were at his funeral.

They were cheering. The rabbi knew this man. The rabbi talked and the people listened. The rabbi, with a sad voice, spoke and said this:

"A man here dies a poor man. He gave ninety percent to the children charity so they would have food and shelter and never did he ask to get credit for it."

And one woman started to cry and then the men started to cry and soon the whole group, who wanted to see this man dead, started to cry. It was said it was the day that the world heard the cries and the streets got flooded by the tears.

On the next two days Craig went to class it was Monday as Craig's birthday was on a Tuesday a school day and had to be celebrated a few days early it was a Saturday. Craig, without any thought, gave away the money. Knowing some classmates were not as lucky as Craig, Craig's father working for Xspeen. A company of science research to help planet earth. Craig saw that some students were very skinny and probably didn't have any food on their tables, so Craig gave the money away. Craig never turned around and saw Doc's face. Docs was so disgusted with Craig. If Craig had just turned around and saw his face Craig would have explained what he was doing, but Craig was in his little world, like Robin Hood giving to the less fortunate.

Craig had created an enemy, not a bully. Doc does not look or talk to Craig. But the bullies on the next day were born. The student who the classmates hated became his friend and like wild animals they made Craig the outsider. Craig's brain was becoming more developed, always learning his mind, still seeking knowledge. They wanted Craig to fight, making him as low as them. Craig refused to fight, knowing it was wrong. The person gets a free shot and hits Craig. Craig was becoming his own psychiatrist.

(Craig speaks}

"As I realize fighting is not the answer, but the dreams are as real and they take over for the moment."

Five months later, Craig had his first violent dream. Craig was having a stupid argument with a student. It did not make any sense and then he fought him, giving the person two black eyes and Craig was victorious. When the time came, Craig said to himself, "I want to make this dream come true." Craig forced the issue, it was so stupid, it had absolutely no merit, whatsoever, just like dreams that don't come true. As the student was about to plant his fist into Craig's eye, Craig's arms were frozen. Craig's brain turned off all the switches. No muscle movement, whatsoever, as the two boys went to talk to the principal. The boy Frank Swinger, said,

"I don't understand why he is crying, he started it."

Only if he knew it was a dream, and this dream could have been worst. The principal, Roy Mon, takes Craig to the hallway and talks to him to see what was going on. In Craig's dream he did something and still wants to see the outcome. It was very disrespectful. Putting his hand in his pocket and the finger out. The principal said in a firm voice, "put it away or you're going to lose it. I see what you are doing."

"I think Mr. Mon should have given me a back hand. My father would have said I deserved it." As Craig's dreams were more detailed than others. More action, more violence as the bullies were making a very dangerous person. Craig's dreams were no longer about animals or life, nor love. It was becoming darkness, hate, destruction. But every time, when Craig stepped over that line, a beautiful face, a faint face that comes into Craig's head. Then he starts dreaming that he's running but he can't move. The legs just won't move. The legs become heavy and numb. As Craig looks back, he sees a young face, a beautiful young girl, sad. As she talks, no words come out, but Craig can hear what she says. She said, "don't be cruel, your heart is pure, and you have a good soul. Don't turn, be strong be your own leader."

Craig's brain looking feeding on knowledge. He hated school because they studied only one small part of a topic. He wanted to learn from beginning to end on one subject. There were two things that kept Craig from turning one hundred percent evil. It was that girl. Every time Craig crossed the line, he saw this face; Alice. A warm, kind, gentle face. And when she speaks, there are no words, but Craig hears them very loudly. She tells Craig, "You are a kind man, gentle soul, doesn't let the darkness take over." Craig keeps on thinking of every time, when he does something wrong, she feels the pain and Craig sees the pain. And the punches that the bullies give Craig, the pain bounces off as she is with him always. Craig took the pain that the bullies gave him, and he became stronger, but the pain that he gave this beautiful, kind, and gentle girl were so much greater than any bullies could ever give. The bullies have won, they made Craig one of them. But Craig was extreme. In Craig's mind, he said to himself, "I take this invisible knife and I slash and I slash and I slash your heart and it bleeds. I grab your soul and I spit on it. I am mean and I am a cruel person. I love no more." And for that very moment, Craig's eyes are full of tears. As they fall on his bed. His pillow is soaking wet from the tears. And he knew he could never talk to this girl this way, who he hurt so badly. Craig feels so sick inside, knowing that he destroyed the only thing in his whole life that made him happy.

Craig stops thinking and his tears made his shirt soaking wet. For some reason, a face that he saw was in tears too, she was in pain. As Craig opened his mouth and says, "I am so sorry," he saw her cry and disappear.

Not knowing, that on Craig's pants leg was a very tiny device made by Xmose. He was listening to everything that was being said.

During the month of May, they get a new girl in class. She moves in on the same street as one of the classmates. How should Craig know? She was tall, and hot. Hilda Queen. Craig was using his charm to get a girlfriend, but he got shot down. "Oh well," Craig said to himself.

CHAPTER 10

At the end of the class year, Mrs. Riley took the class to Bell Tower beach. Mrs. Riley looked old, but she was in her late forties and a heavy smoker.

During the day at the beach, Craig entered the arcade and the classmates ganged up on him and wanted him to smoke. He says no way, they wanted him to smoke so he would be a part of the group. Craig took off. When it was time to go home, the classmates came back to Craig and accused him of telling Mrs. Riley that they were smoking. She knew they were smoking. Craig knows this never did happen. Stupid as the smart ones were, they did not have the brains. They thought that Mrs. Riley was born yesterday. The classmates might have a change of clothes, they might have a gallon of perfume. Mrs. Riley smoked way before they did, and she knew all the tricks. She was teaching for a long time too, so she was not stupid. For that, the classmates hated Craig. The classmates probably believe this lie he was accused of, and they probably still believe it to this day.

As the screen flickered, a picture appeared. In the lab where Craig was laying, it was Craig at Bell Tower beach. The bus pulled into a parking lot. The classmates leave the bus. Five of hottest girls were wearing their bathing suits, they call them bikinis. Craig just stared at the most beautiful sight in the world. The five of the hottest girls in his class wearing bikinis from top to bottom. The girls were showing off their stuff and, boy, they had stuff. Craig had a smile on his face a mile wide.

Craig was walking toward the water. He reached the water, and it was freezing. He decided he would go inside the building where it was cool. Craig had a pocket full of quarters and he was heading for the arcade. Inside a huge room were video games and pinball. Some pinball games looked so old, hundreds of years old remakes. And they were the cheapest ones too. The new pinball you needed to be quick, very quick. And Craig was not that quick. He put in a quarter, and he was using a pinball machine that was dated Nineteen seventies. Then a classmate goes over to Craig and they were all smoking. A few of them walked over to Craig and said, take it. Craig looked at them, "Get out of here I'm not going to take it." This person tried so hard. Craig being somewhat smart left the building and went to the water.

The time was ending, and it was time to go home.

Mrs. Riley round up the classmates and they headed home. A classmate comes over to Craig and accused of him of ratting on them for smoking. Craig said no. The hot classmate Sally wearing the bikini, the beautiful parts protruding in the open air. Craig's mind really somewhere else, he didn't hear Sally. She was yelling! "I don't believe you because you're not a part of the group." As alone Craig was, his brain kept on working. Thinking of the sexy classmate and what she was wearing. "I don't care what they are saying," Craig says to himself. "I know what I was thinking. Lucka, Lucka, lucka, lucka. As I stop for the moment, and I gaze upon the beauty. Their beautiful parts protruding from the top and I could see a lot of detail. It was the second-best day that I had in my life." Clean observant, but his mind stills need food. "Didn't know as much as the other students know. I am a slow learner, but a wise one nevertheless." The brain is a very powerful tool.

Craig sitting in his bedroom, on the floor, eyes closed. He opened his eyes and gets up and he opened his closets doors and he was looking for something. He said out loud, "Where is it?" At this time Craig was looking for the game that Alice gave him. It got lost. When he could not find what he was looking for, a piece of his heart broke off. He was looking for a certain game. Now he says was it only a dream ? this was only a dream, never happened ? And he laid on the floor, eyes opened up as the rivers started to overflow, his eyes burning like they were on fire. Craig feels thousands of people pounding on his heart, crushing his love. Yet deep down in Craig's mind the game does exist. He knows it, he saw it he had touch it. He will find it once more .

Craig knows down deep inside this was not a dream. The game does exist. The name gone for good in the brain. Got erase by someone or something why! .'

"Doctor. We need to find the answers."

"I know," said Doctor Framharr. "But his dreams are important. It's the way that his mind works, they are the clues. What we think is not irreverent."

"Ok Doctor," said Sakra.

CHAPTER 11

Dream-BIG SISTER Show (feeling sick for being a total A--)

When Craig went to sleep that night, he had a crazy dream. He dreamt that he was on the Big Sister show.

Craig gets a phone call. Mother yelled, "Craig! Craig! You have a PHONE CALL!"

Craig dashes into the house. "Hello," Craig said to the producer of Big Sister.

"Hi, Craig. My name is Dogqwin, producer of Big Sister; we read your application for the Big Sister show. We want you to be in it."

"Yes! Thank you, sir! This is going to be great."

Not even three minutes goes by, and the Newspaper people and television reporters are rushing over, Channel Four CBS, as known WBZ, Channel five ABC, Channel seven NBC was there, and Fox 25, all interviewing Craig. "You are going on Big Sister, tells us all about it."

"Well," Craig said. "I am not running for president of the United States. If I had, I would win."

One reporter from Fox 25 said, "How?"

Craig said, "I would say these famous words. 'Read my lips, no new taxes'." And Craig whispered, "Suckers."

The computer kicks in reading Craig's thoughts of his dream.

Second part of the dream. MS. Jackie Qinn from the talk show The Yacker was hosting the show again, a blazing hot Asian woman. Craig remembered her on a news show, The One Hour show. Wait I think it was Zonnie Qinn .

The house guests are lined up and Jackie says, "Do not talk or say anything, do you hear me! Or you won't be going in." Craig starts making funny faces to the audience, they started to crack up laughing, and the house guests are biting their tongues to prevent laughing. Ms. Qinn says, "Craig, get in the house now." Craig runs in. He finds a room and the rest of the house guests follow.

Meanwhile, outside the house, Jackie Qinn talks to the audience.

"Well, we are back for another season of Big Sister. I think this one is going to be a whole lot different this year. People buckle your seat belts, I am telling you."

Inside the house, the house guests are sitting in the living room, and they are introducing themselves. Up in the corners were cameras. They were facing down. The couch was an ugly green color and they had three love chairs in blue and two red chairs. The first person who introduced herself was a hot blond-haired girl.

"Hi. My name is Gail and I am from Canteen."

The second girl, skinny with long brown hair said, "Hi, my name is Mary. I am unemployed."

"Hi, my name is Sue, and I am a student in college." Sue was tall and she had an athletic body and she was wearing a short blue dress and pretty bright yellow medias.

"Hi, my name is Craig." The entire house guess says the comedian "No I am a Schleper r. I schlep things for people. Before I stop, I would like to give a shout out to my favorite chess hero, Susan Polgar. A part of a generation of Grand Masters chess players. You know she was named after her great grandmother, and she was also a Grand Master chess player."

"Hi, my name is Jack ..."

Craig starts to cry; he was in tears.

"What is wrong, Craig?" asked Nancy.

Craig said, "I am remembering when I got off the airplane, a little boy got arrested."

Jack said, "Well he did something wrong."

Craig said, "No, he did not, he was greeting his brother."

Mary replied, "Greeting his brother?"

Craig said, "Yes, he said, Hi Jack, Hi Jack, Hi jack, ha haaaaaaaaa oh, oh; oh I'm 'p'eeeing in my pants."

Moe. Moe was a weightlifter and a wrestler for the minor leagues.

The next person to introduce themselves was George, a painter, and Fred, a golfer, and was also a writer for a newspaper. Steve was a runner. John and Frank work for fast-food chains. One was McGoldens and other Burger Queen. And Nancy has red hair. She was wearing bright red Medias and a very short blue dress and she had red high heels, eight inches high, and she was a single, hot nurse.

Craig looked at Nancy and sees how pretty she is, but something in his head says stay away, she is not the one. Craig was getting confused, even in his own dream.

Outside the house they were forming groups. Craig stamped his feet and yelled, "Boom, boom, boom!"

Fred asks Craig, "What are you doing?"

Craig replies, "I don't want to be considered a floater, so I am making noises."

Big sister talks on the intercom.

"Craig, please come to the diary room."

Craig walked in slowly. He opened the door, he is on his hand and knees. He cries out.

"I did not do it, I swear, the devil made me do it."

Big sister says, "What Craig?"

Craig says, "I don't know."

Then Craig out of no were starts to cry. With cried no tears coming from the eyes.

Big sister says to Craig, "What is the matter?"

The computer is going in and out as it can't handle Craig's thoughts. As of the presents time the computer is talking.

Craig said, "I just farted, and I pooped my pants, Ha, haaa oh, oh, oh I 'm 'p'eeeing in my pants."

Big Sister held a Head of Household competition, and Mary won. She had made her decision that she was going to pick Steve and Moe, and Moe was furious. Moe was yelling at Mary and swearing.

"Why did you pick me? I did not get you mad at me. Are you a blaming Fingool?" He goes and punches the wall, putting a hole in it. Mary got so scared she actually peed in her pants. Six of the security men, bigger than Moe, took him out of the house. The woman producer comes in, consoling Mary and taking her to her room to get her changed and calm her down. Steve is downstairs, saying, "Were the filth, flaming, filth is Moe!"

Frank walks in the house minding his own business. Steve goes, "Where is filth, flaming filth is Moe."

And Frank says, "I don't know."

Steve, from out of nowhere, punches Frank in the arm. The security men again run from the back room and throw Steve out of the house. The computer starts to talk reading Craig's thoughts.

"This seems like I am watching and old TV Show, Jerry Springer."

'Note what the doctor and the nurse does not see is a small tiny man inside the video monitor. He is watching."

Craig goes into the diary room to talk to Big Sister.

"I can't believe these two men. What the hell were they thinking? Big Sister, I need to light up the house. I am going to say a joke. For the people who this affects, any money that I win will go to the charity."

Craig exits the diary room.

"Hi guys can you please come into the living room. I have some sad news.

When I was in the diary room giving Big Sister my thoughts of what just happen, the producer that runs these cameras was listening to the radio and she started to cry. Big Sister had the intercom on, and I heard everything. The producer's name is Billie Jean. She says, 'Billie Jean ! what is the matter.' Billie Jean says, 'Johnson and Johnson stopped making bandages'."

Craig started to cry.

(The whole house says) "Craig, why is Johnson and Johnson stopping making bandages?"

"Because they Band Aids, ha, ha, haaa oh, oh, oh I'm p 'eeeing in my pants."

After Craig's joke, Big Sister said this group needed something, so they bought five extra cheese and onion pizzas, ten coke zeros, five regular coke classics and people said that the soda was made by caveman, that is how long this great soda has been around. It was, and still is, the real thing. '

In the lab that Craig was laying, A picture appeared on the screen as the nurse and the doctor watched it. They see Craig's face as he smiles when he says coca cola.

Big Sister put a message on screen that 'two people had left the house, please if you have any problems or concerns come into the diary room and get it off your chest. Please'.

As the house guests talk about what had happened, Mary leaves the table. Craig goes over to her. "I'm sorry, I was not there." She replies, "It's ok. He is gone."

Nurse Sakra talks. "Doctor. Where is her face?"

"Craig is dreaming of that girl from the first grade, you don't see it. All the girls have the same face. Everything he is saying is how he is feeling. He is so disappointed; He has failed her. He feels so badly for all the stupid things he has done. He feels like he ripped her heart out."

When the doctor stopped talking, the picture on the computer proceeded.

The next day, Big Sister is just dying to hear what Craig has to say. "Craig, can you please come to the diary room."

"Yes, Big Sister. Can you please give me five minutes, please five minutes? Ok guys, we all watch Big Sister, right? I am going to imitate one house guest, try to guess who this person is. Ready. So I am on this treadmill, wiggling my touches. Big Sister yelling, blank come into the diary room now. She replies no, I got small friends in big places or was it I got big friend in small places. You can't make me come in there. I want you to try. I will sue, sue, and sue!"

And Sue comes running over, "Why you want to sue, Sue?"

"No," said Craig. Craig goes on, "Wait. She takes off the fifty thousand dollars' microphone." Craig makes a sound then splash. And 'Big Sister and "BBBIG BROTHER' yelling at her get blank in the diary room right now!"

Fred said, "Yes, I remember her. Her name is, Janet Goose head. She was madly in love with Gessy, the big body builder, the bonehead."

"Yes, Fred you are right," said Craig. "Janet did not realize he did not care for her the way she thought, and he really did not care for her as she thought. If she only knew, and if I was there at that time, and she was one hot woman of beautiful color. We could have the first, small sister or brother in the big house."

As Craig was walking into the house, he felt sick to his stomach, his face turns white as a ghost. He entered the diary room. Before Big Sister could ask Craig if he is ok, Craig starts to cry, and these were real tears. He felt like he took his own heart from his chest and smashed it on the ground. Craig sat down and it took him five minutes to calm down.

"I feel sick. Not sick what you think, just sick."

Big Sister said, "Please tell me."

Craig's eyes opened up, like a dam that just got busted open, water rushing down, and his eyes burning like fire; the throat swollen, hard to talk. And Craig said,

"I just said something. That I just hurt someone so special. I just took her heart. I ripped it from her chest. I threw it on the floor. I smashed it and I smashed with my hands, and I ripped it to nothing with my hands."

As that special someone was in America watching the show, she saw Craig, she heard Craig, felt so sad and she changed the channel, not knowing what he has said; she will never know.

Gail won the second Head of household and she nominated Frank and Nancy. As the power of veto got back to the game, Gail won the power of veto, and she did not save anyone.

Live eviction was taking place and all the house guests were sitting in the living room and Craig was sitting on the couch near Gail. She was wearing navy blue Medias and a red mini skirt, and a tight, short sleeved sweater. Jackie sees Craig smiling. Jackie yells at Craig, "Craig, why are you smiling? I just notice you smiling."

"Well, Jackie. I went to molding school and they said if you're in front of a camera you smile, and I am in front of the camera. Lucka, lucka, lucka, lucka."

Jackie quickly changed the subject. "I am very busy, so let's hurry and cast your votes, because it's an odd number of voters, one of you is going to be a lucky son of a B. So, the first victim is Mary come into the diary room and cast your vote."

Mary votes for Frank.

"Thank you, Mary. Now quickly send in Sue."

Mary yells out, "Sue, get your ass in the diary room now." Sue stood up and she ran like a bat of hell to the diary room.

Jackie says, "Sue, who do you vote for?"

She was out of breath. Jackie said,

"Come on, girl. I don't have all day. Let's go."

Sue said, "Frank."

"Now if you can manage to send in Craigal the bagel, maybe he has the cream cheese, thank you!" Screamed Jackie.

As Sue walked slowly outside, she managed to say Craiggee, Craig knew what she was saying. Craig entered the diary room, feeling a little weird how Jackie is looking at him through the small monitor in the corner of the room. Jackie being a married woman, giving Craig the eyes. A young man old enough to be her son. Craig didn't mind. He loves older women too. But he stopped in his tracks. This time he sees a heart dripping, not blood, it looks so different. It was love. Again, Craig feels like he was cheating on a friend that was lost.

Craig said, "I vote for Frank."

"Please get Jack."

Craig goes to the meeting room. "Your turn Jack."

Jackie says, "It is official. Frrrrank he is o-u-t- out of here. Hi Jack, Hi Jack, Hi, Jack, I hope no police officer heard me."

Jack said, "Very funny, Jackie."

"Before you speak, there Jackie boy, it really does not matter what you say. I got the votes right here right now; you can say Mr. Mcgoo. It would not matter at all."

"Ok," said Jack. "I vote Frank any ways."

"Ok, please send George in. Hi Georgie porgies who do you vote for?"

"Frank."

"Ok, now get back to your seat. Well, the votes are all in; it looks like Frank is our biggest loser. The loser gets one minute to say his or her goodbyes and no freaking crying. We all know it is all a fake and the viewers at home knows it too. Frank, you got exactly one minute starting now."

Frank saying goodbye.

"You got thirty seconds. If you're not out here, you will be going to be walking home and we will be canceling your plane ticket." Frank dashes out of the door. He trips over the step. He goes flying on the floor, and the people in the audience started to laugh as it was so damn funny. Frank had to leave quickly to change his pants as he peed on national television.

Craig had made it for the third week on Big Sister and now for the head of household competition. House guest, one at a time you will go to be fitted for your balls.

One by one a man was drilling holes into ten pin balls.

"I said to myself, yes, this is up my alley, no pun intended."

When Craig got to the man drilling the holes, Craig asked if they're going to have oil on the lanes. The man said yes.

"I will take this ball please, and I would like it to be fingertip." The man smiled knowing he has a bowler. The ball was pretty good.

"I used the same one at home. It was called Zone Triple X. Brought back from hundreds of years ago. This ball is one that the people die for in getting. I knew the ball, but not the driller. The driller did a great job drilling and this was a live television show."

A voice over the speakers say, the lostest score sits down.

Each house guest throws a ball down and the lowest drop sits down.

The computer reads Craig's mind and says Five is the lowest. Gail, Mary, Sue, Alice please sit down. Craig gets back feeling really good, throws another strike. Now the house guests are complaining that Craig's balls can do tricks that are not fair.

Craig said, "My ball, ha, ha haaa does not do tricks. I throw a hook ball. Your ball could do the same if you picked out the right ball and got it drilled with fingertips." Craig with a strike, wins again. Craig is now the new head of household. Craig speaks, "Do you know why I love bowling ladies?"

They all said, "No why?"

"Because I love to play with my balls, Ha, ha, ha, ha, ha oh, oh, oh, oh I am 'p'eeeeeeeeing in my pants."

Big Sister calls Craig into the diary room, the head of house room is ready. Craig asked

Big Sister, "I want to do the biggest farce, in the Big Sister history."

"Go ahead, Craig. I am listening."

"Tomorrow, I want you to call me in to the diary room. If you can write this part down so I can pull it off, it will be great. I bring all the house guests to the living room; I will say Big Sister has done the Pandora's Box earlier this year. You all know what happens when the head of household opens the Pandora's Box, good or bad things can happen. This case they both do. The head of household got a great gift, but it comes with a penalty too. After the Head of Household tells you your punishment if you like you can ask him what he has won, and he must give you an answer.

One by one, the head of household will touch you on your shoulder, you must go inside the house into the living room and when any house guest walks by and say what's up, or how are you doing, you must clap your hands five times ,hop on foot five times and yell Scooby doo, the last house guest's must slap their hands ten times and hop on their foot five times and count out to fifty slowly and by ones slowly. And yell out "Scoobyee, Doo, and Yabba dabber doo."

As the computer finish the thought of Craig it went straight to the dream.

"Ok Craig, what did you win?" Jack said.

Craig speaks, "I won the ultimate veto. This veto will last me for the finally three. This veto I can save any one or two people from the chopping block if I choose to do so. I can also choose who to take over in its place as well... If I want to save Sue, I can save Sue. If Sue and Nancy are on the chopping block, I get save both of them at the same time and choose the other two I want out. Yes, I can pick who I want out I have the ultimate power and I can still play for the veto competition and I can still become head of household too. However, I can't change my own nominations. I can pick two who I want to save and the others I am blind folded. I have to eat peanut butter and jam, "Smuckers" jam for two weeks and sleep in the have not room with cold showers. But I made a deal with Big Sister. I have fair skin; I will be washing their cars so I can get the hot showers.

If Big Sister is up to it. She might ask me to give her a little strip show too."

"That's bullshit," said Fred. "We should leave now, who you want to be the other two!"

"Fred there are going to be ways for you to stop this so it can be fair, so relax." said Craig.

Craig goes up to the head of household room and starts getting his things together. Sue comes up with Mary, Gail, Alice, and Nancy. "Craig can we talk to you?"

"Yes, ladies."

"What, who are you going to nominate?"

"I don't know," said Craig. "I like to be in the house with the hot women, Lucka, Lucka, Lucka, and Lucka."

Craig went to the Have not room. The floor was wood.

"I actually love this room."

Craig took out his tap shoes and started dancing. Big Sister allowed Craig to keep his disc player and tap shoes.

Craig took the duct tape and wrapped the tape around his waist and covered the CD player. And Craig pressed play.

The first song comes on, Michael Jackson "Billy Jean".

Big Sister calls in Fred to the diary room. Fred opens up. "This is totally bull." And he storms out. Big Sister calls in Nancy. Nancy says, "Maybe I can use this for my advantage. I like it."

Meanwhile, Craig is in the room dancing like the "King of Soul."

And Big Sister gets everyone's thoughts about Craig's farce. Craig leaves his room and goes outside and taps Fred's shoulder first. Fred swears and goes in the house. Craig walked in with a smile on his face. "What's up Fred?" Fred claps his hands five times and hops on his foot five times and says Scooby doo. Craig runs into his room so fast. Closed the door and starts to crack up laughing, nearly 'p'eeing in his pants for real. When he got outside and Nancy walked by Fred, she says to Fred, "What's up?" Fred again claps his hands five times, and he hops on his foot five times and yells out Scooby doo. Craig runs right back into his room. Nancy does not see Craig and Craig cracks up again. Talking to Big Sister in the Have not room, "I can't believe I am pulling this off." Craig goes outside, sees Jack and nonchalantly Craig taps Jack on the shoulder.

Jack was not very happy in getting hit. Jack walks in the house slowly and says, "What's up?"

Of course, Fred claps his hands five times and hops on his foot and yells, "Scooby Doo."

And Jack touches Fred on the shoulder. To relieves him.

Fred said, "You are an ass and now I going to get you back!"

Fred walks outside and back inside again, walks near Jack.

"What's up?"

Jack counts to ten and does all the farce and Fred goes back and forth in the house getting Jack back. This went on all day and Nancy was the last one to get hit. Feeling a little silly she completed Craig's farce.

It was the day for nominations. Craig picks the two people who he wanted to save, Gail and Alice. The others he closes eyes put two keys is the bag and with the eyes still close he slides the rest of the keys into slots.

Craig goes outside and speaks to the house guests in funny talk. "Hey guys, the nomination ceremony is about to begin, being, and begun and right now, rrright now."

The house guests walk in the house real pissed off.

"We should all leave right now, and you can have all the money."

"Listen George, I am sure Big Sister will change something; it's something new they are trying, give it a chance. I saved two people and the rest I do not know who I put in the bag, I was blind folded. Before I can continue, I will start after these commercial messages."

Big Sister on the intercom yells out

"Start now!"

"The first person I save is Gail." Gail says, "Thank you, Craig." "The second to be saved is Alice." "Then Alice turns the keys box to Sue. the next one to be safe is Sue, Sue takes out Mary's key, the next one to be safe is Mary, thank you Craig. Mary takes out Nacy's key. The next one to be safe Nancy, the last one to be safe is you Jack, Thank you Craig. Well George and Fred, I'm sorry I did not know who I was picking. I was blind foolded if I did not say this before. I did not know who I picked, Good luck in winning the veto competition.

"Craig, you can't save any of us," said George. "Yes," said Craig. "Sorry, George. I cannot. You need to win the veto."

As the day went on all the house guests go into the diary room real pissed. Every single person said they were walking out. Big Sister pleaded with them. "Don't, good things will happen. I will tell you what I'm going to do, perhaps on the next veto competition please stay."

As the veto competition taking place, Craig wins the veto.

The House guests are in an uproar. All the house guests do not want to leave; they are thinking how to kiss Craig's ass for them to stay. Nancy walks into Craig's room. Craig is pretending he is asleep, but she does not know Craig is awake. She tries to get information from Craig. She says,

"Crrrrraig, tell me are you telling the truth about the veto?"

Craig responds, "I think Nancy is hot, I want to bang her."

Nancy smiles very softly she says, "Shit. I am giving him a wet dream." She continued.

"Nancy wants you too, but please tell me is the veto true?"

Craig answered, "I am getting so hot." Craig raised his arms and the eyes are closed as he reaches to kiss her on the lips.

She manages to get away just before Craig reached the lips, and Craig opens his eyes and starts crying once more. He hears a faint voice. "Why Craig?" Even in his dream within his dream he sees her.

"Doctor. I see the faces now. I really never noticed it before. More so now. All the girls have the same face. The day when she left only that image is in his head."

The doctor answered, "I know, she holds the key, but what?"

It was the face of the birthday party, when he saw her face with the tear. As the face became blurry, he cannot see, but he could see the tear clear as day.

During the veto ceremony, Craig speaks to the house guests. "With my power of VETO!" With a deep voice of importance Craig speaks and smiles. "I can save one of you, so please state your case."

They both spoke. "We are going to be leaving any ways. It really does not matter when."

Thursday came and Big Sister today was on live, "We are going to have the live eviction please get ready." As the house guests scrambles to get ready for live TV.

"We are going to be live in three, two, and one."

The camera went live to Jackie; the camera went live in the house.

"Hi, House guests."

"Hi, Jackie."

"Craig, I hope you been taking your gas ex pills."

"Yes, Jackie I have not been farting for five hours now," and when Craig stopped talking Bam ba boom. Craig laughed and the house guests said to Jackie, "thank you for jinxing us."

"Sorry House Guests. I am glad I'm out here not in there. Ha. Ok, remember if there is a tie, too damn bad for the both of you. You are o-u-t out of here, you got it, good. Gail you are up first, please come to the dairy room and cast your vote. Gail likes Craig very much who you think will Gail vote for. Your vote."

"I vote for George W Bush."

Jackie says, "Sorry, you can't vote for an ex-president even if a republican."

Gail said, "George."

"Please get Alice right now and I don't have all day. We got one vote for George, who will Alice vote for. People start your bets now." Jackie screams and yells! All bets are now close. Jackie talks to Alice. And Jackie asks Alice, "Who do you vote for?"

"I vote for Georgie Porgie."

"Ok please send in Sue. We got two votes for George. Who will Sue vote for. Hi Sue."

"Hi Jackie, I just love your dress."

"Well, thank you. Who do you vote for?"

"I vote for George."

"Can you send in Mary. Well its three for George. Who will Mary pick."

"Doctor. Even in Craig's dreams he is joking this is so remarkable."

"Yes, Sakra. Craig is one unusual person."

"Mary who is very hairy and loves her dairy how are you?"

"I am ok, Jackie."

"Who do you vote for?"

"I vote for Fred."

"Thank you, can you please send in Nancy. Hi Nancy; I see Craig might have eyes for you?" Jackie says this in a tone of sexiness.

"No Jackie I looked into Craig's eyes. I see it belongs to someone else. I can feel his heart, it belongs to another woman I don't know who."

"OK Nancy your turn to vote."

"I vote for Fred."

"Can you send Jackie Boy in?"

"Yes, Jackie."

"Well, we got three for George and two for Fred can this be a double banger.

Hi Jack, Hi Jack, Hi Jack. Ooops, I hope the police didn't hear me."

"Ha, ha, ha Jackie good one," said Jack.

"Who will Jack pick?"

"I pick Fred."

"Ok Jack. Please hurry and sit down in the living room. I am very busy. I'm going to be on the Yacker tomorrow.

Well house guests, guess what we got? Not one but two jurors. Yes, a three-way tie Fred and George you are Out of here! you got a total of sixteen seconds to say your goodbye and no cries, starting now."

George and Fred said, "Bye, bye, bye."

"Good luck. Yaw right. Frig you people," said Fred underneath his breath. The two men open the door and walk to Jackie.

Jackie said, "Please sit down. Well, how are you two losers doing now? You two are the Jurors and you got the whole house to yourself. You can raid the refrigerator all you want."

George says, "Well that's nice."

Fred says, "I hope there is cable in there."

Jackie says, "Yes there is and they got the Play Boy channel on it for you two."

George yells out, "YA WHO!"

Jackie says, "Here is what the house guests had to say if one or both are out."

Gail goes first, "Ha, ha, ha, ha Fred and George, I think Craig wants all the girls to be the last to stay for some hanky panky."

Alice said, "Hey Fred and George what a plan, it was all my idea to get you two out of the house, Now I might have some fun with Craig now."

Sue, "Hey Fred George, sorry for you, you had to go; I think Craigal the bagel with the cream cheese wanted just the girls in the house."

The next head of House Hold begins. It was touch and go, Nancy won.

Nancy being little older, her pictures were hot; She was wearing hot mini skirt and her legs, "Boy I love legs." She had six pictures of her wearing the most gorgeous medias, Blue, Red, Hot yellow, bright white, green, and hot ivory green.

"Doctor. Should we skip this part I think this dream is not going to help us at all?"

"No nurse we must see everything! I don't think it's going to be that kind of dream."

Nancy took Craig into head of household room. Craig was nervous that he was he going to spill the beans; he needed to keep a straight face. Nancy asks Craig who she should nominate. Craig said, "Jack and Mary and get out Jack."

So, Nancy put Jack's name in the bag with Mary, when it was all said and done, Mary cried and said, "Why?"

Craig looks at Mary. As the computer is reading, what is on the mind of Craig the video screen.

"I look at her she stops crying as she just put two to two together."

The veto game started, and Nancy blew it away, during the veto ceremonies. She kept the veto, and they voted for Jack. Now Craig is in a house with five women. Almost like home with his four pain-in-the-ass sisters. Craig went to his room with a huge smile on his face; he was saying his favorite words of excitement that is 'cucka shit cucka shit cucka faha.'

The Head of Household challenge was a hard one - who left the house first. The first video was Steve.

"Steve, what the f is you doing? Get over here now," said Moe.

Steve said, "No way. I want to punch that mm Filth in the face, and I am going to be happy doing it too."

The second video was Frank.

"Hey Frank, Frrrrank I think you got a phone call you need to go inside the diary room."

The third video was John.

"Hey guys," said Craig. "Where's John?"

Gail said, "Might be in the bathroom."

Craig said, "Yes he did smell little like shit. Ha, ha, ha. You get it?"

The girls said no.

"John it's a slang word. I believe to be over three thousand years old another name for the toilet. John. Ha, ha ah oh, oh, oh I'm 'p'eeeing in my pants. I pick the order that left the house first. I was wrong I put down John first and Frank second and Steve third. Steve was first, oh well." As I think about it, it was Moe who left first .Got thrown out of the house.

Alice picks Nancy and Sue and when the veto was done, Mary won the veto and she decided not to use it. The two girls looked at Craig. "Are you going to use your powerful veto or never use your powerful veto? The game is almost over." Craig said please excuse me. He ran right to the bathroom so they could not hear him laugh so hard, so hard he nearly' p'ees in his pants.

"Alice had made supper, it was a nice hot roast beef medium well. Roasted potatoes, carrots were well done, cooked well. Alice is a great cook. For just some reason I forgot what she does, the most beautiful thing in the house. She is very kind; sweeter than sugar. She has a magic touch. Every time I was thinking of a girl who I forgot; deep inside I never truly forgot her. She would hold my hand and the pain it would disappear like magic."

The live voting happened again. It was Thursday.

"Hello, House Guests."

The house guests all in unisons say, "Hi Jackie!"

"Well, its getting down to the nitty gritty. Who do you think is going to be the finally three?" As the house guests talk over who they want out. Craig who does he want to leave? Jackie starts with her evil laugh.

Nancy and Sue yelled out, "Not me, please!"

"Hello House Guests, its time; you all know and I should not have to repeat myself, but I am going to say it anyway. The head of House Hold, that's you dear, are not allowed to vote, your rights of being a voter is no longer in effect. There won't be a tie so don't worry, one of you girls is going to be safe. Gail, please come in, you are up first. Hi Gail. Who are you voting for?"

"Can I vote for a Demacrapper?"

"No, you can't it has to be Sue or Nancy."

"I pick Sue."

"Thank you. Now please get Mary. Sue now has one vote, who will Mary pick? Please place your bets. All bets are in; the betting is now stopping! Hi Mary, you cutie hairy thing you. Who do you vote for? Wait! Wait! Wait! I know who you look like now, cousin it, and there we go. Ha, ha, ha."

"I vote for Sue like screw (long pause) you." And Mary smiles.

Jackie said, "Please send Craig in. Well, it really does not matter what Craig says, it is official; the guys are going to have a gang banger in the juror's house."

"Hi Jackie."

"Hi Craig, just want to say it really does not matter what you say we got the verdict. You can say snot rags it really does not matter."

"Ok Jackie, I vote for Sue."

"You should have voted for Nancy! Now Sue is going to be mad at you. Hello house guests when I read the evictions you got seconds to get out of the house because I really need my sleep for my big show for tomorrow. Three to zero a kill. Sue you got seconds to say your goodbye starting now, go! Go! Go!"

Sue said, "Bye, bye, bye, boo who, boo, booo, whoo, not enough time to cry, bye good luck."

"Why Sue was a great player?"

"Yes, Nancy, she was," said Craig. "Hey Nancy, you got great pair of legs."

"Why thank you Craig. Why don't you ask me out?"

"Ask you out?" said Craig.

"Well ask me out for a date."

"I can't. My heart belongs to someone else. I don't know who. My heart belongs to this one girl, and I don't know who she is. But I do, it's crazy, this girl turned on all my lights, she has your color hair, same color hair too."

Craig is seeing long brown hair, no longer seeing red.

"But you are not her. You don't go to my school; you are much younger than she. And I am double your age. She was an angel. Sweetest thing you could ever see. And I, Craig am a vicious animal, I destroyed this girl's poor heart. I cry every night. I wanted to tell her I'm so, so, so sorry and she does not see, nor does she hear me, and she does not even want to look at me and then I go and make a stupid comment about another woman in this stupid house. I felt like I stabbed my own heart with the spear. My heart chattered to a billion pieces. My first love and I killed it. I feel so sick inside."

"Maybe she will watch this show Craig or one of her friends. will tell her what you said and how you feel," said Alice.

"Well Alice, I don't l know, I know; we can't sing songs in the house, but I going to say it. As it is only words. It is by a man who lived hundreds of years ago. This is an old song. They say he was an animal."

"What? An animal?" said Gail.

"Yes, Alice he was in a rat pack."

Gail said, "A rat pack? Is he a rat? I did not know rats could sing."

"Me neither. I saw a picture of him, he looks human. His name is Frank Sinatra," said Craig softly. The song it goes little bit like this.

"I got the world on a string sitting on a rainbow, got the string around my finger, what a world what a life I'm in love. I've got a song I got to sing, I can make the rain go got the world around my finger what a world, what a life I'm in love. Life is a beautiful thing as long I hold the string, I be a silly so AND so if I should, ever, never, will I ever let it go."

Craig stops singing and tears rushed down his face.

"I am a stupid romantic fool. I know I can never have her."

Alice said, "You know, Craig, maybe someday she will forgive you."

"She can't forgive me, because I can't forgive myself," said Craig. "I am a total jack ass."

The next head of household was a bowling game again. "House guests this is not going to be your normal bowing game. There are four lanes. You have got minutes to score the highest number of pins blindfolded, using the guide to make sure you're straight. Good luck, you need it."

Craig put on the blindfold, can't see but he counted his steps and knows where the ball should go. The ex of head of household is screaming.

"I can't believe it, a strike."

Nancy said, "Who, who, who?"

The ex-head of household said, "I will be quiet." The buzzer rang. The house guests took off the blindfolds.

"House Guests with the most points goes to Craig, with a 95."

"Thank you, Alice," said Craig.

Alice gives Craig the Key to the head of household room. They both go inside the closet where they keep the dry goods to talk. Craig goes in as Alice needs to talk to him.

Craig said, "Ok, what's up?"

"Who do you want to leave?" Alice asks.

"It has to be Nancy and Mary. Please don't say anything. "AS they both exit the dry food closet.

Alice says ok. Hey Craig well guesses what? Alice said. Yelling this at top of her lungs Craig coming out of the closet. Ha, ha, ha, ha, oh, oh, oh I'm 'p'eeeeing in my pants.

Craig laughs and said, "Very funny."

"Well, that's nice of you Craig, you have the Veto. It is only good for three people once there are three, doesn't make you a winner."

"Yes, you are right Mary." That night Craig was thinking who he should pick. Craig went to the refrigerator and took out five steaks, five potatoes; cooked some carrots, made a nice garden salad. He made a great meal for the four girls, and they thanked Craig. The nominations were tomorrow. As Craig was lying in bed, Alice comes over, thanks him for saving her and Gail.

Craig woke up and it was late in the afternoon. He went downstairs, right into the diary room to get the Nomination box. As Craig puts Mary and Nancy's keys in the bag, he felt bad.

"House guests it is time. This is my Last speech. I can't save you two as I was blindfolded. But this time I was not. I feel sick. I had made new promises and I have to break. But there is one promise I can make, and I will never break it again. That is! The girl who I hurt; that very girl who I destroyed her very heart. I won't do or say anything to make you cry or feel disgusted with me anymore. Oh, I am so, so sorry. I'm in the Big Sister house thinking of one person that I had destroyed." Craig paused. "Please excuse me."

Before Craig left to go to his room, he took one of the keys out of the box. Craig went upstairs. His eyes open like the dams had huge holes in them. The water rushing down so fast destroying everything in sight. Rain started to fall. Downpours from the sky. As the water hit the eyes, the water became hot. As it burns and burns, no eyesight. As Craig got himself together, he went downstairs and said sorry.

"I had to do something."

The girls understood. Craig speaks with a hoarse voice, "Nancy are you sure?"

She said, "I am sorry, about your feeling for that girl maybe someday that special someone will come back to you."

Craig replies, Being sad and down. "No, it will never happen. When you get bitten by a mean dog, you stay away. When a person takes a knife and starts jabbing into your heart and all your love is drained away, the person who I had something for. I go and I take my friend ship away and it..... and I throw it away and I go physically takes it and smashes it to nothing. I had murdered my own love my friendship. I and feel so sick inside.

Mary, I am sorry I picked you; you and Nancy must win the veto tomorrow."

"Craig, you got lucky in winning the super veto," said Mary.

"Please excuse me ladies," said Craig. "I need to go to the bathroom."

Saturday came very fast, and Ms. Jackie is on the big screen.

"Hello house guests in a few moments the two of you are going to vote, be smart damn it, this could be a life saver for one person.

If there is a tie, well again, tough sugar pads, and Alice, you are up first. Alice, who do you pick?"

"I pick Mary."

"Ok please send in Gail. Hi Gail please pick who do you want to get kick out."

"Oh no I forgot who to pick I don't know is it Mary or Nancy? If I get it wrong, I am screwed, Nancy, I pick Nancy."

Jackie said, "Are you sure?"

Gail said, "Yes, I am sure."

"Well house guests we now have shown here, when we did this show we never had a tie. Now over one plus years it's a tie, the two people who are headed to the big house, Nancy and Mary." Three Company. Jackie appears on the big screen, "Now Craig, please don't get any ideas. Big Sister does not want to pick up any hospitals bills you know what I mean."

"Well Doctor. I think this is going to be one of those dreams after all."

"Wait Sakra, it's not over yet."

Craig speaks with a soft and happy voice. "Hi ladies, guess what?"

"What Craig?"

"You two are lucky people, congratulations for making it to the final two."

"Wait Craig," said Alice. "What do you mean the final two?"

Craig walks backwards to the entry door to go outside the house, the two girls follow him. Alice and Gail kept on approaching Craig.

"What do you mean?" yells Alice.

Craig opens the door and walks out of the house. He has already packed up his bags and gave it to Big Sister.

"Hi Jackie. What's up?"

"Well Craig are you ready to vote? I show is over and we are going to pick a winner who do you want to win?"

"I have to flip a coin, not so sure. But they are going to hate me."

In Craig's mind he knows who the winner is. It was a beautiful, sweet angel. The girl that was in his heart the very first day they met; the special girl who Craig goes and destroys with a lot of regrets.

Jackie says, "You are absolutely right, Craig, they are going to hate you.

Welcome back house guests. Craig please take a seat."

The Jurors saying, "Yes he did not win, yes."

"I see you are happy that Craig is out here."

All said, "YES!"

"Well let me tell you this; Craig is a big winner in more ways than one, more after these commercial messages." Here take that, hey take this and don't take a piss. Ovil Moker sugar bomb makes you feels good.

"Ok, you over there, go head ask your question, ten seconds for each."

"Um what can I say I can't think of anything?"

"Nothing times up," said Jackie. "Up next is Jack."

"Well, are you? Were you? Could you have?"

"Sorry times up next, nothing to say. Ok Craig your turn."

"Alice please pick a between number 1 to 100."

Alice says, "69."

Craig says, "Thank you."

"The winner of Big Sister is Alice."

The band starts to play. There was whistling. Jackie hands over half a million dollars check to Alice. Jackie says.

"One thing before we go, can anyone here tell me what the biggest farce in the Big Sister house was? Here is what the Jurors had to say."

"I don't know, what farce? You got me Jackie."

"Alice, Gail, do you know what the farce was?"

Gail and Alice said they didn't know.

"Craig took a punishment for pulling off the biggest farce in history of Big Sister; we are going to award him 30 thousand dollars for pulling it off. Here you go your slimy devil you."

"Thank you, Jackie," said Craig.

"Doctor," said the nurse, "in his dream there were two men, they did not seem to be a part of the dream, but they were."

"Yes, Sakra. I saw it; I am glad you did too. They were looking straight at us knowing we are watching them, very strange indeed."

CHAPTER 12

Craig's real pain (hurts and beauty)

During the Summer, Craig's Hebrew school class was having a car wash for a fund raiser. It was ninety degrees outside, and it was super-hot. Craig was so focus on washing the cars, he did not see the most gorgeous girl in his class, Rachel Wildfire, near has feet. Craig stepped on her foot, causing it to swell up like a balloon, and being a tough ass, Craig said, "you should be wearing shoes." But his heart was torn. He could only think of the two girls that he had hurt. Here comes her brother who pushes Craig, and Craig's father stops by and yelled "What's going on". Rachel's brother did not say anything and as Craig entered the van, Craig's father said,

"Why didn't you pop him one?"

Craig did not say anything because it was his fault that he had stepped on the foot of the most beautiful girl in class and he never said sorry. Craig, looking way back to his memories, feels like maybe he is a cruel person and needs to be left alone.

Seven grade pops in. Craig took out a piece of paper and started drawing crazy symbols.

Doctor cries out, "Record this, record this!"

The nurse replied, "Already am, sir."

The doctor said, "I can't believe this, he is writing the formula for the Nuclear Atomizer that was destroyed in the fire at Alice Mcgoodle daughter's Mansion."

"It was a shame what happen, she was a brilliant scientist."

"Yes, she was. She was very special, a gift that Craig gave to Alice so many years ago she gave it to her daughter; the special gift for a special friend for a daughter. Oh no! He just has thrown it away, the most important paper in the world."

"Doctor, do you think she might be still alive? They didn't say that the body that was found was hers, there might be a chance she was at the right place at the right time and was protected by the force field."

"Ok Sakra. I will be right back."

The computer speaks, reading Craig's mind.

The doctor goes into another room with thirty computers. A man name Simon was scanning the areas for life. Three areas were known for successfully activating the force field. Israel, Ireland, and the crazy town that Craiglived in Town of Hope. Simon scanned the house and did not find any traces of DNA that matched Alice's daughter, the only thing that the doctor could wish for was that she could be safe.

Ten minutes' past. The doctor said, "Let's continue."

CHAPTER 13

Age 13

On the summer of June 15, Craig was riding his bicycle. He always followed the rules. On the highway there was a huge pothole. Never fixed in three years or more. It had got deeper and wider. Craig rides his bicycle, and he pulled off a little so he would not fall into a deep hole. A car going fast, a person not paying attention on route 140, hit Craig and dragged him fifteen hundred feet up on Mullen Street. Craig's bicycle gets total led. Craig's legs are all messed up, there's a hole in his pelvis and a chipped bone in his neck. An ambulance rushed Craig to the hospital. When Craig wakes up, there was a nurse. She looks like a television star. Perhaps she had the same hair cut as the actress and she looked like this woman, "Farrah Fawcet" pretty hot. Craig being lucky thirteen and being in the I, C, U.

Nurse said, "I.C.U."

The doctor said, "Yes, I see you, too."

While Craig was in the hospital, Craig's grandmother was dying of cancer in the house. Lying in bed she senses something wrong. She knew something was wrong. She had given Craig her last bit of life to keep this poor soul alive.

Craig never said goodbye to his grandmother.

CHAPTER 14

The Start of the Genius

Seven grade, the bullies became more frequent, it was mostly one grade higher. But Craig took it, Craig took those punches; he was eating it.

"Doctor. Look at him, the brain, and the brain waves are actually eating the pain."

The brain wave on the screen took shape. Huge mouths, pointed teeth, eating strands of brain waves that were pain caused by the bullies.

"Yes, Sakra, they are, the brain is feeding off the pain, making Craig even more powerful than they know. But wait look, look way up in the corner. Look very carefully, do you see it?"

"Yes doctor. I do see it, it's her again. Was she there all the time?"

"I don't know," said the Doctor. "We can't go back but we will keep an eye on this corner."

Up in the corner of the video screen was a small face, blurry so they could not make it out. It looks like a woman, the girl in first grade. It moved like she was alive in the picture, moving slowly.

Craig bought weights and started to lift. Got strong but didn't want to show it. Craig stopped and thought about first grade, not about the beautiful girl, but his passion for dance. Craig was brought up with all kinds of music. Glen Miller, American Patrol, the songs that taught Craig his shuffle step ball change. Very old music, other songs Craig likes was the Fifties, sixties, and eighties disco, too. Even in the twenty second century they called her Lady Goo, goo, gaga, "Lady Gaga her song, Poker face". Sounds so dirty. Craig loves it. We are talking about thousands of years ago and this music still lives on, "Chattanooga Choo Choo". And Craig thought, "I can't forget Benny Goodman Swing, Swing." Craig remembers second grade and when he took up tap. He was dancing with five girls, even at that age they were hot to him, and he was the same age as them. Craig was getting very advanced but didn't know how to control his thoughts. Craig was thinking some of the old reruns from way, way, way back. Like the Jackson Five, watching this kid named Michael Jackson dance. Craig out loud says, "I want to be famous just like him."

Chapter 15

The start that changes the world

In the Eighth grade, getting picked on by bullies just washes over him. In study hall, Craig takes out a notebook and makes crazy symbols again.

"Nurse, Nurse! Record this, record this now!" screamed the doctor.

"Yes, doctor," said the nurse. "I am recording this."

The doctor said, "Craig does not have a high I.Q., but he is writing this as if he has a higher I.Q. than Albert Einstein."

"He was afraid to study, if he did he could be very dangerous."

"Yes, he could. He could have done a lot of damage if he knew what he wrote. Sakra, look at this part of his brain wave. Very interesting."

"What doctor?"

"Let me read it. Craig was a C student in all of his classes except one."

"One?"

"Yes one, Biology. That explains it all."

"Mr. Flatterson can I ask you something please?"

"Go ahead, Craig."

"Well, I been drawing these crazy symbols and they look like they could be very important?"

In a firm voice Mr. Flatterson said, "Let me see, Craig. Where did you get these writings from?" Then, very loudly and with a lot of anger, "Where did you get this!" Mr. Flatterson grabbed Craig's arm tight and dragged him to the intercom. The woman speaks, "hello."

"I need someone to look after my class, this is a code 68 -P."

"Ok, someone be there right away."

The guidance counselors come running into the room. Five police officers come running into the room, they handcuffed Craig, they pulled him out of the classroom as if he just killed someone and the police took Craig into a room that was heavily locked. Nobody in school knew what was inside. It was always bolted shut. It was a huge room, with white walls and no windows. There was a huge box with wires. And a few lights and paper.

The policeman uncuffed Craig and an old man with white hair said, "Good morning, Craig."

"Good morning, sir."

"My name is Detective Gunn. You can call me Peter. Sorry if we scared you, but we need to ask you a few questions, ok? This won't hurt, this here is a machine nothing else."

This is a high tech lie detector.

"Craig, we are going to ask you a few questions. Ok?"

"Yes, Peter."

"What are the names of your parents?"

"Their names are Hanna and Abram Galuta."

"How old are you?"

"I am fourteen."

"Ok, where did you get these writings?"

"Nowhere. They were in my head, I just wrote them down."

"Thank you, Craig, that is all."

"Well gentleman, either Craig is one damn good liar as he just passed the highest lie detector in the world, or this man has an IQ that is very high."

Mr. Flatterson speaks out very loudly, "Are you telling me, Craig, just wrote down a formula for shrinkage, the one that Doctor John Mcgoodle could not do?"

"Apparently yes; Craig, in minutes, wrote down a formula that would have taken years to do," replied Peter.

Mr. Flatterson said, "Give Craig the shot, tell him he will forget everything that happened here today and now we know what we have to do."

"Yes."

As Peter took out his needle he said very softly, "Craig, this shot will make you forget what happened today. If this had gone out to the wrong people, this would and could have been pretty bad." The doctor gave Craig the shot and said very softly, "Craig, you are going to do great things."

"Doctor Framharr, why are they going to make him forget this?"

"Nurse Sakra, they are not. Only what took place at the meeting. This solution will speed up the process of what he knows and when he makes it. It takes many years to complete so we need to keep an eye on this."

Craig found himself in the French class. Mrs. Berchieno took Craig to the front desk where she was sitting. She said, "Craig you're failing French."

Craig said to Mrs. Berchieno, "I am not going to France. I don't need it."

She looked at him. "You might in fact need it."

So, Craig said to her," I got a joke, would you like to hear it?"

She said yes. "Two wrestlers wrestling, the Frenchman and American, the Frenchman has an American in a submission hold. The American says, merci, merci, merci and the Frenchman says, Pas de quoi, Pas de quoi, Pas de quoi." She laughed so hard. For that joke she says.

"I am going to pass you, and I thought you did not learn anything."

CHAPTER 16

Beauty is not all what is crack up to be

Craig had to stay after school today to make up what he missed. Waiting for the late bus, with Craig, was a cute long blond-haired girl. Looked so innocent but she was cruelest person in the world.

A girl bully named Lane Verberg.

Craig was brought up to be a gentleman and never to hurt any girl and she started to attack him. She was saying all kinds of horrible things. She said, "I am a German, we kill all your people." She kept on attacking him saying more and more hurtful things and laughed. As much as that hurt Craig, he was looking straight into her eyes as she says, "are you going to hit a woman, a girl?" Well, she was not a woman and at that moment was not a girl. But what Craig did, though, to make her shut up, he planted one right on the lips. She yelled out that she was going to tell the principal. Craig said, "Go right ahead, are you going to say the cruel things that you just said to me too?"

"Doctor. I want to read what she is thinking. The waves are awfully strong here."

"Go ahead nurse."

"Craig if you weren't a bad kisser. Well."

"Doctor. I think she liked the kiss. I hope Craig did not give her any special gifts."

"I don't think so, no, that was a onetime only. His heart was in the first grade, and he will always love Alice. In his heart, she will never be gone. She is his Angel, his guardian's angel. How much Craig thinks about her, the tears that flow from his eyes? The pain that he caused her. He feels very sick inside as I can see this on the wave pattern."

CHAPTER 17

Craig Becomes the Scientist

Hours passed, Craig is in his room; the nagging mother called Craig downstairs, "Craig, set the table. Your father will be home shortly."

"Why don't you have Sara do it?"

"Your sister is studying for a test."

"Ok, can I watch my favorite TV show? Doctor Who is on tonight."

"Yes, you can," said Mother.

A few minutes later, Craig's father walked in and said, "Hi honey!"

"Hi dear, supper will be ready in a few minutes." Craig sets the kitchen table. His three older sisters were out with their friends for the weekend. Craig put on the television and changed the channel for the Doctor Who show. Sara comes running downstairs to eat. She said, "Do we have to watch this show?"

Mother said, "Yes. Craig set the table; I told him he can watch his show."

It started out on a green grass hill. The Tardis appeared and a man named Craig Glatky was running, as he was being attacked by metal spiders. They were the size of small dogs. There were about twenty chasing him. As the Tardis fully energized, Craig opened the Tardis's door. And started pushing buttons and he pulled down the lever. The

Doctor comes into the room and he looked and said, "Very interesting." He then asked.

"Who are you?"

"Craig," said, Craig. "I was getting attacked by metal spiders and I saw this police box. I just saw this police box and I opened the doors and just pressed a few buttons."

The Doctor looked at him. "There is only one type of person who can operate a Tardis, which is a Time Lord." The Doctor checks out his heart, surprised he has two hearts. The Doctor tells him this is not going to hurt. The Doctor puts his hand on Craig's forehead and he sees an imploded Tardis and this man nearly survived; you are a very lucky man to be alive. As the Tardis stopped, the Doctor opened the door. It was plain white. Craig entered the room and pushed the walls like they were huge doors, as they were. The Doctor goes in the opposite direction and he sees a small door to the left and a door far from the right. The Doctor and Craig split up. As Craig opened the door, he looked to his left at a glass window. Craig looked down and saw people with knives and people on the beds, they were getting metal parts put on them, the birth of the Cyber men. He left and came across a stairway, so he walked down it. He saw a glass door leading outside and beautiful green grass. As he opened the door there were three attack dogs that looked like German shepherds, but alien. The mouth opened and huge sharp teeth were hanging out, saliva dripping out of their mouths, and the dogs were bigger than normal. The dogs were close in size to Craig and the show ended. Craig said, "Damn, next week is going to be good."

The father said, "and you like this show. This show is nuts. It is for crazy people, you're not crazy."

"Dad, it's science fiction, it also deals with science facts and with fantasy, the Tardis is bigger inside than outside. The Tardis is based on Topology theory."

"Yes son, at the lab we are studying the theory. And we are almost there. We don't have enough power to go into the future but if we do there is no way to get back to the past. However, we can see by one's brain waves of their life to see the past as it were alive."

"Cool," said Craig.

"Craig."

"Yes, dad."

"Your school called today."

"Yes, what did they say?"

"They are doing a science contest project; I got all your materials in the van, set it up down in the cellar. This project is going to take you a few years to complete, so take your time."

Craig finished his supper. It was a steak dinner with a bake potato and a garden salad. Craig always floods his salad. He liked the dressing more than the salad. The steak was a T bone medium rare. And of course, to Craig's right was a can of Coke Zero. Craig never knew why every time he drank a coke he smiled. As Craig goes outside it was getting dark. Craig opened the back door to the van and saw a ton of boxes. He emptied out the van. It was about ten o clock on Friday night. Craig entered the cellar and set up the boxes. Craig took the two tables and started to set up near a wall at the far end of the cellar. Craig never noticed two outlets for gas before...

They had two cages outlined with plastic and holes, there were two burners and they had two gas connectors for gas burners, as Craig saw in the box. About 10: 30 at night, Craig opened a box and it's a metal detector. "That is weird," Craig said. "Why in the world do I need a metal detector?"

Craig went upstairs, brushed his teeth, took a shower and went to bed.

CHAPTER 18

The Start of the Formula

Craig woke about six o' clock and he started to make the first batch of the formula. Craig went to the office to tell his dad about his progress and the father did not hear Craig open the door. Craig overheard a plan to take over Eastern countries and so Craig went downstairs and changed the formula.

"Doctor we can't see what he is changing!" screamed the Nurse

"I know; I don't know why," said the Doctor. nervously.

Craig with a different voice said, "I will tell you why, because it is what I want you to see. Let's keep on and you might find the answer."

Craig went upstairs. It was Saturday. Craig's dad and Craig went to Saturday serives. Craig was so involved with his project. Craig's father called him over.

"Son, I got you a metal detector so you can leave your work for a while, clear head and explore outside see what you can find."

CHAPTER 19

Time Capsule

Craig said, "Ok thank you, this explains a lot."

Craig took out the metal detector. It was about seven o clock in the morning, and he goes out in the back yard to see what he can find, if anything. Craig started from the house and slowly he walked toward the wooded area. In the middle, to the right of the back yard, a strong signal was coming from the ground. It looked like a lot of metal. Craig laid the metal detector on the ground and found two big sticks. Craig took the two sticks and with all his might shoved them into the ground so they were sticking up. He runs back into the house, runs down the cellar stairs and lays the metal detector on the floor near the wall. Craig's three sisters were over their friend's house for the weekend and Craig was home with his little sister Sara. Craig runs back outside to the shed and grabs a shovel. And he started digging. Craig could hear Sara yelling from the house.

"Ma, Ma, Craig is digging up the back yard!"

Craig's mother told Sara to go and help him. She looked at the mother like she was nuts. Sara walked out and she asked her brother,

"Craig. What the hell are you doing? Craig what are you doing?"

"There is something down there made of metal. I am going to find out what."

Now Sara is interested. "Can I help." As she burps, Craig says, "Yes ok you can, pig."

"Thank you; I know I am a pretty intelligent girl."

So, they started to dig, and the hole got wider and the hole got deeper. Craig hits something. "Sara, please wait I hit something." As Craig pushed away the dirt there was a box. It was big and it had bubble wrap all around it. Right underneath the box was a piece of plywood, still preserved with a handle right in the middle. Craig and Sara took in the box and put it on the kitchen table. Craig took off the bubble wrap and there was a key in a plastic bag. The key was in perfect condition as was the lock on the box. The box had words on it and said time capsule. Sara shouted, "Ma, Dad! Craig found a time capsule."

They walked in and Craig opened the box. There were movies and there was a box which said blue ray, it had a plug and it look like what we used. And it had loose cables to hook the box and blank DVD disk saying 'play me first' on the cover. Inside the box was a letter. Craig read the letter. Craig opens the time capsule. There was a long letter describing what was in there. A time capsule that was buried thousands of years ago now being dug up for the very first time. It said, Hi my name is Craig Galuta; I made this time capsule in the year two thousand and fifteen. I never made a time capsule before so I don't know what to say. I will give you all the details in case you don't know what to do. For the electronics If you don't have any electricity or if you do and it's not compatible with my equipment maybe there would be a way for you to see this. I don't know when this time capsule is going to be opened up. I have many videos from my time. Movies that I bought, and television shows and music that I enjoy that I have recorded. You can see in this big metal box. I have tap shoes. I took tap when I was real young, I started when I was five. And I love tap so much I bought shoes that would fit me so I could still tap. Underneath the hole is plywood, it could be gone by now I don't know. I have a bag, there should be thirty ten pin bowling balls in it. Tomorrow, I go on my last bowling tournament as my hands don't work so well anymore. I became a pro bowler in the two thousand fourteenth bowling with the greatest of all time hall of famers. Like Little Bo Park Jr III, his father was a great bowler and a hall of famer. Also, I have beaten another great hall of famers, Walter Ray Williams, another super star. Here is my time capsule. I have two DVDs of these two great men giving bowling tips. I knew how to bowl but their tips were like money in the bank, I hope you enjoy them as I did. I also have in this time capsule, I won this in a raffle at the pro-am tournament. Hope it's still in great condition, an autograph shirt of Walter Ray, anyways I was on fire until I messed up my hands. I was considered the underdog. Before I came pro, a man name George he was a senior pro bowler and he showed me the way to hook my ball. And later Little Bo Jr the third showed me what Bo Jr press what I learn and force it. and pressed it so I could not forget what I have learned. He tells me glide like an airplane. A great teacher. I got their DVDs, the two hall of famers DVDs, watch them learn from them and so, if there still ten pins and if my balls are any good, please use them or I gave you trash and you can bury them back or use them as a walkway oddment. My bowling bag I give you, you might have to dig further down, I have autographs of all the pro bowlers I have met and bowl with. Take care Craig.

So Craig hooked all the cables and turned on the blue ray. "Wow, I can't believe it works."

"Neither can I," said Abram. "This blue ray is ancient." They put in the DVD. A face appeared.

"Hi my name is Craig Galuta. I am thirty-five years old. Right here to my right is the house that I bought off my sisters, I had won my first PBA tournament and I won over nine hundred thousand dollars playing against top notch bowlers. They were and still are hall of famers. I was on a role. My hand is not one hundred percent, now and tomorrow will be my last tournament. Underneath this box lies 30 of my bowling balls that gave me at least one three hundred games. But I am using three of them for my tournament tomorrow. This ball here I won doing a charity tournament. I was not a pro bowler at that time. But I have beaten not one, but two pro bowlers and their averages were two hundred or more with no handicap on a 3,6,9, tournament. And on the same tournament day I have beaten two more pro bowlers and grand total of six pro bowlers". They had an average of 200 or more. I got out of work I arrived at Manchester, New Hampshire, about three in the morning. I had about three hours' sleep. I had a chance to close my eyes for a while, at seven p.m. They had an elimination round, one ball lowest score sits down. The pro bowler that runs the house puts me on lane one. I hit a nine drop. Some pros got a five drop and they sat down. I landed up on lane 15. I was the underdog, with no sleep and I was getting tired headaches. I dropped an eight and the pro that was recently on PBA Television championship, throws an eight and we both sit down. So, at that time I decided to become a pro. They call me PBA Craig. If you look at these balls and they still have ten pins if you can use them great, or throw away. I know I just said that I just love to talk on the video camera. When I was younger, I was a tap dancer, love to dance. My beautiful wife Alice, she is in the house cooking dinner. Background Alice yells,

"Sweetheart, dinner almost ready."

Craig yells back.

"Be there in a minute dear. We are going to be having our first child soon, boy or girl I am so happy to be a dad."

Alice walked over.

"You still working on that crazy time capsule?"

"Yes sweetheart; say something so the people may see it in a hundred years or so."

"Hi my name is Alice. Yes, I am having a baby. Actually, I am having three, two boys and a girl. "

"Wow," said Craig. "I did not know. Mazel tov. I hope you enjoy my music and movies; I also have video on different places that I travelled, so enjoy the past. Oh, wish me luck tomorrow on my bowling tournament, oh wait I already had it before you look at this. I just hope I do well that's all. Take care. My name Craig, oh wait one more thing before I go, I also play chess, if you play you take after me. If any of my family sees this of course."

It was eight thirty in the morning dad speaks. "Wow, he is your great, oh so many, grandfather."

"Wow!" said Craig.

"And we saw our great so many grandmother too. I wonder what the babies' names were, and grandma she is so beautiful," Sara said.

"You know, its eight thirty. Let's go the Big B and buy some soda and popcorn, we can have a movie day at noon. I will buy pizza and at super time Chinese food," Dad said.

Craig and Sara said yes!

Craig and his father go to the store and they buy popcorn and they bought Coke Zero and Craig has a smile on his face when he takes it and Craig's father buys the regular coke for his little sister. And Craig's father buys Bud Weiser beer; they say this beer company is older than Coke and others say they are very close in age. Craig's father knows Bud was made in 1856 and Coke 1866, still pretty close in age; But Coke is still the real thing.

And then father buys Tab for mother. Craig gets home and with bags in hand he runs to the door. And of course, the bags rip open. Paper bags stink.

Craig's Father said, "See I told you, never run with bags in your hands. Don't you dare open the bottles or I am going to have your head."

Craig with a smile on his face says asks why.

"Just listen to me and stop asking questions."

Craig picked up the soda and smiled. "I know why," he thought with an evil little laugh. Thinking that he should open the bottle near his little sister with a huge smile on the video screen that the Doctor and the nurse is watching.

The nurse speaks, "Doctor. Craig was a normal child just like any other brother."

The Doctor gives a smile and said "Yes. He was something of a good person in heart, but something destroyed him. I don't know what. I think it might be what his father said, let us keep on watching."

They put in the first movie, "The Sorcerer's Stone." The beginning of Harry, Harry, Harry Potter and when that movie was over they had a bathroom break and went to the second show. Even better. And when that show was over, they had another bathroom break and Craig's father calls in for pizza, Extra cheese with onions and green pepper. And the other pizza, mushrooms, Craig likes fungus. At six o'clock Craig goes back down to the cellar to add more chemicals on his project and Craig's father calls take out for Chinese food and the delivery was fast and they saw one more Harry Potter movie. It was "Order of the Phoenix." Something about Lestrange Craig thinks she was hot. After Craig finished the Chinese food, he went upstairs very fast, brushes his teeth and takes a shower and lies in bed. Craig dreams.

CHAPTER 20

J.K Rowling (Harry Potter Dream Order of the Phoenix)

It was dark and cool night. Harry Potter just lost his g-d farther Sirius Black. At the Weasley house, a group of the Order are talking about what to do next. A man comes along, Lord Gakee, young man but very powerful. He reaches the door and knocks.

Mr. Weasley yells out, "Who is it? Who is it?" in a quick sharp voice.

A calm relaxed voice said, "I am Lord Gakee and I want to help Harry, Harry, Harry Potter." With all their wands up Mr. Weasley opened the door. They saw a sweet young man. Mr. Gakee speaks, "Harry, what if I can tell you I can bring Sirius back, would you give me that chance?"

Mr. Weasley talks, "You can't. He is dead!"

Mr. Gakee says, "No, not really, I was too late I could not save him; I saw Ms. Lestrange, she missed Mr. Blacks heart by inches. I can get him out of the archway of death."

"How?" asked Mrs. Weasley. "The archway is quite unique. If someone who is very bad and the other person who is good and the person who puts the person inside does a 180, turns good or bad depending on who put the person in, they will come out if they change

They heard a crash and fire hit the house. Harry is about to run out of the house, Lord Gakee holds him back. "Harry please. Harry let me go and do my thing."

Lord Gakee runs out of the house. Lestrange thought it was Harry at her back chasing her, but it was Lord Gakee. She was laughing saying, "I killed Sirius Black, I killed Sirius Black." And Lord Gakee is yelling back to her, "I want to make love to you on your back. I want to make love to you on your back."

She just stops so fast and as Lord Gakee reached her and slammed her down on her back. As he was right on top of her, she said, "Who are you? Who are you? What is your name? and get off me."

Lord Gakee says, "I am Lord Gakee, a very powerful wizard, yes more powerful than Tom."

Lestrange says, "You dare to call the lord by that name!"

Gakee says, "Oh please he is a two faced fool, all talk, a sad little boy. But you are very, may I please."

"What? Please? Please what?"

Lord Gakee in a soft low voice, "I am not using any charms, and I am not using any kinds of potions. I would like to give you a little, to give you a kiss." He said very slowly and romantically.

She said, "Get off me now!"

"Why Ms. Lestrange, you are very nervous, and you are afraid, your heart beats very fast."

"I was running, you nit wit." She tried to yell out.

"Oh, go right ahead give me the kiss." She closed her eyes, she was squeezing them ever so tightly, like it was going to hurt her so badly. Gakee gives her a kiss on the lips, and she changes, the death eater mark is gone, her face changes, but Craig, who is lord Gakee, does not see a face. It's blurry once more. Craig sees an outline of a girl who he grabbed the soul and heart of and stepped on it until it was no more. The girl from the first-grade incident, beautiful, kind girl of any man's dreams. Craig just throws it away like yesterday trash.

Meanwhile at the Weasley's house, Sirius Black popped in and Harry turned around.

"Sirius, is this you?"

"Yes Harry, it's me."

Mr. Weasley said, "Wait Harry, ask him a question only he knows the answer to."

Harry speaks, "Sirius in the Order, in your mother's house, when I said I wanted to join you did something."

"Harry, I gave you a wink."

"Yes," said Harry.

Moments later someone was knocking on the door.

Mr. Weasley with wand in hand. "Who is it?"

"Please I am unarmed, my wand is in my pocket, my hands are up."

It sounded like Lestrange, but the voice was a little different.

Sirius said, "Open the door its safe." As Ms. Lestrange entered the room, everyone gasped as the Order looked at Lestrange as if they had seen Cinderella. Sirius spoke, "How did you change?"

Lestrange replied, "I just got kissed by a very handsome man and he took off saying he must try to save Tom."

"Is he crazy?" Mr. Weasley said. "He is evil; He is trying to kill Harry."

Harry said, "I think I somehow know what is he going to try to do."

Mr. Weasley says, very doubtfully, "What?"

"Mr. Gakee is going to travel back in time to make Tom good."

Lestrange took Harry to the side.

"Harry later on, please talk to me. I have something you might want."

"What?" asked Harry.

Lestrange said very softly, "A horecock ' Trying to be funny '

"A horecock ' trying to be funny ' What is a Hore cock Sounds dirty ."

With a speed of light, Lord Gakee arrived at Malfoy Manor.

He clapped his hands once to go inside where Tom was yakking away, trying to find a way to kill Harry, and as Tom sees a man pop in, Tom's wand was up, and all the Death Eaters had their wands up also. Lord Gakee took all the wands with a swipe of his hands. Lord Gakee says, "these wands are so outdated; I feel like I am in the dark ages." Lord Gakee takes all the wands and breaks them in half. He said, "These are not going to be any good to you anyways. Now Tom."

Tom looks at him, "Don't you dare call me that."

"Tom, Tom, Tom, now shut up let me talk. If these people knew who you really are, do you think they would be at your side? I am going back in time, and I am going to try to save you. If I do or If I don't, you won't remember me being here anyways, and of course, you all have your little wands back too," said Lord Gakee. Three quick claps and Lord Gakee disappeared. And he reappeared in front of a small house. There lives Tom Riddle's father and mother, and the father is yelling at Tom.

"Tom, get your ass in your bedroom now! If you come out, I am going to whip your little sorry ass."

The mother says, "Honey please, Tom did not mean to do it".

Mr. Riddle says, "I did not know I married a bitch, I mean a witch."

"Please stop," said Mrs. Riddle in tears and Mr. Riddle hits his wife. Mrs. Riddle cried more loudly. Lord Gakee knocks at the door. Tom's father comes to the door.

"Hi, Mr. Riddle. Could I please have a word."

"No, get lost!"

"Please, I know Tom has special gifts, with these special gifts you can be a very rich man, a happy man."

Mr. Riddle said, "I am already wealthy," and slammed the door in Lord Gakee's face.

As Lord Gakee walked around the house, Mr. Gakee saw a young boy crying as he heard his mother crying.

"Tom," said Mr. Gakee. Tom looked up and Lord Gakee talked to him and said, "I see why you kill that asshole father of yours, but to take this grief and hurt other people is not the right thing to do, think about it boy."

Tom, for a moment, did not know what the crazy man just said, and he thought about it. Tom heard voices. They were two rattlers, two big ones. One snake said, "I'm hungry. I need food." The second one said, "I can eat a cow."

Tom spoke in the snake language.

"My father might be good to eat."

The snakes move up their heads and say thank you. They climbed up to the windowsill and entered Tom's room. Tom opened the bedroom door. Tom Riddle's father said, "I told you to stay in your room." The two snakes, unseen, got nerer the father as the father gets out his belt. The father yelled out, "You are going to get boy." Tom in snake language said, "Kill, kill, and kill." The two snakes bite Tom's father and he falls and the snakes have their dinner.

Lord Gakee comes to the present and he says Ga Gee invisible and clapped his hands once and turned himself invisible. There he saw Tom Riddle, no change, and he is just as evil, just like before.

Lord Gakee changed himself younger and he goes to the school that Harry is in. Hogsnorts ""trying to be funny, the school of Magic and Wizardry. The teacher who was taught the dark arts, worked for the headmaster. Doris was a good woman, a very sad childhood life. She was the hottest girl in class, but no boy would have asked her out.

Lord Gakee took a seat and Doris talked.

"We are learning all about the hooters, that are the Owls."

Harry cried out "No, we need to learn more powerful spells to protect ourselves from Voldemut .

"Oh, you silly little boy. He is dead, dead as a door nail."

"No, his is not. I fought him, you stinking woman, I might have won the battle but not the fight."

"NO! you did not Harry, and I don't like the tone of your voice."

"Please excuse mam. Yes, Harry is right, Tommy is alive and yes, I saw him too. He is just an ass like you, but you have a very good excuse."

"What? Who are you? How did you get into my classroom?"

Lord Gakee took his wand. How mid evil it was. All the kids had one. He pointed it up into the air and said some words, Ga ga youngga ha, ha, ha and flipped his wand to the teacher and she becomes young, the same age as the rest of the class.

The class gasp as they did not realize how beautiful she was.

"What did you do to me? Tell me now!" She took her wand and a mirror appeared.

"No young student has this kind of knowledge to do this. Who are you?"

"I am Lord Gakee."

Lord Gakee appeared his normal age, and he gave a kiss to the younger Doris.

Craig woke up from his dream. It was seven o clocks in the morning. Craig wondered what else is in the box that he dug up. There were a lot of papers and disks inside.

Craig goes to his computer, and he types in Craig Galuta. The search ended and Craig was reading about the past.

Something caught his eye. Something about Craig Galuta's death. With speed, Craig took his mouse and he clicked to see how his grandpa died.

"One week ago, after a strong PBA match against the two top PBA champions. Craig Galuta wins the last television champion ship. On July 1st a rig, an eighteen-wheeler hit Craig from behind and killed him instantly. Craig leaves a wife, two sons and one daughter and Craig, being very paranoid person, wants us to put this in the paper now. Craig was friends with journalists from this newspaper and a few police officers and Craig's wife is about to give birth and did not want any complications during the birth. Craig did not want his wife to know that he got hurt or died before the birth of his children. Craig had a feeling that the children can sense the feelings of the mother.

If there was a tie on this championship the pro bowlers would travel out of the country and throw one ball for a tie breaker. This is Craig's message for his wife.

"Dear Sweetheart. I had one of those dreams again. The dreams are much stronger now than before. Sorry that there was no tie breaker. If I had won, I did it for all of us. You are always in my heart. If I don't make it back, I love you and our children. I am so sorry that I was not there for you. I hope our children grow up to be kind and sweet like you. Look for what we have and look at what we love. I am sure our driver will take you to the hospital as planned. So sorry that I was not there to see our little babies be born. Love you."

Craig went outside and he looked at a huge pine tree right smack in the back yard. Craig ran to the shed and grabbed the shovel and digs near the tree. Right on the tree trunk Craig could make barely out was carved CG plus AMG. Craig took three steps and started to dig. Craig found a briefcase. Craig opened it up and yells out Holy shit. Craig saw One hundred dollars' bills inside the briefcase, it must have been millions and millions of dollars. Craig wanted his wife to be taken care of without having to pay any taxes on the money.

"I am so glad we kept the house."

Craig ran to his bedroom and lays the suitcase on the floor.

"What would my grandfather do with all this money? We don't need it. I know."

Craig took his bicycle out of the shed and rode to the post office, took two overnighter boxes and files home.

Craig split up the money. It came to one point five million dollars for two boxes. Before Craig sealed the two boxes, Craig puts in a letter in each box. It read 'my grandpa gave this to his wife over a thousand years ago. I found it and now I give it to you. May you use it for your clients to use it in good health'. The first box is addressed to "My One Wish" and the second to "My High Hopes foundation".

These two groups give a wish for children who are very sick.

"I hope this money will bring some happiness for some child."

"Hi dad. I need a ride to the post office I need to mail this right away."

"Ok, let's go."

At lunch time Craig and his family were eating lunch.

"I found something that Grandpa gave Grandma and she never opened it up," Craig said.

"What son?"

"Well dad, you will never believe me. It was three million dollars."

In the high pitch voice the mother talks.

"Where is it, let me see. I need the money."

"I don't have it anymore. I gave it away to people who need it more than us. I gave it to charity."

"How dare you do that. That is my money!"

"No! It's Grandma's money and I think Grandpa wanted me to do that. How can you say that? Some people might not see tomorrow. A child who looks happy today, will never be happy again. Can you really say you need this money, as we have everything? More than money. We have our health. You should be ashamed of yourself. You are the one who should be teaching us kids to be more caring not the other way around."

Craig's father was impressed. The next part of the formula is not to be put in for about five hours. Craig opened the time capsule and saw for music cd's. Craig put one disk in and the first song played was Beat It, by the king of soul. The second song was by a very hot gorgeous woman, Madonna, Vogue. Craig goes to the computer and Google's "Madonna Vogue". And YouTube had the video of this song and Craig goes and does the dance.

CHAPTER 21

Summer started the new school year, ninth grade, and Craig looked in the time capsule, he didn't put it back. He found another video of grandpa. He put it in the blue ray, a DVD which he labeled 2. Craig put numbers on the CD's as they were all blank.

"Hi this is Craig, again this video might be the sixth. I don't know, I didn't number them. I know the last one might be me telling you what is in my time capsule. Today I talk about when I was in ninth grade. I bowled what is called candle pins, they are small balls and the pins look like candle sticks. I took my own balls. Maybe I might find them, and you might get to see them; I don't think candle pins are around as it was dying out. Anyway, during what we call gym class, I get one hundred and thirty-two score. The coach puts the pressure on me and said get a strike, I throw an eight and get a B in gym. I was not a class pet, and I was not a jock, I hold my own. I did not drink nor smoke. They might call me Mr. Goody two shoes." Craig stopped and said to him, "Wow Grandpa sounds just like me."

Craig ran downstairs and he starts to dig the hole again. Craig's mother comes running out. "Craig why are you digging up again?" "I think grandpa might have candle pin balls down there. I need to see if he did. I heard this year in school they are going to bring back an old bowling game; I think it might be candlepins." Craig dug and dug, the hole got deeper, just a little deeper than before, and he hit something. He found candle pins balls in a plastic bag were in a bowling bag. He opened the bag and saw a score card. So excited, "Ma, Ma," Craig cried. "Look what I found, AH ha, ha." Mother comes running out.

"Craig what did you find?"

"I found the balls and I found his score card too." Mother said no way. Craig opened it up. Surprisingly, the paper was still good as the bag was sealed tight and the bowling bag was waterproof. In nineteen ninety he bowled a one hundred thirty-five game, a one hundred and fifteen and a one sixty game. "I hope I can bowl as well as him."

"You can dear, with practice." Craig pulled out more bags, a whole lot of them. Vipers, "Oh look at this. Boston Red Sox Yes."

"Wow. Orange balls. I think they are comic balls. I think these balls can glow in the dark."

Craig's mother looks up towards heaven and says, "Thank you grandpa for your blank junk, it's not like I have enough junk all ready." The wind blew a soft breeze and through the wind it sounded like laughter.

Craig took the time capsule, and he opened the box again and sees another video. Craig labeled this one three. "Hi this Craig again. Do you know they call me Craigal the bagels and I got the cream cheese." As Craig heard this, he says, "Oh no shit, even Grandpa's day they said the say the same thing. Things just don't change."

CHAPTER 22

Trip

Craig on the DVD is talking. "My wife and I we are in London."

As Craig looked around and then said to his wife, Alice, "Hey sweetheart, look, two people are fighting. Let's zoom in, I think he is someone famous."

Alice says, "We should stay away."

"No way," Craig said softly and loud.

A tall thin woman with long blond hair was talking very loudly so all the people around could hear.

"Paul you are a nobody and you're a has-been. You don't sing with anyone new or famous. People don't know who you are."

She looked at a person with a video camera.

"Here they come now, the paparazzi and I bet they don't know who you are and they know me."

"Who are you?" Craig said to the woman.

And Craig looked at Paul McCartney.

"Sorry, I heard this fighting," Craig said. "Say, are you Paul McCartney? Did you do an awesome song by the greatest singer, Steve Wonder, Ebony and Ivory, together we sing in harmony."

Paul said, "Yes."

"Wait Paul, there is another one, please wait for a second. The King of soul. People call him the King of Soul, Michael Jackson." Say, Say, Say "what you will. As Craig turns around like the king. But Craig says wait, wait. There is another one too.

"Paul there is another song. I want you to help me sing this song please."

Craig was all excited seeing Paul.

"We can go right to the end part. I will start. I'll be singing the kings part, the dog gone girl is mine."

"No, no she mine."

Craig says, "Wait! Wait! Wait! Paul you really want her."

Craig pointed to the woman who was yelling at him. Craig says loudly,

"You can have her. See Yaw!"

Craig turned telling his wife lets scoot now. Paul yelled, "Wait get back here! That's a dirty trick. I don't want her, get back here now!" As Paul chased Craig and his wife down the street and he caught up to the wife who still has the video rolling. Paul catches up to Craig and taps Craig on the shoulder, Craig thought he was going to knock him out but instead gives him a high five. Paul says,

"I could not have planned this any better. Thank you. Look right over here, this is my favorite pub. I be happy to buy you and your wife a cold one."

"Thank you, Paul. We don't drink, but if they have coke we take that, soda, soda coca cola."

Craig goes in the time capsule and takes a DVD. It was Walter Ray William's video, this has 's inside a two DVDs horseshoes, and how to bowl.

"What in the world is horseshoes?" said Craig.

When Craig learnt about an ancient game, it looks so fun. And after he watched that he put on the bowling video. Craig received a lot of information by watching and listening to a man who was alive over nine hundred years ago.

CHAPTER 23

Saturday, Craig was with his father all day. They went into the Xspeen Company and his father showed him where they conducted the experiments. They took an elevator down one floor and the room was huge. The building went thirty-five miles. There was an opening that Craig could barely see. It was for a vent and had a closed square made of tin for the intake of the air. The size was about three feet by three feet in diameter.

"So, let's take a ride," Dad said.

To the right was a golf cart. Craig and his father drove looking at different tables with computers and what Craig saw was a vent, yes indeed a vent.

"This room is top secret. Don't say anything to anyone about this room, not even your mother or your sisters."

Craig said ok. Craig couldn't understand what he saw, anyway. He saw the huge square made of tin for the vent and his father turned around.

-Craig's farther was showing him the experiments they were doing at Xspeen . To give Craig brief tour of what is to become.

Son it is ten thirty, we did not have any supper; I am going to call your mother, we are going out for supper. "Ok dad. "

Craig's father pulls out his phone. Says, Call dear. Phone said calling Pear. No call dear. Phone said calling fear. Father says I hate the freaking phone. He dials the phone manually; Hanna picks up the phone. "Hello!"

"Hi sweetheart. Craig and I did not eat any supper so taking Craig and we are going to Belling Tower to eat."

"Ok sweetheart. I will be waiting for you."

"Our Company just bought 85 percent of the Garden of Eden restaurant," his dad said to Craig.

"Wow!" said Craig

"I have 45 percent shares of this company and they close at eleven. I hope to get there before they close."

"Let's go!" said Craig

Craig jumped in the van and put on his seatbelt.

"We hired a new manager two weeks ago, she is well known as Ms. Former U S A, and they have ten years waiting list for hiring any new employees. All the men are dying to work there. I was told she is a looker," Craig's father said.

"She is a looker dad?" said Craig.

"Son, do they teach you kids anything in school?"

Very surprise they were slow it was 10:55 p.m. and the place was dead. There was a sign upon entering the building. It read, If you come in, you must be eating or drinking or you can't stay and hold up our seats I'm sorry. They had all kinds of men just look at the new boss. She is an eye opener.

The grills were clean they were ready to leave at eleven sharp. The hot skinny Hostess with long blond hair said, "Can I help you?"

"Yes," Craig's father said wearing his work badge. "I'd like to place an order please."

"Oh," she said. The hostess took the two men and showed them to their seats. "Please sit down." The Hostess, tall, hot, wearing the company issue mini skirt, wearing black un collant. "That's why it's call the Garden of Eden," the Hostess said, "I will get the waitress."

The hostess runs into the kitchen yelling, "Turn on the grill, turn on the grill. We got two people." The voice of a girl said what the frig-

--swear bleep it's ten fifty-five, come on. The manger comes out of the office, the new manager Shelia. She was also wearing manager's issue uniform. Being six feet tall and a former U S A pageant winner, she got the top of the line wardrobe. One-piece black dress, six inches above the knee, it might have been seven, it was so sweet. She was wearing the Italian black collants with the non-slip dress shoe.

Shelia says, "What is all this yelling about?"

"The head cook says nothing."

The manager goes outside. She sees the stockholder, she asks him, "Hi sir, can I…"

As the manager was talking to Mr. Abraham Galuta, the head cook, a woman, dark skin, blazing hot, comes out the kitchen. Craig sees a name, Sam. In place Craig waves to her and blows a kiss to her, his father was talking to the manager. Sam goes back in the kitchen, and they could hear her yelling at the other cooks, "the little boy blew me a kiss."

The whole kitchen was laughing, and he could hear them saying, "Sammy has a new boyfriend." The manager said, "Please let me get the waitress."

The waitress comes out she is also a hot woman, dark skin skinny but looks like a weightlifter. She has big arms for lifting the trays . She was in great shape. Her name is June. She was also wearing the issue uniform that the Garden of Eden has issue for the ladies, a black hot tight black mini skirt with pin stripe collants. She was wearing a low

heel shoes for not slipping on the kitchen floor.

"Hi, my name is June, may I help you. Sir may I get you a drink?" said the waitress.

Mr. Galuta ordered a bud and Craig ordered a Coke Zero. Craig smiles and blushes. And she smiles too. The manager comes out. "Sir, the grill is ready in a few minutes sorry for the wait."

"No, it's ok, I should have realized the time and you want to go home."

"Yes you are a looker," said Craig.

His father kicked Craig in the leg, and said, "I don't know what he is saying."

The manager had a great sense of humor and laughed, "Thank you."

The waitress comes over to take their order.

"I will have the Chicken Dipper."

Craig says, "I am a meat eater, sweetheart. I want the steak. Any will do, I am not fussy."

June says, "Ok I will get your steak on the grill, ok it will be about five minutes."

The waitress comes back over. "Sir, we are out of Bud, if you got the time we got the beer. Miller beer."

"Ok. I guess a Miller must do. I do have the time, but this Bud is for you."

"No," said Craig. "Have a Coke and smile, See Dad, you don't smile. I'm smiling, you're not smiling when you drink your beer. When I drink my ice-cold Coke, I have a smile on my face. "

Craig and his father ate their meals. The girls were totally awesome.

The waitress handed Craig's father a paper to sign. Craig's father handed June five hundred cash tip. And her eyes lit up like a Christmas tree. She gave him a big thank you and she went to end her shift.

Chapter 24

The Beginning to the End

The next day when it all started a manger name Bizeno. The young man came from Japan to work as a manager for the Garden of Eden. A very funny man with a very funny accent. He had been working for the company for twenty years. A really nice guy who spoke very little English. In the background you could hear some of the workers singing his favorite songs. Like Born in the USA and Sweet Caroline. With two new kitchen help, the other two guys had gotten hit by a flying pasta plate, thrown by the two crazy busters. Now on leave because they lost their minds. Bizeno told the two new guys to clean out the freezer and make it neat. The two men were inside the freezer. Bizeno, who never goes in the freezer, goes in. He helped the two young boys clean the freezer and when he put things against the wall he unknowingly hit the hidden switch. The freezer door locked, the two twin waitresses leaves the building in the nick of time. They heard a loud buzzer and the lights in the restaurant turned red.

Bizeno screamed to the boys. Get over here quick! The floor is opening up. Bizeno tried to open the freezer door but it won't move. The boys got to the other side and when the floor stopped moving, there were stairs leading down. All three of them started to walk down the stairs.

"Stay close," Bizeno said.

As they walked, they came across a cage, it had plastic all around it with holes and metal bars and there was a man, five inches high, lying

86

on what could have been a bed. Tim yells at Biz not to open the cage as he might be mean.

Bizeno said, "Oh come on man, he looks so gentle, and he can't hurt a fly." Bizeno opened the cage and taps the man, he did not move. Bizeno talked to him, "If you can understand me, are you ok. What is your name?"

There was no movement and Fred said, "Let's get out of here; this place looks like it goes for miles."

"You're right. Let's keep on walking straight," Bizeno said.

Bizeno was walking faster than the two boys; Fred was the slowest and he was behind. The creature opened his eyes and escaped the cage. Jumping on Fred and climbing so fast, it bit him on the neck, killing him instantly. Then the creature jumped on the next kid, biting him on the neck as well and killing him very quickly. Bizeno was still walking fast. He said, "Come you guys, walk a little faster. I want to get out of here." Then the creature jumped on Bizeno.

The creature said, "You are not too bright to leave the cage door open. Yes I can hurt a fly and I just killed two and the third is you."

A quick bite in the neck and Bizeno was bleeding to death. The door from the freezer entrance already shut. The building to the Garden of Eden implodes.

A phone call to Mr. Galuta. It was the lawyer of the new manager of Garden of Eden.

"Mr. Galuta the lab got breached. Three people are known to be dead, not by explosion, but by Experiment. We had to destroy the restaurant."

"I see," said Mr. Galuta.

Meanwhile Xmose got his hands on the formula and started to make more of what he was. In this lab they had everything.

Xmose was being smart and made one thousand like him, like clones with different faces. He also had a way to speed up the project and to speed up time, and other invention that were made. The worst of all were the explosives.

CHAPTER 25

In senior year, Craig finished the science project and the science fair was about to begin. No person was to talk about what they were doing until that very day.

"Hi Bill," said Craig

"Hi Craig," said Tim.

"Hi, Tim," said Craig.

"Hi, Craig!" said Bill.

"What are your special projects guys?" asked Craig.

Bill said, "I made a device that does illusions."

"I can take matter that does not move, move," said Tim.

"Wow, great. Mine is to shrink huge matter."

"Well Craig, it looks like you're going to win."

"Well Bill, I don't know yours, and Tim sounds good too."

A man on the loudspeaker starts to talk, "Welcome to the science fair. Everyone has done so well. We usually have only one winner, but this year we had decided to have three winners. It is a three-way tie for Bill Beluga, Tim Tyler and Craig Galuta; I have passes for you three to take a tour in our top secret building of science, the Xspeen center, as your work will be in process."

"Wow, that is so cool, I all ways want to go inside," said Craig, already knowing what is inside.

"Me too," said both Bill and Tim.

The tour was after the graduation, July 10th, and Craig met up with Bill and Tim the day before. They were very excited for the tour. They walked into the woods and came across a strange dirt path.

Across the other side of the world, the beautiful princess, Alice, found a man, George Mcgoodle. As time had shifted for these men they did not know, how many years have passed they did not know. Alice married George and they had a daughter. A smart scientist who created the most powerful energy known to mankind. As this time a few minutes before after time went crazy as the world is being change. All around the three men the world was being destroyed by Xmose.

In the distance they heard a loud explosion. "Tim did you hear that?"

"Yes. Sounded like an explosion."

"It's getting late, we should be headed back,"

"Yes you are right, we should be headed back. Ah it's raining hot pebbles, we need shelter and quick!" So the three men ran and found a stone shed in the middle of nowhere.

"Guys," said Tim, "you think the roof of this shed will hold?"

"Yes Tim, the roof is made of slate it should be fireproof." Craig said. Soon it was midnight.

"Guys, its late and it's still raining with the hot pebbles."

"Yes," Tim said. "Craig. Let's sleep here and before we go, I will call on my cell and tell my mom what has happen and let your moms know as well."

Tim turned on the cell phone and it was dead; the phone was fully charged and it was just dead. Tim and Bill went fast asleep, and Craig closed his eyes. Morning came, and the three men walked outside and smelled a horrid smell, like dead people. Everything around them was burnt; toward the right was a statue figure of a dinosaur.

"That is crazy. This dinosaur it was not there before," said Bill

Bill went over to it.

"Guys, who do you think put this here? Is this some kind of joke?"

"No Bill, it's not no joke. Let's get out of here now!" yelled Craig.

As the three men started to walk so did the dinosaur.

It was a T-Rex; Tim heard something and looks back.

"Guys we should run and now," Tim said.

Bill and Craig looked behind and they saw the dinosaur right behind them. The three men ran fast. So fast that they did not see a hole that was just in front of them, and they into the hole.

The three men landed on something soft. It was weird because they were in the middle of nowhere. As the light shone, they looked up and saw a clear blue sky. They were on a street called Middle Lane Rd. Craig's Great Aunt Maggness lived in a house three houses down, but she passed away over 20 years ago, a great woman.

"Well, guys, we are somehow in Boston," said Craig.

"What?" said Bill. "Boston? Are you going nuts Craig? How can we land up in Boston? We were in High Dale just a few moments ago?"

"Well, Bill, this house that we are looking at is my great aunts."

Tim said, "Yes Craig. I remember. Right here right?"

"Yes, Tim, this is the house."

Bill said, "Let's knock and see what happens?"

Craig went to the door and rang the bell. Craig's great Aunt Maggness comes to the door.

"Hi, Boys. Come on in. I made some cookies."

"No, thank you," said Craig."

"Oh, come on," said Bill.

The three men walk inside. Craig saw a stairway leading up. Craig opened a door leading somewhere else.

Craig knows something is not right here. Craig can't put it together. The inventions that just got invented how can they be fully working. Craig closed the door and runs downstairs, As the two men are about to eat the cookies, Craig threw the plate on the ground, the cookies burned a hole on the floor. the two men drop the cookies on the floor, and they ran out of the door. The aunt screamed with a loud piercing noise and the whole neighborhood started to chase the three men. They came to a huge hill. As they climbed the hill, the top opened and they started to fall. Two arrows fallen, From Tim's belt the other Craig's baggy shirt. "Are you two OK," asked Craig.

At the time when the three boys ran from the Aunt's house, the illuion machine only saw large people attacking, but they were actual Xmose's army. They were small and fast.

"It's only I, Bill did not make it," Tim said.

"I just saw Bill running with us."

"Bill ate the cookies. He told me how to fight the illusion just before he died Craig this is what you have to do."

The Illusions were powerful, but the poison that was given made it stronger for Tim can handle as the arrow from were the heart was finally fallen off.

Craig and Tim ran for miles and they came across a small hill as the reach the top the fallen into a deep hole.

In a place with solid blackness, where they can't see anything, a small light began to become brighter, so it was easier on the eyes. A small man, the size of Craig's thumb, came in and started to talk.

"I don't know how you managed to survive the bomb and I don't know how you survive my other traps, but here it ends. You two will die here."

"Who are you?" asked Craig.

The man said, "I am Xmose, the ruler of Xmotoians. We were created by humans, we were bred to kill. I took the formula, and I created my people."

Craig thought, "I am responsible for this."

"Why do you want to kill? We can live in peace forever."

The Xmotoian's said, "No, we were created to take over your planet and we shall."

The two Xmotoians took spears that had the illusion poison, and they threw them. One hit Tim on the chest and Craig got hit on the left side of his chest, but he had been lucky. There was a silver dollar in his pocket. The second spear hits Tim and now Tim is fully unaware of what going on.

In twenty minutes had gone the two boys' walkout. They were sitting in a jail cell made of toothpicks. It was too funny to escape. The Xmotoians solder told them to walk up the stairs and leave. They saw the stairway but it did not lead anywhere, except a hundred feet drop to death.

"Come Craig," said Tim. "Let's leave now."

"No, Tim!" Craig cried out. "It's a drop. The stairs go nowhere. We are going to fall to our death. We are going to die."

Xmose heard this. He called out his people and they started to run towards Craig. Craig tried to pull Tim to follow but he pushed Craig off. Tim had the arrow in his heart, and he only saw what the illusion poison wanted him to see. Tim ran up the stairs and he fell to his death. Craig had nowhere to go. In the middle of the field was a vent leading down. Craig was far enough away that Xmose did not see where Craig was going. Craig lifted the cover and climbed down on a ladder.

The hole was lit up by small lights all around and Craig ended up in the lab.

"Gail Mcgoodle is gone. She might have been a great help. Do you think Craig stills has the gift?" said Sakra.

"Well," said the Doctor, "I don't know, but Craig is our only hope."

As Craig was lying on the bed, the doctor talks to Sakra.

"It is not certain, but it looks like the two women survive the blast. Officer Jones is doing his research."

Sakra with a sad voice, "The time capsule was destroyed. What a shame. All that history gone."

"No. It was protected by the force field. That is how Craig and the two boys survived."

The chemical from the blast did not reach the boys. They were very lucky that the rock debris.

CHAPTER 26

The Rise of Xmose

Meanwhile up one floor. Xmose was talking to his people and planning for attack. "Go now. Find this suitcase. We need what's in it."

Twenty-five of the Xmotoians were getting ready to go outside. There were no people around. All the townspeople were afraid and had left the only place that was safe. Craig's family left for a safe place, but it was the final resting place, as Craig's father was responsible for the destruction of the planet and making Craig responsible too.

Craig woke from the bed that he was on and he went to the computer to work on a formula to make the Xmotoians live longer and be a little friendlier.

Not fully understanding just happen in the head of Craig's knows he must do something to correct a big mistake.

After Craig had finished the formula, a voice came over the intercom. "We are the Xmotoians. We will start our attack three weeks from today. You will all die, the doctor gave the formula to the professor Doctor. Flattworth."

Craig yells out, "Let me go up there one more time and let me speak to them, maybe I can say something."

Doctor Framharr said, "Craig you can, but it won't work."

Craig being stubborn went up and to see Xmose. He walks about a mile or two wearing a metal vest.

Xmose said to Craig. "You're back?"

"Yes, I am. We can live in peace. Why do you want to die, it's plainly senseless," Craig said with a concerned voice.

Xmose said, "We are bred to fight, fight to the end. No human will survive, all dead as we are the soul survivors!"

As Xmotoians surrounded Craig with theirs spears, Craig ran right on them, squashing them like grapes. Hearing them yelling retreat, retreat as they started to run in the other direction to keep alive. As Craig went to safety, he heard on the loudspeaker, another voice, not the leader. He said,

"My name is Xzeem. I just killed the leader Xmose. We lost a lot of lives today. We have had enough killing and we choose to live in peace. Do you accept?"

As Craig climbed down the ladder, tears rushed down his face, thinking in ten seconds he could have wiped out life that he had created or help to create.

Doctor. Framharr came on the loudspeaker and said, "We accept your terms."

Xmose was on Craig's pant leg very much alive.

The Doctor said, "Let us go. We will eat something; the war is over."

Craig and the Doctor left the room and Xmose jumped off Craig's leg and he goes to the computer. He jumped on the computer and started typing. He saw the formula that was not used for him. Xmose put in a small device on the computer and downloads everything on the computer.

Xmose saw something. "Ha, Ha, ha!!!!! I can't believe this." Xmose was a sick man, and he pulled down his draws and peed on the computer and the computer started to short circuit and he ran to the elevator door. On his two-way radio, "I got the formula. I'm uploading it to you. Use the two dead people. Use their blood and I shall be there in forty minutes. You will never guess what I found out."

Chapter 27

The Journey It Finally Happened

There was an elevator about twenty feet away. Xmose activated the elevator door and escaped.

"Calling Xzeem! Come in."

"Yo."

"How long until the formula will be ready? I don't know how much time we have. We might have hours or seconds. I don't know."

"It should be ready in two hours, sir. I can't rush it."

"Ok. If I die, give me the shot anyway."

"Yes sir. How long do you think it will take you to get here?"

"I think about an hour. I'm riding a little faster than the human running. I gave them a little surprise."

"Hey, Doctor! do you hear that? It's the fire alarm!"

"Yes, Sakra."

Everyone, who was in the other computer room, were about to enter the mess hall when they heard the smoke alarm. Craig noticed the computer was going up in smoke and they also smelled something gross.

"What the heck is that smell? I know it's not the computer!" said Craig very loudly.

"I think someone, or something just pissed on our computer."

A loud voice came over the intercom, with a loud laugh.

"Yes, it was me. Xmose! Yes. I just piss on your computer. I am very much alive and well. How is it, that all of you people are so stupid and created us to be so smart? Maybe we should keep you all alive so you can be our slaves. You humans are plainly a joke."

"Doctor. Framharr starts to talk.

"Well, Xmose, the jokes on you and you think you have the upper hand. You have actually two weeks to live. We got the reading when you changed the time."

"Well Doctor! The joke is on you. I got the formula for our cure, and we will live for a much longer time. Oh, by the way. I downloaded all the information on the experiment that stands right beside you too."

Craig looked down at his pant leg. He saw a tiny microphone and it had a camera. Xmose was watching him and listening to him.

"Doctor! What is Xmose talking about? I am an experiment?"

"Well yes, Craig. Your father, your great grandson, dug up your grave and he took a cell that was located near where your heart would be and we planted it in your mother, your grandson's wife. Your wife also got dug up and Alice was going to go into your grandson's wife as well and both of them would become twins and rule the planet. As you were our secret weapon. Alice's cell was very active. It disappeared and we thought it got destroyed, but it landed on the back of Doctor Matterson's shirt. It must have fallen off and landed on the seat of his car. When his wife took the car, the cell managed to go into her.

"You somehow sensed this and failed Kindergarten to meet her."

"I wonder if she is still alive," said Craig.

"Well Craig, she is; she is in Ireland. The force field was activated, and she is safe and her daughter too. But when you see her, please don't tell her that she is an experiment. She might get a relapse or something."

"I won't. How can I escape this building and how can I survive outside the force field?"

"We have a special suit that you can put on. It is bullet proof. No spears or sharp objects can penetrate this. The helmet will close when you go outside the force field. It will only open in a safe zone. If, by chance, you are in an illusion, the helmet will stay closed, and you will think otherwise. This suit is programed to feed you. And it has a built-in bathroom, so when you need to go, you can go and the waste will come out the back end. Take this pill. Good. This pill will make all foods or drink taste like shit, if you eat anything out of the safe zone that has poison in it. The illusion that Xmose has is very powerful, and he will stop at nothing to have you killed. You will stop eating any food or any drink and the poison won't harm you. When you see a blue object that object is good, there are several refrigerators with special pad locks and you will know the combination when you get there. Xmose and his gang don't know what they are, and they hold no importance to them. When you get to the end, you will see a blue door. Press the combination to open the door and press button 6 and that will take you to the lobby to leave the building. There is a car outside. It's battery powered and has a gasoline charger so you can keep on going without stopping. It has GPS and is fully automatic. Just type in where you want to go, and you are off. You can sleep and you don't have to do anything. I don't think there is going to be any water out there, but if so, your car can become a boat."

"Well, that is good, but I want to use the computer first, if you don't mind. I need to find out something."

"Of course, please."

Xmose reached his camp and was all smiles.

Xzeem had a big smile on his face too. "Well boss, it's ready right now! Are you ready?"

"Yes, give it to me."

Xzeem gives Xmose the shot. A small prick and he was in pain, screaming so loudly, swearing everything in the book.

"What the hell did you do to me?"

Xmose began to grow. He grew to five feet eight inches tall. Xzeem gave himself the shot and he started to grow, too. Xzeem gave a few of the Xmotoians the shot and they too grew, and now they need new clothes, too.

Thirty of them had made batches of the formula and they gave themselves the shot and started to grow. The whole group of one thousand, less twenty-six, ready for battle. Meanwhile, one flight down.

Craig walked into the other computer room that was not damaged. Craig typed in his father's name. Craig found his grandson, Abraham Galuta.

Craig stopped and yelled out.

"Wait a minute! Wait one minute!"

"Yes Craig?"

"You wanted me to take over this planet? Why would I want to waste my time to rule this huge piece of rock? I would be bored stiff. I would have everything; I would not need any money. I could take any women that I wanted, if I damn choose, because I would be the ruler. My life would be threatened, though. For every person could be someone who wanted this power. So, I am glad this did not work out."

"Craig is very practable. Running the planet would be more of a headache than a luxury."

Doctor. Framharr stopped and thought. Craig is more human than he realizes.

"Wow. I never thought of it that way."

Craig gets a message on the screen.

"This is Doctor Galuta. I am going to put in a code on the talk show the Yacker. The code will be shown briefly. It will be the episode of 28th of October. Find it. If my experiment fails, this and two others will stop the disaster."

Craig types in episode 28 "The Yacker" Bless the YouTube episode 28 the Yacker.

Craig watches the screen. A pair of numbers flash onto the screen, 28 and 62. Craig wrote these numbers down and put it in his pocket.

Craig said, "Thirty-five miles. I have to walk thirty-five miles to the door leading outside. Why in the hell couldn't you make a door closer? Or put a few exits in the middle."

"Craig."

The sweet, soft voice of Nurse Sakra said, "We had to do it for safety reasons."

"Craig," said the doctor.

"Yes, Doctor?"

"Please put on this suit. The pill should be all set now. You can leave. Please be careful. We do not know how advanced the illusions are."

"Well, let's see, shall we? Maybe I can use it for my benefit."

Meanwhile, up one floor.

Xcroanas and twenty-five other soldiers drove small trucks. To a human, the wheels would look huge and the trailer enormous. Xcroanas drove the crane to a loading dock ten feet from the elevator door. Xcroanas typed in a few numbers on his pad and the loading doors opened. The truck had booster rockets, and the truck flew. Going past five large vehicles and then landed safely down.

When Xcroanas reached the ground, the area looks perfectly normal. The force field preserved everything. The people who had left the town, looking for safety, died.

Xcroanas found Craig's house and blows away the front door. He entered the kitchen. There was the suitcase that Xmose wanted. Xcroanas drove the truck into the house and removed the suitcase. Using the crane, the solders hooked up the suitcase. Half-way up, the suitcase came crashing down and luckily nothing got broken.

"You idiots!" cried Xcroanas. "Be careful!"

"Yes, boss." "Xcroanas, when you get back, we need to make you and the other solders larger and make a larger transport so we can leave here."

"No need, sir. I passed five transporters when I left. They are very large."

"Good, we will be expecting Craig very shortly. Short, ha, ha, ha."

The trucks sped away. They had triple their speed. Rushing through streets and wooded areas to get back to the base quickly. The trucks had blasters and vaporized trees and any obstacles that were in the way.

"Hey Xzeem. Did Xcroanas come back yet with the suitcase?"

"He is already here. They already got their shots, and they are now looking at the videos. We are going to kill Craig very quickly and easily."

"Good. Let's start the illusion. We should make some houses so if we need to retreat, we can."

The room turned bright red and buildings started to appear. Up on the ceiling, freshly painted light blue for the sky.

Craig walked inside the elevator door. Xmose had not deactivated it. Doctor Framharr screamsed.

"Yes! Xmose did not deactivate the elevator."

Very softy, Doctor Framharr said to his coworkers,

"In case Xmose is listening. Craig will destroy them. He has to."

Craig is inside the elevator which has two buttons, one and two. Craig pushes the number two button and says out loud,

"That's nice. Now I have to take a crap."

Inside the elevator there was an intercom, and the light was on.

"Craig, this is Xmose. We can see you and hear you. Don't you dare take a crap on my floor." Craig replied,

"Your floor? Are you serious?"

"Oh, just get up here so we can kill you quick and easy."

"If you wish. You know what I did, I wanted to help you. Give you a better purpose in life. If you solely want destruction and death, so be it. I have no choice in killing you. It would be a waste of a great achievement."

"Bla, Bla, Bla."

Xmose shut off the intercom and started talking.

"Ok. Listen up. In a few minutes, Craig the human will be coming through those doors. Let us toy with him for a bit. Let us use the illusion random function."

The elevator stopped. The door opened.

"Wow, the smell of clean fresh air. I think the Doctor did not know what he is talking about. I am outside. The sky is a beautiful blue and there's heat from the sun. The building all around me looks normal. Excuse me, sir. Can you tell me what the day this is? I simply forgot."

No answer. The man kept on raking.

Craig looked at his watch and it was about seven o clock, Monday morning. And when he looked up, there was his school.

Craig went inside. The classmates looked real enough. Craig went to his home room and sat down and very quickly he goes right to the classroom.

Craig was in his English class. What Craig did not know; he was in his first day of school. And he was going for the ride of his life.

"I am your new English teacher this year. My name is Ms. Moon. And don't you dare make fun of my name, or you will be in a living in hell. I am going pass out a total of five books. The first one, here it is. Everybody got a book? Good.

The author is "Craig Steven Glatky". This is a very usual book. No title, now open the book. No chapters."

Craig yelled out, "No Chapters, no title?! What kind of book is this?"

"Yes, Craig no chapters. The book is labelled One through Five. Five books are one story. It starts out in a Mansion and only horror thereafter. On the last page of every book, it gives an outline, page by page, and line by line of importance. This story is a mystery and a horror. I feel like the whole class will like this book."

"Craig, I hope you read this book. I know you hate to read."

"Yes, Ms. Moon, but how did you know?"

"I know everything. That is why my name is Moon."

"Well, Craig. Ms. Moon is right. You hate to read," said Bill.

"Yes, you're right. I hate to read."

Time passed and Craig was walking home. He never walked backwards. Craig always kept on walking forward. His house appeared and he went inside. Not hungry, nor did he see any parents. Went right to his room that it was supposed to be. Craig turned to the last six pages. He read the outline.

When Craig just closed his eyes for a second, the next day appeared. Craig opened the front door. Instead of walking to the left, he walked to the right. Craig walked about 4 miles this time and his school just appeared again.

Craig opened the door and landed right in the English class again.

"Good morning class. How is the story? You should be on page 98 by now.

Craig, I've a question for you. Did Mr. Cadpis die before or after the devil came through the porthole?"

Craig said, "Right after Cadpis died is when the devil fully appeared."

"Very good answer, it looks like you are really reading the book."

Craig stepped out of the classroom and he found himself outside the school once more.

"Hey Xmose, come on, let's make this harder. He is not reading the book and we must make the questions harder."

"Are you serious? Perhaps I should kill you for being a stupid dude. The humans are the stupid ones. Are you a freaking human? There are no words in this book, Nit wit. It has empty pages. He only sees what he wants to see."

Craig gets inside his house and goes down to the cellar; the door does not want to be open. Without any thought, Craig goes upstairs and sleeps. Five seconds later and he's fully awake and ready for school again.

"Hey, Xmose. I got a great idea."

"What?"

"The nurse, what is her name? Yes, Sakra. Let's get a sample of her blood and make us a woman Xmotoian. We will use the face of the girl in first grade, that was in Craig's head, add a few years to it and see what happens. As it will be our last resort for killing him."

"You surprise me. That is a great Idea! Midnight tonight, take three good men and get the sample of her blood."

Time now seemed to be a little slower than usual. Normal time its 1 o clock and Craig felt a little hungry. The school had not appeared yet. Craig kept on walking. In a small cage was a box. A metal box with a keypad. Craig thought about the combination. The keyboard had zero to nine and a plus and a minus and a divide symbol and a x for multiply. That's weird. Craig decided what numbers meant the most to him. seven and six. So Craig pushed the number seven button and the plus sign and the number six button and he pushed one and three and the door opened. Inside this small refrigerator was a bagel with cream cheese and lox and a Coke Zero. When Craig ate the sandwich and drank his Coke, he had a smile on his face.

"Ah the real thing. Wait a second. I was going to school again, wasn't I? Oh, this must be an illusion. I must keep this to myself and play along."

Craig walked about one mile and he reached the school. It was about three in the afternoon in real time. Eight o'clock in the morning on the illusion time. Craig opened the door, went to the home room and he sat down. In front of his eyes, the room changed and he is in the English classroom.

"Class. On Monday we are going to have our first test on the book that you should be now finishing up. Here is the second book.

Now take this piece of paper, we are going to take a test."

"Um, excuse me, teacher. You said Monday for the test."

"Just do the test and shut up!" the teacher shouted. Craig smiled. "I love tests!"

With no expression, no comment, the teacher just passed a blank piece of paper.

"Now answer the five questions and you got thirty minutes to do it."

Craig is confused. He does not see anything on the paper. But he takes out his pen anyway and answers to nothing. Craig thinks,

"What can I put on the piece of paper? I know what."

Craig wrote: You are a bone head. Stupid is, as stupid does. Your mother eats crap. You smell like dead dog piss.

Craig passed the paper in. The teacher corrected the paper very fast.

"Great job, Craig. One hundred percent. I am so glad you are reading the book."

"Well, thank you. I think this book is so great. I can't wait to read the second book."

Craig opened the second book as he saw nothing in it. Craig just sat in the classroom and watched what happened. There was no change. An hour passed. Nothing happened. Craig opened the door to see where it led to. It was outside. No hallway, just outside. Craig walked out and the school disappeared faster than it appeared. Craig kept on walking to the right. Craig walked six miles.

It was ten o clock real time, Xmose boosted the time. Craig opened the door to his house. He entered the bathroom, does his thing and brushes his teeth. Took a shower, as if it felt real.

Craig decided to go and walk outside instead of sleep; changing his routine. When Craig opened the door, the room was slightly lit. Craig looked to the right and he saw buildings, looked like someone's house. To the left, more buildings that looked like real people's houses. Craig decided to keep on walking. Craig walked for about an hour; it was eleven o clock, feeling a little tired, Craig's house appeared and Craig went in. He found a bed and laid down.

"Xmose. Its midnight. We are going in."

"Good, and don't fail me."

Xzeem went down the elevator and turned on his torch. He found the door leading out. There was a keypad lock. Xzeem took out a decoder and opened the door. The hallway was bright, and it led into a huge room, hundred feet by hundred feet with a bunch of computers. Xzeem went to a computer and typed in a word to find where Nurse

Sakra was sleeping. To the far right, near a corner, was a door with a small red light above it. Xzeem and his three henchmen went through the door.

It was a narrow hallway that looked like it could go on for miles. The hallway went about thousand feet. The hallway has a floor that was a belt driven. and slits for chairs. Xzeem and the henchmen were standing on the belt chairs pop up. On the right arm rest was a keypad. Xzeem pressed three numbers that was where Nurse Sakra's sleeping quarters were. The seat had automatic seat belts and the four were fastened as the chairs moved fast on the belt.

The chair stopped and the seat belt disengaged. The four Xmotoians got off the seats and went to the nurse's door.

"You three, stand guard. I am going in."

"Yes, sir."

Xzeem opened the door; it was not locked. He looked at the beautiful nurse. He had a chance to get what he wanted and kill her, but he decided not to kill her. Just the next worst thing that he could do. He gave her a kiss on the lips and he makes love to her. Xzeem put the needle into her body. The needle is so fine she does not feel it. Touching the bone and getting the blood made a very strong ingredient for Xmose.

The Xmotoians have a little different body structure to humans.

"Let's go now. Let's go now!"

With a big smile on Xzeem face, the seats appeared, and he typed in number one for the Lab. A speed preference appeared. Xzeem types in 80 mph. The seat belts fasten and the chairs speed away. It took only a few minutes to get back. The four ran to the elevator door and they were on their way back.

"Hey, Xmose. I got what we wanted. Let's start making the women."

"Very good. Why the big smile? You killed the poor nurse?"

"No. I gave her a nice present. If by chance we die, we shall live."

"And you think this is going to work? How?" said Xmose.

"It felt really good, and I think it might work," laughed Xzeem.

"I don't know. We have to see."

In the lab part of the room, Xzeem and Xmose started making the women. Using Craig's memory for the special girl that he hurt. Making the nice, beautiful girl a monster. How could the Xmotoians be so cruel.

When the first experiment woman appeared, she was mostly, not mostly, all of this new humanbeing so beautiful. Xzeem felt that he was getting too old and he does not have any time left, does not get jealous at what Xmose is about to say.

"You are remarkable. When you kill Craig, I will make you second in command."

"Great. When do I kill him?" she said a huge smile and sharp teeth showing.

"I need to give you a name. Ze'ma. Your name is Ze'ma."

The next day, Craig woke up. He had eight hours sleep and he was off to school. Craig walked about a mile and he reached the school.

The teacher not the English teacher, it was the gym teacher. Xmose wanted to see how strong Craig is and how he reacts with pain.

Craig can see what is going on and he plays the game.

"Ok Class. We are going to run three miles around the tennis courts, and we will see how fast you can run."

Craig said to himself, "this is going to be a waste of my strength." The coach yelled out go. Craig ran slowly, halfway across the second tennis court. Craig is huffing and puffing. And walked the rest of the way.

The Coach yelled out, "Great job, Craig. You're the fastest one here." Craig thought,

"Are you for real? Xmose is not too smart after all, and I am going to make them look so damn silly they might just give up."

"Xmose!"

"Yes."

"Craig can't run for a long distance. He is out of breath. I think the poison that we gave him when we met is taking affect."

"Good, Xzeem."

Craig was a little sore from running, not! Putting on a good show for Xmose. Craig turned around and walked the other direction towards the door. Craig looked at his meter. It was 20 miles away. It was about nine am in the morning. It will take him another thirteen hours to reach the door.

Craig walked. At one o' clock in the afternoon, Craig came across another metal box. It was blue and it was safe. Xmose was too busy making the women and he did not notice that Craig was eating. This time it was a very good chicken salad sandwich and potato salad. And yes, there was a Coke Zero inside. Also, inside the refrigerator, was a toothbrush and floss and a bottle water. There was a bucket nearby. Craig brushed his teeth and flossed, spitting out the water in the bucket.

Craig walked about nine miles, it was six o'clock. There was a restroom and a metal box. Craig used the restroom and then used the metal box. There was a roast beef sandwich and chips and yes, a coke zero.

"Where is Craig now?"

"Craig is at the twenty-mile mark, and he is eating. He has a goofy smile on his face. I don't understand why."

Xmose pressed some buttons on his small device that he had in his pocket. Craig's house appeared. It was a safe place to sleep, but for how long, Craig did not know. Craig wokes up and the watch said six o clock in the morning.

"There are twenty miles standing in my way to get out of here."

Craig started to run a good pace. One mile to go before he stopped and a huge hill appeared in front of Craig.

Craig started to walk up the hill and a dirt path appeared. It got dark but it was light. Like he was outside. It started to rain.

"Funny. I am not getting wet," Craig said to himself. Craig did not say anything when he reached the mansion.

Craig reached a mansion; it looked like a castle. Something out of a story book. Craig rang the doorbell. Nothing happened. Then Craig used the knocker and the door opened.

"Hello, any one here?" Craig yelled.

No answer.

"Hello, any one here?" Craig yelled again. Craig entered the home and yelled. Again, no one answered.

The front door closed and Craig tried to open it, but the front door won't open and Craig felt pain in his chest. The door had very mean faces, scary faces, and a laugh.

"You got five lives left."

"Five lives left? I must be in some kind of game."

Craig is now in a lobby. To Craig's right was a stairway leading up with mean faces. Towards Craig's right of the stairway were two doors with mean faces and straight ahead, a door to the left of the stairway with a happy face.

Craig approached the door and it opened. The hallway looked like it could go on for miles. Towards Craig left, every eight feet, was a door. Craig opened one door. An empty room and one door to Craig's right. About a thousand feet away he could make out something. They looked human.

"Hello. My name is Craig. Where am I?"

No answer. Craig ran. As Craig ran, the further away the people got, and the door that was on Craig's side did not move.

Craig opened the door and walked down the hallway. Counting the doors, and he guessed right, he opened the door and he saw four people. The girl was very thin with very long red hair. An old man, about sixty with balding a U-shape on top of his head and he was very short. And two young children, twins.

"Hi. My name is Craig."

"Yes, Craig. We were expecting you," said the girl with the long red hair.

"Expecting me?"

"Yes, Craig."

The old man with his hoarse voice said,

"You are supposed to lead us out of this house. We are all afraid to leave. You are our only hope."

Craig saw the five books that he was supposed to read in his class. Craig opened the first book and was surprised that there were letters in the book. No chapters, no hints that were in the back. But when Craig touched the book, he absorbed the information. All five books.

Craig knew who was going to die and who was going to live. And Craig was going to change the story as he thinks.

"Now you four must listen to me very carefully, especially you two young ones. If you don't, you will die. Please listen to me."

The young boy and girl said yes, but they don't listen, as they look at each other cross their fingers behind them.

"Please take a torch."

Craig talks to Zed, the old man.

"Please hold the young children's hands and don't let go."

Craig opened the door and entered the hallway. Something made Craig reach into his right pocket. There was a weapon. A small pistol made of plastic. A small video screen on top, it had a number, two thousand.

The hall suddenly stopped and it split two ways. By reading the book, it did not matter which way to go. So to make the twins feel important, Craig asked them which way to go.

The young girl yelled out, "Left!"

The young boy yelled out, "Right!"

"What are these two kids doing? Do they know what's going to happen?"

The group started to walk on the left of the hallway.

Down in the living quarters of Nurse Sakra and Doctor Framharr, the group of scientists were at the mess hall eating lunch. Nurse screamed, "Ow!!"

"What is wrong, Sakra?"

"My left arm is sore."

She lifted her sleeve and saw a small red dot turning black and blue. The doctor looked at it and said,

"Well nurse. Looks like you got a bite or someone or something put something into your body. Please go to the sick bay and we'll check you out. Officer, make sure the elevators and stairways are sealed, so nothing comes in. Just leave the intercom on, incase Craig comes back."

As of right now, Craig has no way of coming back. Deep in the house, Craig and the four new companions walked. The hallway became pitch black.

"Hey guys, please turn on your torches. The danger is coming."

Out of nowhere, a small creature appeared in front of Craig. Still armed with the small pistol, Craig shot the creature. With a low clicking sound, the weapon goes off.

The two twins cried as if the sound was so loud and they had never heard a weapon go off.

"Hey, are you two ok? The sound was not loud, why are you crying?"

The boy spoke very fast. So fast, Craig could not understand him.

"The noise was very loud, what was it? The crying of someone being in pain, who was it?"

Craig could hear what they were saying, as the special suit translated everything being said.

The hallway started to descend. And the hallway splits up again, the left side had light and looked safe, but the right side was pitch black.

"Now everyone listens up. This here is a trap. We must go to the right side of the hallway to escape."

The boy twin whispered to the old man.

"I need to tie my shoe."

The old man let go of the twin's hand and the boy twin pulled out a fake hand. The boy twin and girl twin were wearing white gloves and suits.

The twins waited as the three walked down into the darkness and then the twins started to run in the bright hallway. There was a very loud scream. Like someone just got killed.

"Twins are you ok?"

"Oh dear!"

"What is wrong, old man?"

"The twin boy's hand. Just his hand. It just came off, off, something ate the boy right under me."

Craig walked over.

"This is a fake hand. The twins are dead. We must keep on going. I have no clue how to get out, but I know we must keep on going straight."

The torches were not giving out much light, the three people kept on walking. A huge creature appeared. There was a small light to show where it was. Craig got out his pistol and started to shoot the creature. It took five shots to take it down.

"Are you two ok?"

"Yes."

"Craig. I am very scared."

"Yes, I know red. This house is one big trap. How did you four get in here?"

Craig knows how, but he wanted to hear from the source.

"Well, our great, great, great grandfather passed away and he left the house to us four.

My twin brother and sister and my uncle Zed. We were very close to grandpa. We would help him. But we did not know he was dealing in magic. Wait I remember something?"

"What, please tell me?"

"He mentioned that if we ever get inside the house and he is not here, we must find a light or something to kill the sprits."

"Ok great, that is what we are looking for. Great."

A big brown door appeared in front of Craig. The door was pretty huge. It stood ten feet tall. Craig pushed the door, and it opened.

Apparently, he was outside; but still in the house. The house was an illusion within an illusion.

"Please come with me. We must walk straight. We shall follow the path. We can turn off our torches for now."

The mansion was getting bigger by every one hour. Further and further and deeper into the house they went.

Just in front of Craig was a Grizzly bear. The bear was terrifying. Craig found himself a sword and he took it out, ready for battle. Zed, the bald hair man, jumped in front of Craig and started pounding the bear. Zed grabbed the bear's neck and killed him. Craig was very surprised.

"Ok, let us keep on walking."

As Craig walked, it appeared to be five miles in the house. A wooden door appeared, and Craig pushes it open. They were back in the house. Craig looked back to see if the door was there, and it had disappeared. Craig continued to walk and it got pitch black and he turned on his torch.

"Zelda, Zed, please turn on your torches. Hey, look at this a room."

To Craig's left was an open door. More like a small closet with a refrigerator inside and a couple of cabinets on the wall. They looked blue so Craig thought they would be safe to eat. And they were. Craig's watch didn't seem to work in the house. But on the padlock there was a time.

The clock had two times, one time was the last time the other box was open, and the new time at this very moment.

Craig pushed several buttons and the door opened. Craig gave the two illusions food, of course it looked like they ate it. Craig took out a meatball sub. Craig breaks open the wrapper and the sandwich was hot. The cheese had melted like it had just come out of the oven. Inside there were six cans of Coca Cola.

"Yes, the real thing. Not my favorite Coke zero, but this is now my second-best coke classic, and this has to do."

Craig opened the Coke Classic. Ice cold. A beaming smile on his face again when he puts the can to his lips and drank it.

Craig put the rest of the cans of Cokes inside his pockets. Craig entered the hallway and heard a voice.

"You dare to come into my home? How dare you. Get ready! You're going to die!"

Craig heard something coming from his pocket, and it felt very funny, but Craig was not laughing. The Coke was vibrating.

"I wonder," Craig said.

Craig took a can of Coke, the can became very warm and it was vibrating very fast. A huge creature. A monster, it looked like a cross between a dinosaur and the creature from the black lagoon. Many hours before…

"Xcroanas, what discs did you look at?"

"Well, Xmose, we saw quite a few. We saw a classroom, a bunch of stupid ass kids, and a half-witted teacher and his wife as a human, pretty damn hot. They called him Kotter. There was a kid they called him the "Barber Barbario." He also appeared in another disc that we saw, three actually. One was Saturday Night Fever, Staying Alive, and Grease. We also saw a disc of men using heavy boulders and rolling them and knocking down objects."

"We can use this to kill that human, Craig! Yes, anything else that will help us?"

"Well, we saw a space television show. We can trap Craig in an illusion, and he can never come out. Oh yes, we saw Craig sitting down listening to music."

"Yes, Yes! Yes! We will play this music and maybe put him in a trance, or we can put him in a television show, and we will kill him with these boulders."

"Not only that but we saw some sheets of paper with holes marking for these boulders that we can use to put holes in these boulders"

"Great, how long will these boulders take to make?"

"It should take about three days or so to make."

"Good. We will use the school illusion with a twist. If he makes it out alive, he will be too weak to fight us and we will crush him."

"How many boulders should I make?"

"Make a hundred and we will use fifty of our solders to roll these massive boulders to destroy Craig, ha ha, ha."

Meanwhile back in the Mansion. Craig shook the can of Coke and opened it up. A bullet of Coke hit the monster and it died.

"We must be very careful, guys, we don't know how many booby traps this house has."

"Yes, you are right Craig. This house does not seem to want to end."

"Yes, Zed you are right."

Craig took his torch out and moved it right to left and straight up. As Craig thought it was total darkness. Craig might have been walking around in circles. Craig kept on walking about fifteen feet and a light appeared. A small table with a blue button shinning bright with a white light.

Right below it, there was a message.

"You have no choice in pressing me. You Press it, you might live; you press it, you might die. So, press it."

Craig presses it. A loud bang, multiplies bangs, like something crashing behind them. Craig and the two companions started to run beyond the button. Craig thought there might be a wall there but it was open. The three ran for about a mile and then stopped. Out of breath, Craig speaks.

"Are you two ok?"

"Yes," said Zed, out of breath. "I am ok and you Zelda?"

With a very soft sweet voice, she squeaks out, "Yes, I am ok."

Five of the Xcroanas sneaked up on Zed and killed him, Craig turned and took out his sword. Craig yelled out, "Who are you? What have you done?"

"We are Xmotoians. We look a little different now don't we?"

"Yes, you do, you got bigger. How?"

"Would you like to know?"

"Well, you just killed my friend. Now you must die."

Craig took his mighty sword and started to swing, killing the five Xmotoians. Their bodies were not made of hard bone matter. Zelda was afraid, she started to run away down the hallway and the floor opened up and she fell into a deep hole. Craig ran after her and then Craig fell into the same hole. It was like a slide. Pitch black with fast moving white dots, the illusion felt like Craig was sliding very fast down and yet it was only a few feet.

Craig stood up as the room became light and Craig was in a classroom. In the front row was an empty seat. Craig took the seat.

There was a man that stood about six five with curly brown hair. At Craig's right was a kid, about eighteen years old, with curly brown hair called Juan Epstein, a cool dude they say, right next to a very tall guy, dark skin, he was six eleven and he was the star basketball player in the class. His name was Freddie Boom shugluga Boom shugluga Boom Washington. Towards Craig's left was a kid about five ten inches tall, brown afro. His name was Arnold Horshack and next to him the man with all the moves, Vinnie Barbarino. We can't say one of these guys are class clowns, every one of them had their style. Mr. Kotter spoke.

"Class, can one of you tell me who was our sixteenth president?"

"Ooh, Ooh, Ooh, M. Koorrtear, please pick me."

"Please Arnold, no sound effects. It sounds like you're having an orgasm."

Vinnie speaks out. "Hey Mister. Kotter, I don't think Arnold knows what that is."

The three boys got up and high fived each other. And Arnold speaks.

"Mr. Kotter, I bet you don't know that who ourr sixteenth presidentname was, Abraham Lincoln, was not his real name it was Abraham Johnson."

"Really Arnold, please tell me."

"Welllll, Abraham was sleeping in his bed all alone one night and his wife was angry with him and when he woke up, the maid was fixing up his bed she saw a puddle in the middle of his mattress. She said to the president. Sir, we had no rain last night and I saw this puddle in the middle of your mattress where you were sleeping and your wife was downstairs sleeping. We should call you Abraham "Leak col – in.""

Vinnie stands up. Gives Arnold a high five and the rest of the class give him one too.

"Great job, Arnold."

"I can't believe Arnold said a funny joke," laughed Juan Epstein.

Xmose said, "This was a waste of my time."

"We need some illusions to destroy him now!" screamed Xmose.

"I got the thing," said Xspeen. "I saw a show. This guy was wearing a suit of some kind and I found out, using our new computer searching for the weakness, we can kill Craig this way very easy!"

"Yes, do it now!!"

Craig walked out of the classroom. Just appearing in front of Craig, was a small suitcase. Craig opened it up and it was an orange suit. The suit just appeared on Craig's body.

Craig said to himself, "I feel a bit strange."

Craig ran a few feet and jumped into the air and Craig was flying. A song popped into his head.

"Look what happened to me. I can't believe it myself. Suddenly I am on top of the world, it should have been somebody else. Believe it or not, I am walking on air, feeling so free, here I am on top of the world."

Craig landed and stood right in front of Craig was one of Xmose's solders.

"And now you going to die ha, ha, ha."

"Oh really? How?"

"By the green rock. ha, ha, ha."

"By what? What is that? A green rock?"

"It's Kryptonite. Your weakness."

Craig was on his back laughing so hard.

"Yes, Yes, yes, you are going to kill me, not by this rock. I am going to die laughing. Tell Xmose, if he thinks he is going to kill me this way, he needs a new brain. Maybe Doctor Frankenstein can help him."

"Who is this doctor?"

"Forget it. This suit has special powers you know. Now let me rip it off."

Right under this suit, Craig had a new suit. The real suit. A suit of the Man of Steel. "You see this suit, the kryptonite that you hold is this man weakness, but with my heat vision..." A beam of heat vision changed the color of the kryptonite to red.

"Ow! You burned the rock right out of my hands."

"That's right, and I changed its properties of the kryptonite too. And now you're going for a little ride."

Craig, with is super-human strength, picked up the Creature and threw him far away like yesterday's trash.

"We need to get villains in here and fast."

"What villains do you want boss? Catwoman? The Joker? The Riddler? Wait they are "Batman villains", Oh I know, The Brainy Yacker and Lex."

"Good, just do it!" screamed Xmose.

Craig thought, "I am still in this reticules illusion. Let me see If I can change it to my liking."

With heavy concentration Craig thinks. A building. A building appeared, it said 'the Hall of Justice'.

Craig thought more. Of Batman and Robin, Aqua man, Green Lantern, and the hot Wonder Woman.

"What is going on? How did Craig get this, this is not part of the illusion is it?"

"Well, Xmose, this illusion is still on random function; we can't shut it off or we not going to get our illusions that we want when we enter the main function."

"Damn it! Ok, we need more villains. Get the Joker, the Riddler, get all the villains we are making The Hall of Doom, wait better the Legion of Doom."

"Ok boss."

Craig thought this was ridiculous. He could think up Superman and look like him, and Craig finds a seat.

In the Legion of Doom, Lex Luther is the leader and starts a plan to kill all of the superheroes, of "Justice League" and every superhero in it.

"Now with this time machine we are going back to where it all began, when the superhero were nobodies."

"Oh, come Lex. We don't have time for that nonsense. Let's steal the kryptonite from the museum and attack Superman and the rest. The Joker and Riddler and I have special weapons to kill Batman."

"OK, go ahead and do it."

The battle took place. Good guys against bad guys; the war was taking place. Each villain got destroyed. Popping off each villain that was made. The Hall of Justice disappeared. But one villain stayed alive. It was Catwoman.

"So, you couldn't kill me, Ha, HA. Ha!"

Craig approached Catwoman.

"You know, Catwoman. I believe there is one thing that is a women's best friend and I am going to give it to you."

"What?"

Craig reached into his pocket and pulls out a fifty-carat diamond.

"Wait! Where did you get this? A good guy that steals. No way."

"No Catwoman. I did not steal this. I own a diamond mine, and I am going to give you this. You don't need to steal any more. But I do want something in return. Because I am Catman."

Xmose was getting very distraught and was just about to flip his wig.

"Let us think, let us find a show that will destroy him. Now!"

Xzeem took the box and stated to press several buttons. The bright light knocked out Craig for a brief moment and the Xmotoians. A man on the loudspeaker said,

Welcome ladies and gentlemen, boys and girls. Look at our new spaceship, the Jupiter Three. We all know that the first two Jupiter's did not work. The ship has been tested and it is time for the Robinsons and the pilot, Don, and their chief science engineer, Craig, to aboard the Jupiter Three and to find a suitable planet for us to live. I believe it is Aires Five just outside our solar system."

Meanwhile, a man who belonged to the Carp gang was going to sabotage the ship. Lucky for this ship there were eight compartments for hibernation.

Doctor Zackery Smith went to the control panel and deleted the coordinates to Aries Five and Smith ran to the robot, reprogramming him and takes out the power pack and he hides.

Meanwhile, outside the ship, Will, Penny, Judy and all the Robinsons were waving goodbye. Don and the chief Science engineer gave a salute.

"Ok, please take an empty capsule, and we are going to be sleeping for a few hundred years."

'Wow, dad, a few hundred years?"

"Yes, my son, a few hundred years."

All the Robinsons went inside their capsules and Don and Craig entered theirs. Putting on their special googles. Smith ran out of a closet and went to the last empty capsule.

The capsule doors shut, and the countdown began.

"T minus ten, nine, eight, seven, six, five, four. Three, two, two and a half, oh, one, blast off baby. And there she goes everybody, the Jupiter Three is off."

Meanwhile the Jupiter goes into hyper drive, and the glass on Penny's capsule cracked. Something tiny hit it, she ages ten years as a heavy object blocks the crack. Doctor Zackery Smith had a screwdriver and he wanted to do more damage, but he did not have the time. the screwdriver was loose, and it managed to hit Penny's glass. Luckily, the toolbox that Doctor Smith had also got loose from the closet, and it blocked Penny's hole on capsule unit.

A loud alarm rang, Doctor Smith the first one to get out of his capsule, followed by John and Don and Craig.

"Who are you?" yelled John.

Looking at Smith.

"Where is the robot?"

"I don't know John," said Don.

Craig was screaming. "I found the robot. No power pack!"

"No power pack?"

"Yes John, No power pack."

Doctor Smith went to the robot, put the power cell in the robot's side. The robot was now on.

"Robot, get us out of this asteroid belt."

"No. I must destroy the Robinsons."

"Wait, John. I must reprogram the robot."

Craig swiftly gets behind the robot and pressed the reset button and the robot went back to normal.

"Now I know everyone here, who are you?"

"I am Doctor. Zackery Smith."

"We did not ask for a Doctor. to come along."

"No, John. I think Smith is here is a spy and tried to destroy our mission."

"You think, Don?"

"That is absolutely right, and we are off course, and you will never reach Aries Five and the earth will die."

"Robot, take Smith to the detention quarters."

"Sorry, I can't do that."

"That is right Mr. Robinson. I programmed this pathetic machine to listen to me."

Craig heard this, and goes quickly back and pressed a few buttons on the robot's side and it was doing another quick reset.

A small keyboard came outside the side of the robot and Craig was typed a few commands.

"Ok John, say your command; the robot is all yours."

"Well, thank you, Craig."

Doctor Smith said, "NO!!!"

The robot takes Smith to a holding cell down two stories.

"John, we have a murder on our ship."

"Yes Maureen, we are safe. Smith is locked up in the holding cell. He can't get out."

"Let me kill him, John. I am a soldier."

"No, Don. Smith deserves a trial like any other human."

"Yes, Smith is no human. He sold out and our Earth probably won't be there when we get back."

"Well, let's keep on going. We will find our way back."

"John, where do you think we are now?"

"I don't know Maureen; I am going to lift up the shields now."

The shields started to move up and off in the distance was a planet.

"Robot, come to the deck now."

The robot moved fast, heading to the open lift. The open elevator for the new safety equipment on the new spacecraft.

"Yes, Mr. Robinson."

"Tell me about this planet?"

"This planet is outside of our solar system. I have no records of this planet. I do however detect life on this planet. The atmosphere is the same as our planet earth."

"Great. Well guys, we are going to visit the first new planet. Stay close when we land. I don't know of the dangers what we will find here."

"Yes, dad!" cried Will.

"Robot, get Smith."

"Yes, Mr. Robinson."

The robot moved a little bit faster than usual. He pushed some buttons on the lift and it went down a little bit faster. Almost the speed of light, the robot gets to the cell door.

"Let's go Smith, you are wanted. We are going to the observation deck."

"Well, this does not look good for me."

The robot grabbed the arms of Doctor Smith.

"Let go of me you ninny."

"I would, but you not moving fast enough, so I am treating you like a little baby. Ha, ha, ha."

Doctor Smith entered the room.

"What do you need me for?"

"Well Smith. You got a little freedom. We are going to be landing on a new planet and you're coming with us. If we should die, you would be left alone and you would die too. So, if we die here, you will die also. All for one and one for all."

"Oh, give me a break."

The Jupiter three landed on a flat surface. The door opened up and The Robinsons and the chief science engineer, and Don, and Smith went outside. A man about six feet tall with slightly curly red hair talked.

"Welcome to my planet. You are either lost, or you have done a huge crime and now you're going to pay."

"No, we are lost. We need to find planet earth."

"John. I don't think he is listening."

"I don't care if you are lost or not. Here in my Hell Planet, I am known as Chef Rams and a few of you who I choose will be cooking in my Hell's kitchen."

"Cooking?"

"That is right old man. Cooking. You will need to past all three or two of my cooking challenges and if you pass, you go off free."

"Smith if you."

"I will pick four people. The tall red head. You the thin man and you two, the one who can't keep his trap shut."

Smith laughed.

"Well, Don Majors, it looks like you met your match."

"Here are the rules. You will all be taken to a kitchen on this planet, and you will be competing against these. They are known as the Hindorions. The teams are equal. You will be cooking a steak, Chicken Prado, and fries and potatoes. All foods that you people don't know. Good luck, you'll need it."

"Well, we are doomed."

"Not necessarily, John. Before I became a doctor, twenty years ago, I was a master chef. I can cook Chicken Predo."

Craig yelled out,

"I can cook steak."

"And cooking fries and potatoes is very simple. I can tell you what to do to so there in no problem." Maureen, Will and the girls went inside of the Jupiter as a bus from the future picked up the eight people to go to the Hell's Kitchen.

"The Hindorions are the blue team, and you are the red team."

Doctor Smith was preparing the chicken and he ran over to turn on the fryer and the oven. Craig had already turned on the gas grill for the steaks. There was a stove. Doctor Smith turned it on.

"Doctor Smith why did you turn on the stove? We don't need it."

"Yes, we do. We are not just going to give these aliens just what was said. We are going to give a little extra. Go into the refrigerator, get out carrots."

Don went into the refrigerator and grabbed bags and bags of carrots and started to slices them on the slicers. In this kitchen they had two nice size bowls where Don put the carrots in..

"This better work, Smith, I am telling you."

"Take it easy, Don. If Smith is telling us the truth, we should not have any trouble."

"You have minutes before we open Hell's Kitchen are you ready? I don't give a rat's ass if you are or not. Open the door Hugo. Hell's kitchen is open for business."

Hugo ran very fast, almost tripping over his own feet, to open the door. People of all sizes come walking in. Never, in one human's life, had they seen so many aliens in one room.

The Chef Ram's yelled out to the red team.

"Three steaks medium rare, two bake potatoes, and one fry."

With just an instinct the four men yelled out.

"Yes chef!" The blue team.

"Three steaks medium rare, two fries, one bake potato." The blue team were quiet.

"Did you hear me?"

"Yes, Chef!"

"Good. Speak up next time, I am getting deaf." The Chef looked at Craig's steaks.

"This is bloody good. Great job."

"Thank you, Chef "

The Chef ran over to the blue team and looked at their steaks.

"This is bloody raw. You can't cook an easy thing, like steak. You are competing with primitive humans lets go."

"Yes, Chef."

The Chef ran to the red team.

"One chicken, two steaks medium, one steak well done, and four bake potatoes."

"Yes, Chef." The Chef runs back to the blue team.

"Two chicken, and two steaks well done."

"Yes, Chef."

Fifteen minutes goes by. The red team has their chicken and steak out, done to perfection. The Chef looked at the chicken.

"Great job on the chicken."

"Thank you, Chef."

"Great job, Smith." The Chef runs to the blue team.

"Don't know what the bloody hell is wrong with you. I can't serve bloody raw chicken to my guests. Turn up your oven now."

"Yes, Chef."

After a grueling day in "Hell's kitchen". Chef comes out.

"After the hard work you all managed to get out your tickets. But the team that had the lowest score was the blue team. Pick two for elimination."

John and Don looked at each other and Craig looked at them both and Smith. Wondering if they will die like this.

At five o'clock in the morning the two teams went into a room. The leader of the blue team steps forward.

"Who do you pick and the reason why?"

"I pick number two and number four. I pick two because he smells bad, and he can't cook a frigging steak. And number four because I was knocking on her door. No reason."

"Ok. Number two you're dead. Bye."

The Chef takes out his laser pistol and shoots number two.

"Get ready to cook for your life. Tomorrow we are going to have some special guests."

Craig went into a room, large in size, it was for the red team. There was one couch and two smaller chairs, and one small chair, big enough for a child.

"Ok Smith you can join us on the couch, we won't make you sit on that chair."

"You're so kind, Mr. Robinson."

"John, I have a bad feeling for tomorrow."

"Don't worry, Don. I think Smith has this cooking down pat."

The four men went to sleep and, about four in the morning, the phone rand and Craig answered it.

"Good morning. Thank you for calling Willy House of pizza, may I help you?"

"Damn. How did I get the wrong number? Sorry."

"Hey, Craig. Who was that?"

"Don't know, John. It sounded like Chef Ramsay."

The phone rang again and Craig answered the phone again. This time he answered it right.

"Good morning."

"Get down here now. All of you!" screamed Ramsay.

The four men entered the kitchen.

"Today you will be cooking for the Cectorions. They are a bunch of mean sons of bitches. So cook your food good. And especially cook the desert good. They love their desert. You be cooking hot dogs. Easy and you going to make a Ccosectize cake. Good luck."

"Ok Smith. I think we can handle the hot dogs; can you make the cake?"

"Not a problem, Major, this is easy. I got all the ingredients here."

John and Don started to boil the hot dogs and Craig was looked at the blue group. They were laughing like the red team were doing something wrong. Smith made extra cake and he ate a piece. The blue team started laughing harder. It was very hard to make this time. Then they looked puzzled. One of their cooks took a piece of their cake and one just died. The body became like mush.

"Smith, how do you feel?"

"I feel good, why?"

"Never mind. Don, Craig, don't eat anything."

' Craig being funny give Ramsay a nickname."The kitchen is now open. Chef Rammy is out. He will be back to tally the votes. When he gets back."

The Cectoreions where screaming. They were very loud.

"The hot dogs taste funny. I hate them. If we didn't give Chef Rammy our word, we would have killed the red team. "

"Hey red team they like raw hot dogs. Sorry you didn't know that."

"Well Smith, I hope the cake tastes good. Smith you don't look so good."

"I am fine. I could not be any fin…"

Smith's body became like a jelly mush. The "Cocceted" had microscopic bugs that eat red blood cells. They Cectorions blood was made of acid.

The Cectorions liked the desert of the Red team and Chef Rammy just came back to the kitchen.

"Well, I gave two teams an easy dinner to be served and both teams screwed it up. Red team did you read the note that I left on your door?"

"We did not see any letter."

"Well too damn bad now. The good news is that The Cectorions like the desert. The Blue team they hate your desert. Both teams lost. I will be picking one on each team to die. Now get the F out of here so I can think."

"Don. This is not good. One of us is going to die. "

"Oh, come on, let us try to escape."

"It won't work, Craig. This door is sealed."

The door was sealed shut. It would not move.

The phone rang. Rammy was yelling.

"Get down here now!"

Craig, John, and Don went to the room were the last person got vaporized. The blue team now had only two people left and soon they were going to have one.

"Ok. I made my decision. The blue team. I pick you, the captain, for letting your teammate eat the cake. You die."

The chef took out his ray gun and killed the captain.

"Now for the red team. Don, you look like you are a leader of some sort. By looking at you a military person so I have no choice in killing you tooNormally, I have a tie breaker and the Red team has more people. The red team wins. You are free to leave."

Chef left the room and he had to send out a suitcase to the Jupiter Three. Will picked up the suitcase and took it to his room. He opened it up and he saw thousands of twenty-four karat gold coins. It added up to four billion dollars of earths money.

John and Craig returned to the Jupiter and Maureen was about to talk. John cut her off.

"No, Maureen. Smith and Don did not make it. Smith ate something and it killed him and Don got killed by Ramsayy. It is just us six now. We should get out of here now."

Don went to the controls and blasted off into space.

"Robot, come to the bridge now." The robot entered.

"Yes, Mr. Robinson."

"Can you detect any planets that are not hostile?"

"Sorry sir. I have to be in close contact to see."

"Ok. That will be all."

"John, I am going to fix you and Craig something right now."

"Thank you, dear."

Maureen set some food on the table. Craig took a piece, and it did not feel like he was picking it up. But his suit with food ability gave Craig the food supplement like he was eating.

"Dad, Dad, look there's a planet coming up ahead." John ran to the bridge.

"Great job. Will, its planet earth." The robot came speeding in.

"This is not planet earth. We are still outside the solar system."

"Robot, this is planet Earth. I know planet earth when I see it. There is our sun too," said John.

"I am telling you, it's not planet earth. I do sense this planet is not hostile," said the robot.

"No kidding," John said sarcastically.

"We will be in range in a few minutes. We are going home. I hope the planet is still alive," John yells out.

"Hi Judy. I feel sorry that Don died. Your father and I could not save him."

"I know, Craig. We had a huge fight beforehand and he was wrong."

"May I ask what the fight was about?"

"Yes. He said I was too old to wear medias. I think I still look great in them. Do you think?"

"Oh yes, absolutely."

"This is John. Everyone get dressed. We are going to land on earth in five hours." John took the microphone and with a lot of excitement said,

"Hello this is Jupiter Three. Come in."

"Hello Jupiter Three. You are coming in clear."

"We don't have enough fuel to land. Can you use the tracker beam?"

"Yes, we can. You will be in range in a few minutes. Thank you for visiting planet Eardth."

John looked at Maureen.

"John, he might not be an American."

"That is what I'm afraid of."

Penny put on her hot purple mini skirt and her matching blazing hot medias and flats that match. Judy put on her blazing bright yellow mini skirt and her bright neon yellow medias and matching flats. Will put on the uniform that he got issued from headquarters. John and Maureen put on their matching uniforms. Craig put on his tux; Very sharp indeed.

"Ok gang, the tractor beam is about."

The ship jolted as the beam took hold.

"Ok, this it. We will not mention Smith, ok. I will talk and I will say we lost Don Majors. Ok. We are about to land."

Jupiter landed smoothly and John opened the door.

Just in front of him was a green man.

"Welcome, Welcome, to planet Eardth."

John whispered, "That robot is very smart. Why did I not listen to him?"

"Hello, I hope you enjoy your stay here. But first I see you have a young boy here. Son do you like computers?"

"Yes, I do."

"Sir. We would like your son to look at our computer, if you don't mind, and please come along as well. Our computer technician passed away the other day. He was very old."

"Ok. Will, your mother and us will follow."

"Ok, that is find. And for you three it is our custom for the new guests to perform in front of us. You can do anything you like."

"Ok. Penny and Judy and I are going to sing a classic song. It's a musical, based on a true story. It's very easy. I will go through it and please join it. Ok?

So, the song goes like this, "It's easy to sing when you know the three words."

Penny says, "like A, B. C's."

Craig said, "Like A.B, C's, it's Doe Ray Me. So let me make it easy.

Doe a deer a female deer, Ray a drop of golden sun. Me, a name I call myself…"

Penny and Judy knew this famous song. As the three hold hands and go around in a circle, they sing the song, and the three were a hit on a new planet.

"Wonderful, wonderful," said the green man.

"My name is Grencha, the Mayor of this land. Now, young fella, it looks like you're the captain of these girls. I want you to sing a song by yourself."

"Really? Ok."

Craig whispered to Judy, "Judy, I am sorry. I just had a song that popped in my head. It's not you. It's just that you got a great name that rhymes."

"Ok this song was written by a person that I know. It is a spoof of a famous song and I made a little change. The gentleman who made this song lived over one thousand years ago. The name is Craig Glatky. So ladies and gentlemen here it is.

'Judy your full of doody people say your full of shit. Oh, Judy you're a cutie and I want to kiss your booty. Oh, Judy you full of doody and the people say you're full of shit and I want to touch your tit. She had a sister named Maria, she was full of diarrhea, and they called her Mary, and she was a hairy fairy, but they also call her Marie, it rhymes with Britney. Oh, Britney you are so pretty, I want to touch your titty'. Oh forget it mayor, I can't sing this song."

Xmose yelled at Xzeem.

"Get the special helmet now. I am going in."

"It has not been tested yet. If you go in, you might not come out, or worse the Illusion might go out."

"I don't care, give me the speaker. Put it on the left part of my chest and tell me how long I have. I will run in and run out. Open the porthole nearest to him."

"Ok, boss." Xmose popped in.

"Hey, I know your Xmose 1."

"If you dare to sing, or try to sing that song again, I will personally kill you myself without these illusions. You got that?"

Xmose slapped Craig's face very hard. Craig's body moved half around, and Xmose ran out and the speaker fell off and found its way onto Craig's body.

Two of solders in disguise had two plow darts. They wanted to shoot Craig with the arrow and finish him off. Mr. and Mrs. Robinson went to where Craig and the girls were and they started to talk. The mayor walked over.

"Please excuse me, Mr. Robinson. Your son is very smart. If its ok with you, can we keep him here for a while to help us to reprogram our computers and we will send him home to your planet, earth? We have the coordinates when your son finishes the programming. We need the help."

"Well, Will. What do you say? Would you like to help these people out?"

"Sure, Dad, I would. They seem very nice. Ma, is it ok with you?"

"Sure, dear, if it's ok with your father."

Mrs. Robinson gives Will a kiss goodbye.

"I'll meet you at home. Enjoy your adventure."

Craig and the Robinsons walked to their ship. The two soldiers were about to blow the poison darts at Craig. Both got knocked accidently by the Eardth people and the darts hit Mr. and Mrs. Robinson.

The ship left the orbit, and they were off. Feeling tired, Mr. and Mrs. Robinson went to bed.

About three hours went by. Judy went to see if their parents were ok. They were ready for supper.

"Ma, dad, what happened? You got old very fast."

"I know dear, quick get Penny and Craig."

Judy grabbed the microphone in the main bedroom.

"Penny, Craig, get down here to the main bedroom, quick."

Craig and Penny ran down to the main bedroom and they saw the mother and father aging quickly.

"Craig, you're the man now here. Take good care of my daughters. We are now leaving them in your care."

"Thank you, Mrs. Robinson. Please can I marry your daughter?" Craig said softly.

"You can marry our daughter," John said.

Craig knew that if they were going to be lost in space he needed to keep their civilization going.

The father and mother, before their eyes, vanished. Into dust.

"You idiots. You shot the wrong person. You were supposed to shoot Craig."

"We got knocked. We were lucky we hit anything at all."

"Damn it. He has more lives than a cat."

"Maybe that is why he called himself Catman. I looked at his background. It is going to be real tough to kill this guy, Xmose, real tough."

"We will see."

"Penny, Judy. You are two very beautiful girls."

"I know Craig. We both had eyes on you from the start," Judy said with a soft kind voice.

"Craig, we need to mourn our parents."

"Oh yes, of course Penny. When you and Judy are ready. I will ask if the robot can make us some rings."

Craig went to the floor where the robot stood.

"Robot, may I ask you something?"

"Well, yes you may. Thank you for treating me like a human. That is very kind indeed."

"Can you make three wedding bands? One for me, one for Judy and one for Penny."

"Oh, you slimy devil you. You're going to be banging two hot females. Yes, I can. Will left a lot of money in his room. It was your winnings from the Hell planet. The Chef Rammy man left you with a fortune."

"Oh really. I am going to take a look. How much do you need to make the rings?"

"I only need a total of thirty pieces, and you will still have a lot of money left."

Craig entered Will's room and he saw the briefcase. Craig opened the briefcase and saw the whole shit load of twenty-four karat gold coins that was worth over a billion dollars.

Craig gave the robot the thirty pieces of gold and the robot made some beautiful rings.

Out in space it was a week. That flew by so fast.

"Hi Penny, hi Judy. How are you two feeling?"

"I feel with my hands," Penny said.

Craig asked Judy, "How are you doing?"

Judy replied, "As I please."

Craig gave a smile.

"Craig."

"Yes, Penny."

"Judy and I are ready."

"Great. I will get the robot. He is programmed to be a justice of the peace.

Robot, can you please come up to the bridge."

The robot came up on the bridge, wearing a black tie. Judy and Penny went down to their rooms to get dressed.

"Robot. I will be back in two minutes. I need to get changed. You got the rings, I hope?"

"Yes, Craig. I got the rings."

"Ya whoooo!!!!!"

Craig ran to the ladder and flew down to his room. With the speed of lighting Craig changed into his tux. Penny and Judy were wearing specially made wedding dressed, made by the ship's computer. A white mini dress gown and shining white medias and white high heels shoes.

"We are gathered here today, in holy matcha mourning, I mean matrimony. Penny and Judy, do you too take this hunk of a man to be your husband? Now and until many more years later when you hit earth?"

"I do."

"I do." said Penny.

She has a huge smile on her face. She had a long talk with Judy about this day, what they were going to do to make Craig a happy man.

"Craig, do take these hot ladies to be your wives?"

"Absolutely."

"Well, that's nice. Keep it your pants, the ceremony it not over yet."

"Yes, Robot. Hurry. Yes."

"Now, I give you the rings and place them on your ring finger. And before I pronounce you man and wives, Craig, it is tradition out in outer space that you smash a glass with your left foot. If you can smash this glass, you can get married. Because fool, you're marrying two girls, you need to smash two glasses. And this is going to be hard. And you got only one try too."

The robot took the two champagne glasses and rolled them up with a napkin. Craig's mighty force smashed the glasses and he just got married to the two hottest females in outer space.

"Hey guys, look what I see."

"What Penny?"

"It's a message from Will."

"Hi Mom, Dad, Judy, Penny, and you too Craig. I just finished up the program and I am sending you the coordinates for plant earth. See you at home."

"Wow, when did he send it?"

"Oh no, he sent it over twenty years ago. We have been out here over twenty years."

"Penny, it might be a mistake. Don't worry. I am programming the ships computers and we have fifteen minutes to get inside our protector capsules."

Xzeem took the microphone and he started to sing with the other two solider. They were singing Craig's song.

"Oh Judy, you're full of doody. Some people say you're full of shit. We want ta. Oh, we want ta to touch your tit."

"Who in the hell is singing that song? Damn it. I thought that song was done with."

Xmose really did not have any sense of humor. And Xzeem and the soldiers went on laughing. Craig went in the protector capsule and sleeped.

CHAPTER 28

Nightmare on

Craig found himself in the cafeteria. Craig was eating his lunch. He heard a bunch of girls talking, very softly.

"Hey, Sue, that is the new kid. He arrived today."

"Yes, Peggy, I know. The rumor is he tried to kill himself with pills."

"No way. I have been having some bad dreams lately again. Take a look at my arm."

"You cut yourself?"

"No, there was a man with blades coming from his hand. He needed more food."

"What kind of food?"

"More people to be scared. I said you don't scare me. You're just a fool in my dreams and he cut me." Craig walked over.

"Hi. Please forgive me. I overheard you. I accidently took the wrong pills. I was taking sugar pills for my sugar. I did not try to kill myself. I have no friends because someone made up this rumor."

"Oh, I am sorry. I didn't know."

"Please tonight, when you're asleep, call my name. Let me be part of your dream. I can stop this man in your dreams."

"Oh, how can you do that?"

"Trust me. I can."

The bell rang and it was time for math class. Craig ate two lunches today. It was hotdogs and cake with chocolate sauce.

Craig's stomach was feeling somewhat funny. After lunch Craig went to his math class. Craig turned around and said,

"Hey Sonny, guess what?"

"What?"

And Craig made a very loud noise. It sounded like a machine gun going off. And the noise was like someone letting the air out of the tire. The smell was bad, like a dead skunk. The noise was heard in two other classrooms.

The class ended and Craig went home, the time was about three p.m.

Craig's mother left for work. She left a note on the kitchen table. She said at eleven o' clock I will call you. And don't forget to take you pills.

Craig ate his supper. The girls went to sleep at ten. Craig brushed his teeth and, like clockwork, Craig's mother took the wrong pills again, and Craig took the sleeping pills right at ten.

The girls were very tired as they did not sleep a wink the previous night.

"Hi Sue. Look at this house. Wait is this the house of that girl who killed herself driving the car?"

"Yes, it is. Do we get Craig into our dreams?"

"I don't know. Craig seemed to be a little off."

"I hear you."

Just by saying his name, Craig entered the dream.

The girls went into the house.

Craig appeared in front of a big white house. In the front, three little girls were playing jump rope. They were saying a rhyme.

"One, two, three, you better stay away from me. Four, five, six. You better find some sticks. Seven, eight, nine. Freddy says he's mine."

"Who is Freddy?"

"Freddy lives in this house."

"So why are you on his property!"

Craig kicked the little girls. They exploded, bones and all. The front door opened. Sucking everything in sight, like someone or something was mad.

Craig walked into the house like there was nothing wrong, the house was sucking everything up and there was no floor. In the middle of the house was a boiler room. Some kind of a factory in front of Craig's eyes. Craig started to walk down invisible stairs and came across a steel floor.

"Hey, Freddy. I don't have much time. Where the hell are you?"

"Oh, dear, you are afraid of me. Yes, I am getting stronger. Wait I hear someone calling me. Someone is calling me. Ha, ha, ha. Nobody calls Freddy."

Freddy moved quickly into the dream.

"Damn it, Freddy Kucka. I only have minutes, before I leave here."

Freddy swung at Craig's body and the blades went through him. Craig turned around.

"Oh, there you are. If you want to live outside this nightmare. Go inside of me and we can do some damage. With your special powers and my evil mind, we can become a force, that only real nightmares are made of."

Freddy thought about it, and he merged into Craig's body.

"Doctor is Craig going to be ok? I took his pills by accident."

"Yes, Craig is going to be ok. I think you might want him dead. We need to have you check out medicine."

"Oh no. I did not mean to take the wrong pills. Oh, what have I done?"

Craig's face changed. Craig aged a few years. He left the hospital on Saturday morning to have some fun. Craig went to the bathroom, and he looked at himself in the mirror. He saw Freddy Krueger.

"Now, Fred, be patient. Tonight, we are going to the night club. I know you like to slice and dice your victims, but I'd like them to harm themselves. Watch as I use your powers tonight."

Craig went to the exercise room and started to lift. For six hours, Craig felt the strength and he also felt the power.

Eight o'clock comes along and Craig walked to the night club. It was jam packed. The dance floor was packed. The power to the lights goes off, but the music stays on.

"Oh, Billy stop, ha, ha, ha."

As the power of "Freddy Krueger" cuts the dress off and the panties; the girl was naked. Then the light come back on. The crowd started to laugh. The girl looked down. She cried and ran out of the club. She does not see the eighteen-wheeler and it smashes her.

"Ok, that is all right. We need a little action pal."

"Well Krueger. Next week is another day. I just want the feel of this."

During the free time. Craig closed his eyes. A bunch of the hot girls in class sat in front.

"Well Freddy, here are some good things to come."

Craig closed his eyes and pressed down nails onto the dresses on the girl's seats. Craig opened his eyes and the bell rang for the next class.

All the girl's dresses ripped off and a few of them weren't wearing panties. All the girls ran out. There was a train track near the school. The girls ran across the tracks, but they never made it across.

"Freddy how is the fear? Am I getting you enough?""

"Yes, but this is getting a little boring."

"What?"

"I said boring."

Freddy was breaking up. He was dying inside of Craig. This was the only way for the nightmare to end completely. To sacrifice people to kill the nightmare.

When morning came, the girls who had brought Craig into the dream, thanked him for getting rid of Freddy.

Craig went into the house that he lived in. It was the same house that Freddy lived in when he was married to his wife. The door slammed shut. The doors disappeared and the windows were all gone. The front of the house was all boarded up like there was a door there. There was no door.

A laughter was heard. You thought I can be destroyed think again.

<h1 style="text-align:center">CHAPTER 29</h1>

X-Men

Craig found himself riding a motorcycle. He had a suitcase on the back of his bike. In front of him were three huge trucks carrying people in them. There was a prisoner in the bus. At the back was a smaller truck speeding in the back and with an arm swooping motion the bus tires pop and the bus does not move. Inside of this bus was a beautiful green woman who could shape shift. She told the bodyguard to let her go or he was going to die.

"No way mutant. You're not going to leave."

Magneto came into the back of the bus and knocked out the body guard. And Craig was just about there.

"You are now free Mystique. Let me free the others."

The security guard woke. Over my dead body. Magneto looked up. At that moment, Craig shoots the guard dead, right in the head. Magneto takes the gun away from Craig.

"I need no help from a human."

"Please Mr. Magneto. May I have permission to speak with you?"

Magneto grabs the gun away from Craig and points the gun to Craig's head.

Magneto presses the trigger.

"You must be a very lucky man. Or a very stupid one. One bullet. Now stand outside, I will be out there shortly. Mystique find out what he wants and kill him."

Mystique went outside and walked around the bus.

"What do you want from me?"

"Mr. Magneto. A year ago, you built a machine to make humans into mutants and you nearly died. I have power, but it's not strong at all. Not nearly strong as you. I have designed a new machine more powerful than the one you built but it will use less power. It is only good for one person, though. I want it to be use one me."

"Let me see."

"There is a reason why I want to become a mutant. I want to be Mystique's equal or come close to it. I think she is the most beautiful woman. But if she is yours, I will stay away."

"Yes, I noticed you blushing when you shot the guard. I did not know why. I do now."

Magneto changed into Mystique.

"You want to date me?"

"Yes." Craig blushed even more.

"Craig I think your machine might have possibilities. Magneto, I got something to tell you."

"I thought I told you to kill him."

"Yes, but he wants to become a mutant. He designed a machine and it looks like it has possibilities. You will use less power in using it."

"Let me see!

Wow. maybe you do have some kind of powers. I will design this," said Magneto.

"Yes, he wants to be my equal so we can get married," said Mystique.

"What married, my number one?"

"Yes, why not. I do think he is a little cute."

All the mutants took off and went to their hide out. It was up on a huge hill and the house looked like some kind of castle. Magneto went to his workshop and started to construct the machine.

"Mystique, what if this does not work. Are you still going to date the human?"

"I just might Juggnot. If a human thinks I am beautiful, not all humans are bad."

Mystique was thinking of Charles Xavier, she had a crush on him from the start. Charles did not give her the time of day and Mystique found new friends.

"Ok the machine is ready. Craig, get down here. Let us see if your machine works."

"Now, Magneto. Look at the video screen. The dot has to line up with the dot in the middle for it to work."

"I see it. Sit down."

Magneto started with his power. The part of the machine that had a circle like sphere started to rotate very fast. Hardly using any magnet force, the machine was fully charged. Magneto lined up the dots and he pressed the trigger.

The lights flickered and went out. It was pitch black. Craig felt powerful. Very strong.

The girl with the power to sense other mutants could not detect Craig as he was shutting off her power.

"Can you detect a new Mutant?"

"No, I can't."

The lights came back on.

"Well, Craig. Sorry it did not work."

"Maybe it needs time to kick in."

"Ok. We will wait."

Craig has gotten his mutant powers.

Craig raised his hands and said,

"Raise before Zod! I hope Superman does not get mad. Ha! Ha! ha! All the mutans had risen."

"Wow. Craig you are powerful. What else can you do?"

"I don't know."

"Can you detect Craig."

"No, I can't. No reading," said the young girl.

"Wow, a mutant that can't be detected. That is very interesting."

And Mystique comes over to Craig and hugged him. With a huge smile on his face, Craig blushed.

With this power Craig sensed trouble coming very quickly on earth.

"Mystique. Let us go on a date. I would like to marry you very quickly. I sense something is going to happen."

"Ok."

Craig gave Mystique a kiss and she changed to a human. A girl with red hair.

"When we get married, I am going to have Charles there and the rest of the X-men. We need them. I am going to ask everyone here for a small truce."

"Wow, that asking a lot."

"I know Mystique but, we can't fight these aliens by ourselves.

Magneto call Charles for a dinner at the Red Meat Cabin and don't wear your helmet. When I ask Mystique to marry me, I want Charles to be the best man. We need all the X-men to defeat the aliens that will arrive on my wedding day."

"Ok, I will do that."

Magneto used a phone that only has one button. Magneto pushed the button and Charles answered the phone.

"Hello, Eric. What can I do for you?"

"Hi Charles. This is part truce, believe it or not. Please meet me at The Red Meat Cabin at six. The dinner is on me."

"Really, some kind of trap?"

"No, not a trap. I have a new guest and he wants to talk to you after I tell you what is going on."

"Ok, I will be there. You're not wearing your helmet, are you?"

"No, I am not."

"Well, I will be there six sharp."

Mystique put on a beautiful green mini skirt dress. She was wearing pretty green medias and green high heels. Craig was wearing a black suit with a black bow tie.

The two sat down and they started to eat. Mystique and Craig were eating a sixteen-ounce prime rib. with a baked potato and a garden salad.

One table down, Charles and Eric were eating a T bone steak and fries and a salad.

"Well, Charles. One of my people is going to be getting married. Do you want to guess who?"

"You know I don't like to guess. I will have to read your mind."

"Don't bother. I will tell you. Mystique. She is marrying a new mutant. He wanted to become a mutant and he has become a very powerful one indeed."

"Over my dead body. Where is he? Is he right over there? I will get him."

Mystique left with Magneto and Craig walked over to Charles.

"Hello Charles. I would like you to be the best man at my wedding.

"There is not going to be a wedding."

"Oh really. Who is going to stop me?"

"Do you really want to know?"

"Da. I want to know."

Charles, with all his might, Could not use his powers on Craig.

"How can you do that? You're blocking my powers."

"Yes. I can shut off any Mutant power that I want when I am close by. You know Mystique likes you and you treated her like a piece of shit. Now I've found her, going to give her the love she craves and I want you to be the best man."

"You will have very powerful offspring."

"Yes, we will. But have your friends close and your enemies closer. Well, I don't think Magneto is an enemy. His beliefs are somewhat right. But when I get married, we are going to be attract aliens and I need your help and the X-Men. I am asking for a truce."

"Ok, you got it."

"Thank you, Charles."

"Craig?"

"Yes, Magneto."

"We are going on a little trip. I just found out Jean Grey is back in town, and she is very powerful."

"Ok, let's go."

Craig thought, Jean Grey powerful? Ha. Not as powerful as me. Magneto, Craig, in the center with was Jean Grey, and on the other side was Charles.

"Jean listen. I can help you with your powers."

"Get out of my head, Charles."

Jean Grey got angry, and she started to use her powers but Craig shut them off. And using his special abilities, he froze Magneto and Charles.

"Ok Jean, listen up. You will be coming with Magneto and myself and you will be on your best behavior."

"How can you do that? I can't use my powers."

"No shit. I am more powerful than you Phoenix. Now I am going to let them go."

"Sorry Charles, Jean is coming with me. Let us go Jean."

Charles looked confused and the house becomes deserted. At Magneto's hide out, Craig was in is room thinking.

"Hi, Craig. I was told you and Mystique are getting married. Why don't you marry me? I am the Phoenix. I am more powerful than Mystique."

"Well Jean, it is like this. First of all, you're still married to Cyclops. And you're not my type. Sorry. When I was younger. I might have wanted to have a ménage, but now my heart is with Mystique. Here is the ring that I am going to give her."

Craig showed the ring to Jean, and she changed into a normal girl. A naked girl.

"Here. Take my coat. Sorry, Mystique."

"What happened to my powers. They are gone."

"They are not gone. You are happy and not on the defensive. Your powers will come back."

"I hope so. I love your ring."

"Well, Ok. Well, let me have it for a second. Please. Mystique. I give you this ring, so you become my wife. Do you except one of two rings that I give you today."

"Yes, I do. I will marry you."

"Thank you, my love."

The news traveled fast. Charles got the news and started to talk to the X-Men.

"Ok listen up. We are all invited to a wedding. Two of Magneto's companions are getting married."

"Wait, are you kidding? This is a trap!"

"No, Wolverine, it is not a trap. Magneto did not have his helmet on. I read him. There is going to be some kind of attack and we are going to help them stop it. It's our planet we are their protector. We are going to have a truce for one day."

Magneto goes to a phone that looked normal and calls for a hall. They also got a caterer too.

"Hey Eric, I want Jimmy and Logan to sing a song at my wedding. Make it so."

"Ok Craig. Not many people call me by my real name anymore, but seeing as you are very powerful, I am going to allow it."

"Thank you."

At the hall, the X-men were standing around ready for battle. As at any moment the Magneto's group would pounce and fight.

"Welcome, Welcome, X-men, please enjoy yourselves. We are not going to harm you."

"Professor, read Magneto now, see if he is going to poison us."

"Silly Wolverine. I am not going to poison you. If I wanted to attack you. You are full of metal."

"I still don't trust you."

The music started. Craig walked out with a fancy tux. Mystique was wearing a glorious mini wedding dress. White as snow. Super-hot legs and she was wearing the hottest white with glitter medias and white heeled shoes. Every man' eyes popped out of their heads.

An old man started the ceremony. He kind of look liked "Stan Lee." A great man back in the day.

"Good morning. We are here to take these two lovely people to be married. I can only hope you can bring love into your lives and the lives of people around you. Craig, do you promise to have and to hold and to have sex every single day with this hot lady?"

"I do."

"Do you, Mystique, take this funny looking man to make him squeal like a pig every night when you get down and dirty?"

"I certainly do."

"Well, Craig, I have something that I must say in Yiddish and now take the glass that is wrapped up with this napkin and smash it. This glass will go up your stinking ass if you dare to break this woman's heart."

"I won't break her heart. I promise you that."

"Ladies and Gentlemen. Wolverine and Sabretooth are going to sing a song to the wedding guests."

"What are you going to sing Sabretooth?"

"The hell should I know, I don't sing."

"Let us sing for he's a jolly good fellow. We both know that one."

Together, Sabretooth and Logan sang. Craig goes over to Sabretooth.

"Why don't you tell him?"

"Tell him what?" said Sabretooth.

"Don't you dare play stupid with me. This is a happy occasion, and this might be the only time you're going to have a chance to tell him," Craig said.

"Tell me what?" yelled Wolverine.

"Logan when you got your metal into your body, Skinner shot you in the head making you have memory loss. You are my brother. I'm Jimmy."

"No, No, it can't be."

"Yes, its true. That is why you can't kill me, nor can I kill you. Our blood is thicker than water."

At that moment, a loud bang came from outside the building. The top of the hall got ripped off. The X-men ripped their clothes off and they had their uniforms on. Craig, with his new suit, became the Dark Angel. Very large robots flew around and destroyed everything in sight.

Mystique got her powers back and she became very powerful. She transformed into Craig.

She could not use all the powers that Craig used, only the power of fire. Craig yelled out, "Hey Me! Use the fires power now!"

Mystique smiled and used the fire power on one robot.

"Now, me together!"

"Yes, Craig, we did it."

"I know. This is going to be weird making love to myself. HA, Ha, ha, when we get out of here."

"I bet you already have."

The battle continued. It was a brutal fight but no Mutant was killed.

After the fight was finished, everyone just left and went their separate ways.

Craig started to walk on a dirt path and then he slid down a steep hill. Just below was water. Craig was in a pond, and it became a whirlpool. Craig took a deep breath and the water dragged him in.

CHAPTER 30

Land of the Lost

Craig was in another world. There were beautiful trees, green grass everywhere. Craig heard a man calling two names, Will and Holly.

Craig got closer. They were two young kids, and the father was nearby. He was Rick the Park Ranger. Craig approached slowly, not knowing if they were friend of foe.

"Hello, Sir."

Craig was about to run in the other direction.

"Hello, my name is Rick and who are you?"

"Oh, my name is Craig, and I am passing through."

"Ha, passing through. Well, I don't think you are going to be getting out of here any time soon," said Rick.

"Why not?"

"Did you go through the whirlpool?" laughed Rick.

"Yes, I did. Why?"

"I believe that was a time tunnel for the past. We are in the dinosaur time."

"No shit. I think this is great. I am going to see a real live T-Rex."

At that moment, a T-Rex appeared.

"I am prepared to battle this creature," yelled Craig.

"You can't kill it," screamed Holly.

"Why not little girl?"

"Because you will be changing the course of human civilization," exclaimed Will.

"I see what you mean. But if we are on the menu. I want to live. And besides, if we die, we don't exist here anyway, so what if we die, we still live, and we keep coming back her. As a loop."

"No, we can't. We need to get out of here," cried Holly.

"Thank you, Craig, for making my daughter feeling good. We are going this way. I am sure you can find yourself another route out of here."

"Sure Rick. I'll be taking off. I hope to see you three around."

"Dad, he gives me the creeps."

"That's ok, Will. We will keep out of his way."

"I don't know, I think he's kind of cute. "

"Always thinking with your pants, sis."

"Oh, Will, you are just jealous that there is another man in here and he might be smarter than you."

Craig walked and came across a mountain side with what looked like a cave.

Craig started up the long trail of the mountain and entered a small hole, big enough to walk in. The cave was deep; it looks like it could go on for miles. Craig walked about five hundred feet to make sure he wouldn't be eaten up by any large animals. Luckily for Craig, had gone camping with is friends still have a bic in his pants. Craig knew never to flick his Bick in public. Craig eneters the cave and notices that there was wood inside this cave very usual. He might think someone was living here.

Craig was fast asleep and suddenly awoken by yelling outside the cave. Craig ran to the opening of the cave and saw Holly and Will being attacked by the T- Rex.

Craig took out his pistol and fired two shots at the T- Rex and the T-Rex went running.

"Are you two ok?"

"Yes, we are ok," yelled Will. "I see you found yourself a cave, Craig."

"Yes, I did. I call it my man cave," laughed Craig.

"Oh wonderful. I hate to ask you. Can we three live there with you?"

"Oh, you want to move in with me? I might be a psycho. I don't know who you are. I don't want to be thrown out of my own house. Ok I'm sorry. Fine. I accept, go get your father."

Will and Holly went back to their campsite. A smaller cave that was not too safe.

"Dad! Holly and I found a cave. It was actually Craig's cave. It lies on a mountain side. Pretty high up and safe from any predator down here."

"Ok, let's go."

Meanwhile, Craig made a bow and arrow and was looking for some food to eat. Craig saw what looked like a cow and he shoots it. With one blow the cow like animal falls down.

"Damn it. This thing is heavy."

Craig pulled the huge carcass back to his cave. Craig found a rope and tied it around the animal. Luckily for Craig, on top of his cave was a pulley.

Craig didn't think about that too much and pulled the seven of gun animal to the cave. Craig reached in his pocket and behold, a nice sharp butcher's knife. Craig started cutting up the cow and made some nice steaks.

An hour passed. Rick and his two children were at the cave.

"Hello. Welcome to my home and now yours. I am making supper. I hope you like steak."

The smell of the steak on the open fire smelled out of this world. Just outside, the smell traveled. Three T-rex's and five other dinosaurs were outside, smelling the steaks.

"Hey, dad. Look outside."

"What Will? Oh, holy shit. Craig, the steaks you are making are attracting a lot of dinosaurs at our camp."

"Well, I have plenty of steaks. I will put more on the grill."

After the steaks were ready, Rick, Will, and Holly were eating their steaks and Craig was eating and making more. When the steaks were finished, Craig threw them outside for all the dinosaurs to eat. After they had eaten the meat. The T-Rex made a funny sound. It sounded like 'thank you'.

The smell went away and so did the dinosaurs. Craig went to the far side of the cave and slept. And the Marshall's slept on the other side.

"Good morning, Craig."

"Good morning, Holly."

"Craig, what do you do for a living?"

"Oh, nothing much. I was exploring the wilderness until I came across this whirlpool and I ended up here. The Land of the Lost. I don't think they are going to find what was lost, ha, ha, ha."

"My dad found a crazy looking tower on the other side of the river. We are going to take a closer look at it today. Do you want to come?"

"I would love to."

Will took his basket and went outside the camp to look for something for breakfast.

Outside of Craig's cave were wild fruits. Everything here was big. The peaches, plums, oranges, and the bananas and Will had to be careful of bananas of some unknown bacteria so he goes and puts on a special glove.

Rick took a pot and boiled hot water and Will dumped the bananas inside and then Rick took out the bananas and Will dumped the glove in the hot boiling water.

"Thank you for the breakfast, Will"

"No problem, Craig. Thank you for having us at your home."

"Dad."

"Yes, Holly?"

"I invited Craig to come along with us to the tower. I hope that is ok?"

"Yes. I was going to ask him anyway."

Craig and the Marshalls started out. They climbed down the side of the mountain and started to walk into the woods. Craig wondered where he was, if he was in the future. Downtown L.A., San Francisco?

"Hey dad, what was that noise?"

"Don't know Will? I never heard that sound before."

"I think I know. We better keep on moving, and quick."

"What is it, Craig?"

"They are called "Raptors". Very dangerous. Quick and a carnivore. They usually hunt in packs and we won't have a chance."

All four of them started to move very quickly to the tower. There it was. A tall black tower. Ten by ten and the four moved in.

"Well Rick, sir, what is this?"

"I don't know, Craig. We never came across this until yesterday."

"Well let me see if I can open this baby up.?"

Craig looked at the tower very carefully and saw no buttons, no nothing. When Craig was about to speak and say I can't open it, he touched the tower and a door opened.

They all walked in. It was beautiful. In the middle of the floor was a table with beautiful colored rocks. Like gems.

"We better not touch this, Craig."

"Why not? If this means getting us out of here, why the hell not?"

Craig saw something like this in his dreams. What colors should he move? Craig moved five colors, red, blue, white, yellow, green, out of know where around the whole room was a bright light and a door appeared in front.

It was a doorway to somewhere in the future. Without a goodbye, Craig went through the porthole and the porthole closed.

Craig was in a huge room with bright lights. Craig noticed, in about thousand feet, there was the door he needed to get out and in front of him, about 100 feet, were thirty of Xose's men with bowling balls in hand.

"Well, Craig. You managed, somehow, to make it this far. Now it ends for you. Here you will die. I have created these boulders and we are going to smash you into oblivion. Xcrotion when I give the word, start attacking."

With a loud yell. Xmose said start the music.

"This music will make you dazed and you will be vulnerable."

The music started to play. It was a song from the movie "Staying alive Far from over."

"Attack, Attack!" cried Xmose. The song got louder.

"Um Xmose, if you're going to kill me with, 'ha, ha, ha, bowling balls you need to at least come closer and hit me."

"Come on, hit him. NOW!" screamed Xmose.

"Your men, Xmose, are not too bright and neither are you. Stupid ass," said Craig.

The song played and the Xmotoians were now getting tired after bowling five balls and Craig was now intercepting the balls. With quick footed movements like playing soccer. Craig used his feet to stop the ball for rolling. Craig took at least ten balls.

"This song is going to do you in now!"

A new song started to play. It was good old country music The Gambler by Kenny Rogers. Craig took a ball into his hands.

"Hey Xmose. I want to thank you. When you made these ten pin bowling balls you must have found my fingers holes' pattern. And it seems you've done a great job in drilling. Thank you."

Craig took his four steps. There were no arrows on the floor to roll the ball, but Craig made do.

Craig glided his ball like an airplane. And smack down goes three men. The bodies turned into mush. The music was played and another three greats songs back to back as more men went down.

"Damn it. Kill him now. The next song will do it."

The next song played. It was another Country song. This was another greatest song of all time, Bob Denver's Country Boy.

This time, Craig grabbed two balls and he used the left to knock down three, and takes the right and knocks down ten.

"I want more solders on the field now."

Twenty more Xmotoians found themselves in the middle of a battle field.

"Craig, I don't know how long this song will last, but this song is going to do it. This song you will make you dead. Xmotoians ! take out your spears."

The song started; it was "Devil down in Georgia".

Ten Xmotoians were about to throw the spears as the song started to play. Xmose with a loud yell said attack, attack, attack. With Craig's fast movements, he grabbed the spear from the Xmotoians and started swinging as the song played and the adrenalin was flowing through Craig's veins.

The song ended and there was one male Xmotoians left. One solider. This solider looked like a kid. Maybe this what they looked like and Craig never took a good look at them. The young child looked straight at him. He knew he was going to die like the rest. Craig looked at him. The Xmotoian dropped his spear with a tear running down his face.

"That was the smartest thing you could have done son. See Xmose? I think some of you might have a chance for peace. Or maybe you are late learners, or maybe you know you lost and want to fight another day."

"I will find your weakness; Craig you will die."

"Well, let me give you a real big hint: the music gave me a whole lot of power. And when I finally meet you, maybe it would be nice to battle you one on one."

Craig walked to the door. There was a keyboard on it. Craig pushed 28, 62 and the door opened. It was an elevator. Craig pushed number six and it goes down, not up.

Stay tuned.

Chapter 31

The Trial

Xmose and his soldiers ran to the loading dock. Craig pushed in the code 28, 62 on the pad and the door opened. Craig walk a few steps , the door behind Craig slammed shut and another door slid open at the same time. The door closed behind Craig and on the wall were numbers like he was in the elevator. Craig pushed number six. The elevator seemed like it was going down.

"This does not seem right. I am feeling like I'm going down. I guess I'll have to wait and see."

The elevator stopped and the door opened into a tunnel of some kind. Lights seemed like they went on forever. Craig thought this could be another illusion. A seat popped up and a voice talked.

"Welcome. Please sit down on the chair and please put your feet on the footrest and hold on tight."

Craig sat down on the seat and a seat belt went over his shoulders and waist.

"Xzeem, are the ladies in the other truck?"

"Yes, Xmose and the radar detectors are fixing on Craig. The tunnel that he is in looks like it goes for miles."

"Good. We will stay back so he won't detect us, and I am going to adjust the illusion box. Yes! Here we are and we are going to make Craig feel really bad before we go and kill him."

Craig is a mile underground and the chair starts to move. The chair picked up speed, going down a steep hill, straight down. The drop felt like it was a hundred feet down. The chair was going fast, straight up in the air and the seat tilted back like Craig was going to tip over. The seat began to drop again and faster the chair went, the chair slid up to the side of the walls and to the left and right, like it was avoiding something. The chair stopped swaying and stayed on the straight course.

Up on the land. Xmose was right behind. The body structure of the Xmotoians can handle the poisons that linger on Earth.

"Now, I got the illusions the way that I want it. The signal is synced into his brain. We are going to make this fool so weak, and the girl will kill him."

"Hey, Xmose. I see a huge vehicle up ahead. We should stay back now."

"No we are going in . We will follow Craig and kill him."

Craig got up from his chair. The helmet covered Craig's head. On the shield words appeared.

"Now you are about to leave the safe zone. This shield will remain closed. Once you are in a safe zone this shield will go up. Please exit and go to the last elevator to the right."

Craig went to the elevator to the right and pressed the code 28, 62 and the door opened. Craig walked in and the door closed and the elevator went up.

It took the elevator ten minutes to travel upwards until it stopped and the door opened.

Craig only saw a large vehicle to the right at the opening of the door. So, he could not see anything to his right nor left as it was all empty.

Craig pushed the same code again on the vehicle's door, and the door opened and Craig entered. a computerized vehicle. A loud piecing noise started and almost made Craig go deaf. The shield on Craig's helmet went up. Now being in the safe zone Craig was able to take off the suit.

"Thank you for joining me, Mr. Galuta. Please put on this watch, it will be my way of keeping you from harm and I can follow you if you decide to leave this vehicle. Please sit down now. We are off. Before I go where do you want to go?"

"Well, thank you for asking. I would like to go to Ireland."

"Yes. I am aware that only a few Countries have survived the bombs. My truck has a special docking unit so you can enter without destroying it."

"That is great, thank you."

"Hey, Xmose, do you see this on our radar?"

"Let me see. Damn it, it looks like a very large storm is heading this way. The fool is driving right into it.

Maybe we don't have to kill him after all. Tell the other trucks we are moving in, and we are going to attach ourselves to that vehicle. Right now!"

"This is Xzeem. Move in on the B Vehicle. We are hitching a ride."

Xmose and the rest got to the B Vehicle that Craig was in.

"Craig, please stay calm. I am putting down the blast shield and I am putting the force field up."

"Why?"

"I detect very bad weather. It is a tornado. A very bad one. It looks like it is about twenty miles long and the speed is up to five hundred miles per hour. Faster than I can move. Now buckle up!"

"Ok I am ready." Craig Enters "Oz"

Craig could not see a thing. Felt a little nudge, and that was it. The tornado had Craig up in the air and the tornado changed direction. Instead of going backwards, it moved forward.

"Hey Xmose. When we land, are you going to put on the illusion machine?"

"Of course. This tornado is giving me a great idea. I am going to put him into a place that is not normal. He will die here. And we are going to put on the force field so this can feel at least real to him."

"So, what are you?" said Craig.

"I am what is called the B – Machine. Or the B vehicle. I am the state-of-the-art land and water vehicle."

"So can I give you a name that I can remember?" said Craig.

"Of course, you can. What will you call me?" said B-vehicle

"How about Kit."

"Kit, I like that. An old television show, a car that talks and the driver was Michael Knight."

"Yes. Do you have any of these shows on your data base? While I am up here, I can watch this awesome show."

"Of course. I will start from the beginning, with the pilot show."

"Great. I can't wait. I love watching old television shows. Hey Kit! This is not the pilot show. This actor is on the Young and the Restless. He is a doctor. Now come on, I what to see "Knight Rider"."

"Yes, of course, I am sorry," said Kit.

"What I hate is a funny talking car," said Craig.

"Oh, come on. You need a little humor," said Kit.

"Yes, you are right," said Craig.

The show ended and Kit landed on the desert floor and Xmose was right behind him with the illusion on and the force field on.

"Kit, where are we?"

"Sorry, Craig. I don't know. My sensor says we are twenty-one miles away from where we were. But on the right path to your destination."

"Can I leave the truck and see?"

"Yes. I will be just behind you."

Kit opened the door. Craig climbed out of the car. Wow, what a beautiful place this is. The smell of flowers and the birds. No birds?

The place looked like a small town. Tree houses, very colorful. Pretty flowers all over the place. A peaceful place.

"Hello? Any one home?"

Craig started to sing,

"Hell is low. Hello, is anyone or anything home. Come out come out whoever you are. Come on out. Please!"

Just as Craig stopped his horrible singing, a huge ball of light approached him. Just before you can yell out Jimmy has crabs a beautiful woman with long blond hair emerges.

"Hello, who are you?" said the hot lady.

"I am Craig. They call me Craigal the bagel, with the cream cheese. And who are you?"

"Wait. Before I answer you, young man. Are you a good witch or a bad witch?"

"Lady, no offence, only women can be witches and bitches and I am no woman! A wizard or a Warlock maybe, but no, I am just Craig."

"Well, just Craig, I am Glenda, The hot gorgeous witch of the North."

Craig said to himself, "No shit. You're pretty hot. "

Glenda, the witch of the North, was wearing a bright white mini dress suit with shinny white medias.

"Well Craig, it is time to meet my friends. Hey, Munchkins, come on out, come on out now, and meet your new friend. I think he killed the stupid Witch of the South."

"Well, Glenda, the hot one, where am I?"

"Wait I will tell you."

Glenda started to sing with her sweet voice.

"Come out, come out and keep it your pants and see your new friend while you have the chance."

Just a few seconds later, a bunch of little children appeared. Well, they looked like children.

"Welcome to Munchkin Land."

"Wait, you say Munchkins?" said Craig with hungry eyes.

Craig was thinking of Dunkin Doughnuts. Munchkins. Chocolate Munchkins.

"Thank you for coming to Munchkin Land and killing the Bitch, I mean Witch," said a sweet little girl from Munchkin land.

One of the small Munchkin's saw the hunger in Craig eyes. Like he wanted to eat a Munchkin. But not that Munchkin. Glenda spoke to the mayor of Munchkin city.

"Mayor, is the Wicked Witch is she dead? Like a dead door nail?"

"Hold on Glenda. Yo! Undertaker, get your ass out here and see that this Bitch is dead!"

The Undertaker of Muncha, Muncha, Land spoke.

"This stinking ass bitch is dead as a door nail."

"Yes, the wicked witch is dead. D-E- A _ D dead." All the munchkins yelled out. Every Munchkin sang.

"Ding dong, the bitch is gone, wait that is wrong, ding dong the wicked witch is dead. Below, far low where the asses go."

After, they rejoiced, a loud bang and a puff of green smoke appeared.

"Oh, look what we have here," Said Glenda.

"Who killed my sister? Who dared to kill my oldest sister, the wicked ugly Witch?"

"Hey, Doris. You should leave now. Maybe another house will fall on you too."

"Fine. I am going. Before I go, I'll be taking back my sister's ruby slippers."

With a quick wave of the wand of Glenda's, the slippers went onto Craig's feet and they became men's shoes.

"What happen to my sister's slippers?"

"There they are. Ha, HA. Ha, and you're not going to be getting them back neither, sweetheart."

"We will see about that," said Doris.

The wicked witch touched the shoes and she gets zapped.

But Craig noticed something strange about this witch. He saw another face, beyond the ugly green face, that was not really that ugly at all.

"I got something I must say to you, Wicked Witch."

"What?"

Craig started to sing an old song.

"Those fingers in my hair, that sly come-hither stare, that strips my conscience bare. It's witchcraft. And I got no defense for it, the heat is too intense for it."

Craig reached the wicked witch and Craig is almost on top of her and when he sings the last verse.

"What good common sense for it do "

Doris disappeared. The face beyond the first, had a smile. There was a twinkle in the eye. No man ever sang a song to her like that.

"I wonder if I can change the bad Witch. I see some good in her. And she is so beautiful."

"Craig, if you are going to change Doris, you will need to get the Willing Flower. This flower is very deadly.

No man every got this flower. You will see men lying there frozen. I don't know if your shoes have that kind of magic to get this flower, but good luck. Now just follow the yellow brick road."

Craig yelled at the top of his voice, "What if the road changes color? What do I do? What if the road just stops, or the witch changes the color? Come on tell me!"

Glenda takes off faster than she arrived. And the sweet Munchkins were all alone. And Craig's mind thinking of DD.

Craig said to himself, "I can go for a nice chocolate, cream-filled doughnut just about now, right now."

"Craig just follow the yellow brick road," screamed the Mayor of Munchkin city.

"Hey guys, this is not brick. They are rocks and stones. Do you know what bricks are?" yelled Craig.

"Yes. I laid them myself. Ok, I am sorry. I ran out of bricks. Just follow the yellow fringing road, man, and if you come across a fork in the road, flip a coin. Now leave. We need to clean up your mess," screamed the bricklayer man. Craig started walking the yellow brick "stone "road.

"Now, what do I say now? Follow the yellow stone road, follow the yellow stone road. Damn it. This yellow road is killing my eyes. They couldn't use green?"

Craig concentrates on the road. Thinking of green, and the yellow stone road became a green brick road. Now I am on a brick road and now its green.

Now, let me see. What kind of song can I sing walking down this road? Wait a second. I got magic shoes. And this place is very beautiful, so I want to see all of it. What can I do to walk faster and also see this beautiful place too? Wait I know."

Craig goes into a deep consitration and think up roller skates. Now he had roller skates on.

"Now I am we're talking."

Craig thinks of song.

"I got it. It's an old song by the "Moffatt's ,Wait what is happing I can't believe this. I got army fatigues on."

Craig was about to sing when he saw two men walk right by him, two older gentlemen wearing military uniforms. They both looked at Craig. Their faces saying 'you must be kidding' just as Craig was singing the song.

"There she just a walkin down the street, singing do wah diddy down diddy do. Holdin my hand just as natural as can be singin do-wah diddy down diddy do.""

Craig's roller skates just disappeared. A loud noise, sounding like a motor cycle, was suddenly right on top of him. The bike stopped right in front of Craig.

"Get on the bike soldier. I need your help."

"Ok, who are you?"

"My name is Israel; they call me Izzy. My brothers are fighting the war and I need your help."

We are at war with the Gizones. They are allies of the Wicked Witch. They made weapons that we've never seen before. So, my four brothers invented a more powerful device to stop the Gizones. The Gizones are using what they call a gun. Not the thing that we use downstairs. My brother Pete got called in late for the war. He was finishing our secret weapon."

"Ok, what can I do?" said Craig

"I need you to take the KX-9 box that my brothers invented and push these buttons. Three, one, six, five, Four. And enter. This is Izzy two- ninety come in Peter 2-one."

"This is Peter 2-one come in."

"Is the plane ready yet, Pete? We need to attack now!"

"Almost Izzy. I need to do some adjustments, a few more things to it."

"Thank you, Peter. Calling Paul, three dash four come in."

"This is Paul three dash four come in."

"Where in Victor and Harry?"

"Victor dash three dash seven been shot in the leg. Harry is flying to him as we speak over."

"Oh no. I hope he's ok, over."

"Yes. He is doing fine. He just took the shrapnel out of his leg and he on the line fighting. Over."

"Wow, I can't believe that. Let us finish this war up now. We need a rest over."

"Wow, Izzy, your brothers are very courageous."

Izzy stopped the motorcycle and Craig got off. The motorcycle sped off like a bullet.

Craig walked a few feet and the whole area changed. There was a duplex on one side street. In the back of the yard were a bunch of people.

In the back yard were two huge trees. One was a red apple tree and the other a green apple tree. There also were two smaller trees, one full of peaches and the other plums. To the left was a grapevine. All kinds of grapes. In the middle of the yard was a small garden. Inside were cherry tomatoes, big tomatoes, summer squash. You name it, it was inside this garden.

"Hi, everyone, this is our new friend Craig. He helped us in this war," said Izzy.

Izzy introduces Craig to his whole family, "Craig this is my wife Fay."

"Hi Fay."

"These are my brother's sons. Hello

"Hi" all three said at one time. You done something great today.

Craig answers "Thank you."

"Thank you "Izzy "It was nothing. it was my pleasure to fight. With the help of your brothers Harry, Pete, Victor we would not have a chance. It was All Victor and Harry and Peter and Paul help in stopping this war. If it was not for Peter making you the airplane you would have no chance, I must go now, take care hope to see you again." Remember without the new airplane with V5 engine we would not be here right now.

"Hey, Craig, before you go, please take some of my peaches, and cherry tomatoes," said Harry.

"Thank you, Harry," said Craig.

Craig took a bite of the peach, it exploded with juice. It was the sweetest thing that Craig ever ate.

"Wait Craig I got something for you."

"Yes Fay."

"I work at the Hostess store and these is what I brought home a box of Twinkies."

Oh wonderful ,thank you ever so much.

Craig started to walk down the street and the scenery changed.

Craig reached a steep hill. Craig's roller skates appeared on his feet and he roller skates down the hill, what a drop. Going down about sixty miles per hour with no stoppers.

Craig came to a flat section and he slowed up, just when he hit the fork in the road. Just in front of Craig was a very, very scary scarecrow. It looked like the same scarecrow that was on the "Doctor Who" show.

"Now, where is my coin. Damn it no coin. Now which way to go?"

"This would be a good way."

"Hey, who said that?"

Craig looked all around. Craig does not see anyone.

"Ok. It is my imagination. Now which way should I go?"

"This way could be good?"

"Wait a second, it was you. And you were pointing the other direction. You're not going to kill me, are you?"

"No. Why would I do that? If I had brains, I would be very helpful, and with no brains I don't think I could hurt a fly."

"Ok. I will let you down."

"Thank you. I am a very bad scarecrow; the crows keep on eating me."

"Well, if you live where I live, you'd scare just about everyone there."

"So where are you headed?" said the Scarecrow.

"I am headed to the Willing Flower. I want to save someone."

"Do you think this flower can give me brains?"

"No offence scarecrow. You are born with brains. And some people who have brains don't use them. Like myself. you're better off not having any."

"Well, just the same. I would like them."

"I will stop over to see the wizard, that wonderful, wonderful Wizard of Oz."

"Oh, goody. I am going to see the wizard."

Craig said to himself, "The fraud Wizard. I can do more magic than he can, and I am no Wizard." Craig and the scarecrow walk.

"Scarecrow. I need to give you a name. So, I don't keep calling you scarecrow, I might say "Scarecrow and Mrs. King."

"Ok, what are you going to call me?"

"I am going to call you Ray. A very good dancer, way back before I was born, was a man named Ray Bolger."

"Well, I use this name with highest respect."

Craig and now "Ray" walk down the green brick road, and they came along a bunch of apple trees.

"Ray. I am a bit hungry. I would like to take one of those apples, but I am in a different place so I am going to try something. Hello, Mr. Tree. May I have one of your apples?"

"No, you may not. Do I go picking things off you?"

"No, but you have something that I need, but let me give you something in return. Maybe you can change your mind."

"What can you give me?"

Craig thought very hard and he clicked his shoes once. A watering can containing 10–20-10 plant food for fruit trees. Craig approached the main tree that spoke, and poured the water on its base. The tree looked like it got fuller and stronger.

"What have you done to me? I feel really good. I never felt like this ever. Thank you so much. Here take these apples and I will give you a basket, too. I will fill it up," said the Tree.

"Thank you, sir, and I leave this watering can here for you. Next week, pour this on your base and you should feel good," said Craig.

Craig walked on and he saw a man. A man made out of tin. A tin can he was.

"Hey, Craig. Why is he not moving?"

"No idea. Oh, look at that. A bee went up his nose. Wait. I think he is trying to say something. You want me to kick you in your pants? No, you don't. You want me to kick you? What? If you could only talk."

Craig looked down and found on the ground a fully filled oil can.

"I found this can. I hope this works."

Craig oiled the mouth of the tin man.

"Ah, that feels so good. I can talk. Please my arms, my legs .my legs, they never let me go.

Thank you, I am the Woods Man. I was chopping this tree and suddenly it started to rain. The old man who made me took off and never came back. I think the Witch ate him."

"I think that is very unlikely," laughed Craig.

"So, where are you two headed?"

"Rayhere wants a brain, and I am going to be getting a Willing Flower."

"Oh, please, can I come along. I need a heart."

"And why do you need a heart? Trust me, you don't need a heart. Once you have a heart, you will break others' hearts and your heart will be broken too. Just like mine."

"So, for you, your heart breaks, nevertheless I would like to have one," said the Tin Man.

"Ok, let's go. We are going to see the Wizard. The old fart.

But I need to call you something, not "hey, tin man." I am going to name you. Let me see. How about "Jack?""

"Jack Haley, a very funny comedian and dancer before my time. I think this name will suit you."

"I like that. So, my name is Jack. Thank you. Oh, and who may you be?"

"My name is Craig, and we are off!"

A loud bang and a bunch of green smoke appeared.

"Not so fast you three. You think you are going to leave here this easy?"

"You can't scare me," said James.

"Ya that's right. We are three and we can get you, you witch," said Jack.

"Hi Doris. You know I got chills that are multiplying. And you are the one I want ooh, ooh, ooh."

"Yes, you want me and soon you will have me. Or is it that I will have you. Just stay out of my way and forget what you are thinking. I don't need to be saved, only you need to be saved."

Just as Doris said that, the inner face looked sad as she couldn't control the mean side of her. And with the green smoke and a bang, Doris was gone.

"Craig calling the good witch, Craig calling the good witch, come in, come in the hot sexy lady."

A white ball of light appeared and the hot sexy good witch flaunted her sexy body and spoke.

"Hi Craig, what can I do for you?"

"Tell me about Doris."

"Well, it started some time ago. When the Wizard came to Oz. Doris saw him and she had fallen in love with this man. The Wizard did not like Doris the way that she liked him. Doris's sister made a potion that turned her into an ugly, mean witch, and a green ugly woman. No person ever saw Doris the way that you see her. So, if you can change her, that would be wonderful. Remember Craig, you're not in Kansas anymore."

"Well, sweet Glinda, I never said I was from Kansas and Kansas City here I don't come. I am from a great state from MMMMM ass a chusets. Because I love that dirty water! Charles. Boston is my home."

"We'll be careful. You don't want to get Doris any angrier than she is. "

The ball of light faded away.

"Well, we are off again, to see if you think he is a wonderful Wizard, the wonderful Wizard of Oz. I wonder if he is any relation to "Ozzy Osborne". Maybe the wizard would go on the "Crazy Train"."

The three walked and they came to a part of the path that was getting dark.

"Crrrrraig. I don't like this. There might be bears or lions or tigers here," said Jack.

"Don't worry about it. I can summon up anything. If a lion pops up, I will summon a raw piece of meat. A Bear, some fish or some honey, because I am funny. A tiger, the same a raw piece of meat. Not talking about a male neither.

"Ok, let us sing a little song now. Lions, not the charity people, and tigers, and definitely not the baseball team, and bears, and definitely not the football team, neither. Ha, Ha, Ha, oh my."

After Craig said his little song, a very loud noise came from behind him and they stopped, and they were afraid. Craig let out a huge fart and the smell went out for miles.

"What was that?" cried Jack.

"I don't know!" cried Ray

"Sorry. Did I scare you two? I had to fart. Wow, even I can smell it. Damn. I must stop eating these apples."

Just at that moment, a lion popped out.

"Come on, put them up, come on. I will have one hand behind my back."

Craig saw a skinny lion, goes right up to him and punched the fool right in the stomach. Softly knowing that he does not look strong.

"Ow. Why you do that for?"

"Well dude, you said put them up and you wanted to fight. So, you should be glad I did not pop you in the face."

"Ok, I'm sorry. I didn't mean to start a fight. I can't fight. I am afraid. I can't sleep at night," said the lion

"Why don't you count sheep?"

"I am afraid of sheep."

"Well, you can count cats, can't you? Pussy cats?"

"No, I am afraid of Pussy."

"I think I know what this Lion needs. I can help him a little, to get some courage."

"How is that?" asked Jack.

"We need to get this Lion a female.

Ok, please stay here. I am going into the woods to look around."

Craig took off into the woods. Deep in the woods he saw a female lion.

"Please excuse Ms. Please don't eat me, but I have a friend that needs your help."

"Don't worry. I am a vegetarian. I don't eat meat. Who is you friend?"

"He is a lion, and he is afraid. I think maybe you can help him a little."

The female lion was pretty hot. Standing on two feet. The front side. You can see the details of the chest. Not too big not too small. The breasts, so beautiful. The nipples looked so hard. And the area was a lot of hair.

"Ok. I will come with you."

Craig and the female lion met up with his new friends.

"Lion, I brought you a friend. Please talk to her."

"No! I can't. I am afraid!"

"Listen up dude. She is not going to hurt you. Only if you F up. So don't F Up!" said Craig.

"Oh, I know this lion," she said. "He had a chance to have me years ago and he ran away. Now I have you right here and you can't run. I got you. Lets go over here so they don't watch."

Both lions, making all kinds of noises, and the male lion talks like Tarzan, "Ah, ah oh, oh."

"Well, Craig, maybe the wizard can give this lion some courage, what do you say?" said Ray

"Well, I guess he can. I think he might have some right now."

The lion became a little stronger. After his wonderful time with the female, he walked over to Craig.

"Well Lion. I have to give you a name as well. I am not going to say 'hey Lion come here'. So, I name you "Bert" after a very famous comedian before I was born "Bert Lathr". He was on Broadway and a very funny man."

"I Like that. He sounds very strong. Bert, my name is Bert, it rhymes with nert, and you better not call me dirt."

The female lion talked, "Bert, you can call me Girt. I hope you not afraid anymore. I think you're going to be closer to me than you think."

"Why?" Bert now shaking terribly.

"I think you're going to be a Daddy. I will wait for you here. Hurry soon, my dear," said Girt.

Bert made a big smile. The four started to walk and a beautiful field appeared in front, just a thousand feet away was the Emerald Square Mall. No. It was the Emerald city.

"Well, well, well," yelled Doris. "They've managed to reach the Emerald city and damn it. He know how to use my sister's slippers. Damn, Damn, Damn. He is protected from any spells that I can cast on him."

"Hi Doris," said the good witch of the North, Glinda.

"What do you want?" said Doris.

"Well, you seem upset. Are you worried?. You think Craig knows how to use your sister's shoes and he does. So, get ready things are going to change."

"Get lost you goody two shoes. I have a plan up my sleeve."

Craig entered and knocked at the door.

"Who is knocking at my door? Go away. Don't come back no more. If you stay, I well only run away, and here I have to stay. Who can it be now?!"

"My name is Craig, and I want to speak to the Wizard."

A small window opened and a man that looked like he needed to be in a home spoke.

"You can't talk to the Wizard, no way and no how."

"If you don't open the freaking door, I will do to you as I did to the witch I got the shoes that I am wearing from." The man looked down.

"Oh, I am sorry, that is horse shit. I mean a horse of a different color. Please come in please."

The man unlocked the door and a bunch of people were walking about. A group of four ladies came to Craig. Luckily for Craig, a group of hot sexy ladies wearing green miniskirts and green medias and green shoes were giving Craig a bath.

Craig was lying in the bathtub, naked, getting washed by four hot ladies in Oz. Something happened in the water and one lady blushed. A smile grew on Craig's face that lasted for ten hours.

"The wizard will see you now."

"Ok, listen you guys. I am going in first. Just stay out here. Trust me. I will say come in, and you can come in."

The door opened.

Craig walked in and a huge face appeared.

"Scarecrow you want brains, Tin Man you want a heart, and the Lion you want courage."

"Hey, asshole. are you blind? The three that you mention are outside."

Craig saw a curtain and walked over to it. Craig pulled the curtain and he saw a man. And he tapped him on the shoulder. The old fart jumped a mile.

"I don't like the way you are talking to me. Go away before I turn you into a toad."

Craig tapped the old man on the shoulder again. The face said, "Don't mind the man in the curtain. Now go!"

"Damn it. How did you know?"

"It does not take a genius. I know you are not much of a wizard. So, give the Lion what he wants, the tin man and scarecrow and I must go."

"You are crazy; men have died getting the Willing Flower. I know Glinda told me all about it. Don't do it."

"Well, I am going to do it and I am off.

James, Jack, Bert. The wizard is ready for all of you."

"Hello, sir."

The three were very scared to now be talking to the great Wizard.

"Oh, please, don't be afraid. I am not going to hurt you. I am a very kind Wizard, trust me.

So, Scarecrow, I think Craig calls you Ray, right?"

"Yes."

"Yes, a great name indeed. During my time, I saw in person a man named Ray Bolger. A great dancer."

"Yes, I believe Craig named me after him. Now watch me go."

The Scarecrow "Ray" does a routine and what a show he does. Almost as good as if Mr. Bogler was still alive.

"Well, you know I am sorry. I am not a doctor. I can't give you any brains but what comes close to it is my two Associates degrees. Now you know Electronics and Plumbing and Heating. Great job. And you did not have to pay a dime. Now that is great thinking. Now Tin Man. I think Craig calls you Jack, Right?"

"Yes."

"Yes. I know of a Jack too, his name was "Jack Haley", a great comedian and a performer. And you want a heart. Well, I told Ray here I am no doctor. I can't give you a heart. Maybe Doctor Frankenstein can, but seeing that the doctor is not here, I give you my heart watch. Sorry, it does not tick any more. It is not a timeex and it took a licking and it stopped ticking. Find someone here that fixes watches, and it surely will tick again.

And you, A Cowardly Lion. A young man that pops up and punches you in your stomach because you want to fight, and you gave up so fast. But you got enough courage in getting laid by a hot woman lion. Well, you don't need any courage, what you do need is brains, and I am no doctor. But I will give you this trophy for at least coming to see me, and maybe we can fix you up with the same or another female lion. I bet you won't be afraid, dog?"

"Well, of course I won't be," said Bert.

"Ok, now you're my guest, please enjoy yourself and explore our wonderful city."

So, the three left and went to the park area where they entered and the witch on her broomstick was writing something.

"Hey witch, if you can hear me. You spelled Craig wrong, it is a C not a G. Please learn how to spell. Or I have to give you my brains," said James.

"To damn bad. I will spell it the way that I want. And for you."

The witch did not see where she was going, and she slammed right into a flagpole and what a noise that was.

The broomstick was lying right beside her. Her face bloody, a few people took her inside to get her cleaned up. She was still dazed.

"Why in the world would you help me, as I want to kill you all?"

"Well Doris, not all people are bad. Even you, who is our enemy, deserves treatment. If this was bad, we would still give you the proper treatment."

Doris stood up, grabbed her broomstick and, with a wave of her hand, she lefts. A big puff of green smoke. At this time, Craig was entering a bad part of Oz. Signs said keep out, leave while you have a chance, you're entering the Night Mares. Craig kept on walking and a girl came up to him.

"Craig, you're my lover and this kid is your son."

"What are you crazy? This kid is not my son. Look at me. I am Black, the kid is white, the kid is not my son. The kid has funny eyes. I don't have. Forty days and forty nights the law was on your side. I told the stupid Judge, the kid is not my son. Girl, I was banging your hot mother and she was my lover. Christy. She has the partly shaved head. She wears the hot sexy black eye glasses, and a pretty mini skirt and hot, very hot, sexy black medias and her hot slender body. And you are nuts."

"Damn you Craig. I didn't know you were banging my mother. From another."

"Well yes, and now I going to turn around, he, he, he. And for you Billy Jean from a movie scene. I am O-U-T, out of here."

Craig kept on walking, wondering if another nightmare would pop up. A group of people were running. They all had instruments. One by one they passed Craig. A man ran towards Craig. Craig stopped him.

"Who are you people? Why are you running?" asked Craig.

A man said, "We are the "Band on the Run "and the jailer man said to Uncle Sam. "Damn, we are the Ban on the Run"."

"Ok, see Ya."

The nightmares were truly nightmares. A land of great music becoming some kind of reality. Craig wondered if there was going to be a chance.

"Who might you be? Wow, you look super? Well, are you Craig?" said a very hot blond haired woman

"Well, yes I am."

"Ok, Craig, now let's get physical, come on I hear your body call. Come on let's get a physical."

"No, let's have something else. Lucka, Lucka, Lucka, Lucka."

Somehow, Craig was changing the Night Mares to his way of thinking, and the land of Oz couldn't do anything about it. Or this was how the Night Mares on Oz was.

Craig reached a house. It looked like his friend Tim's. Tim opened the door and inviteed Craig in.

Tim's father spoke, "Tim, can you come here for a minute? I need to speak to you."

"Yes, dad."

Tim's father was a priest, a very nice man.

"Craig, could you please be nice enough and grab me my can of beer?"

"Yes, sir, no problem."

Craig opened the refrigerator door and saw mold. Craig yelled out.

"Holy moldy!"

Just in front of Craig's eyes he was at McGolden's restaurant. Inside Craig was in the restroom.

Craig said to himself, "What the heck is that smell?"

It was a priest. Making some Holy Shit. The scene changed again. Craig was walking in a field. He saw cows sitting funny in the field. Their two front legs were touching. A huge cow came over to Craig and talked very softly.

"Please be quiet, the cows are praying."

Craig smiled and said, "Oh, holy cow."

The scene changed again and Craig was at McGolden's restaurant again. Standing in line, waiting for the woman to take his order. Craig gave her his order. Craig ordered a big McGoldens and Fries. Goes and sits down.

"Oh, damn. I forgot my Coke Zero."

Craig went back in line and ordered his Coke Zero and sits down but no sandwich and fries.

"How did my meal disappear?"

Craig goes back, "I would like to have a Big McGoldens and large French fries please."

Craig got back to his seat and his Coke was gone. He goes back to the girl and ordered his Coke again.

As Craig looked, his sandwich and fries disappeared again. Craig looked all around and saw an old woman eating his two sandwiches and fries and drinking his favorite Coke Zero.

Craig walked over to the woman and said, "Lady, this is my meal you're eating."

She said, "Where is your receipt?"

Craig bent down and grabbed the ladies handbag.

"Hey, this is my handbag."

Craig said, "Where is your receipt?"

Craig started to walk down the brick road and he found himself in his father's furniture store. Craig was very smart, going to law school in the fall.

"Craig, I know you are a smart man, but this furniture business was in the family for generations."

"Sorry, dad, but I want to go to Law school in the fall."

"Ok. I want you to answer me one question. If you can get it right, you can go to Law school. If not, I need you to go to Las Vegas to go to a trade show and get me information on some beds and carpet samples."

"Oh, go right ahead. I can answer anything."

The father asked the question.

"Son, What What's?" Craig answered, "What?"

The father said, "Sorry that is not the answer."

Craig hopped on an airplane and headed to Vegas. It was a long day at the trade show, writing down all the bed information, new mattresses and getting samples of new carpet. Craig goes to the bar. A very lovely girl, with short blond hair, sat near Craig.

"Hello, sir. I never saw you here before. Would you like some company?"

"Ok."

Craig and this beautiful woman entered his bedroom. Craig went to the bathroom and brushed his teeth and the girl took off her blouse and bra and she said,

"I just got this done just last week." As she was holding her breasts.

"What?" asked Craig as he walked in the room.

She said very loudly, "What do you mean What, What's?"

Craig said, "If I knew that I would be a lawyer now."

In a small town, Crum Field was a man who practiced magic. He was a wizard, fourth generation. Mr. Drake Guayules was a very bad wizard, he could not do any potions right. He worked hard, he mastered the spell to push.

On this particular day, three boys walked by his house. These three boys knew that Mr. Drake Guyables was a strange man, and when a potion again failed, the three boys threw rotten eggs at the man's house. Mr. Guyables heard the noise and opened the door. Without any hesitation, Mr. Guyable's took his wand out and pushed the three boys. A bright powerful green light appeared.

With little remorse, My Guyables was happy, he did, however, feel slightly sorry for killing the three boys. Not!

The sky had gotten dark, very dark. Mr. Guyables house was getting bombarded by hail. He looked outside to see what was going on. As the door opened and flew off the hinges, the house started to shake, and before you knew it, the house was up in the air.

Mr. Drake Guyables felt a little strange; he felt stronger, and he felt powerful. The house landed on a small patch of land outside a quiet place he had never seen before. He stood outside in a beautiful place. Quiet, peaceful.

Mr. Guyables was wearing normal clothes, like a common man, so as a strange ball of light appeared it was the beginning.

"Who are you?" asked Mr. Guyables.

"I am Gail, the Good witch of the North East of Oz." Then a great awful smell of green smoke appeared.

"Gail, I am going to get you and you will die as your sister did."

"My dear Doris, the wicked witch of the South and I will protect my people here and I shall destroy you once and for all."

"Wait a second, are you the one they call the wicked one? I am looking at you; I see a beautiful woman. You can't be that wicked."

The wicked witch of the South disappears.

"My friend, you must go to the center of Oz and leave, go back where you came from, you're not safe here. Follow this road and go now."

So, Mr. Guyables started to walk down the yellow brick road. The yellow was hurting Mr. Guyables eyes. He took out his wand and he waved it. Now the yellow brick road was the color red. Blood red.

"Gail, calling Gail the good witch, I need to talk to you."

"Yes, here I am. Oh, I did forget to ask your name, what is it?"

"It is Drake."

"Well Drake. How can I help you?"

"I saw another person of the wicked witch of the South, why?"

"She is my cousin. During a dance, her boyfriend stood her up. A witch named Carrie stole her boyfriend. She got so full of revenge, she killed him and Carrie and she turned green and ugly." "Well, I don't see ugly woman, I see a beautiful woman. How can I change her?"

"There have been five men who have seen her inner self and tried to change her. They have all failed. I will tell you and you will fail and die trying. Down the South part of Oz lies a flower, this flower is so powerful and can win over her heart, but the flower will kill you."

"I will take the chance."

As Drake walked down the road he came across a shack. The wicked Doris was just standing on the roof.

"I don't know who you are, but I am going to kill you."

"Wait, don't kill me. I am in love. I am in love with you. It was love at first sight."

Drake started to sing the Frank Sinatra song wicked witchcraft. The wicked witch's inner self was talking to her and he could hear it. "Don't kill him. I think I am falling in love. No, I will kill him." As the wicked witch tried her spell on Drake, he took out his wand and brushed away the spell of the less powerful witch.

Drake, with his big smile said to her, "You need to try something more powerful." So with a wave of Drake's wand he put a dozen long stem roses into her hand.

"I don't know what kind of magic you are using, but your days are numbered."

"Ok, but please let me blow you a kiss."

The wicked witch was now very angry and she was coming out of her her skin, "How can I kill him? How? How? He is powerful. I never came across a man like him before."

After walking for days, it felt like days, Drake waved his wand and he got himself to the flowerbed. Drake knew this place was not like any other, and every living thing could talk.

"Hello, flowers, may I have a word with you?"

A flower, the biggest of all the rest spoke. "Why do you disturb me?"

"I need your help to help another person. Only you have a special gift that I need. If you can help me, I can give you something special in return."

"Oh," said the flower. "What can you give us?"

Drake took out his wand and he waved it and plant food appeared.

"Please take this," Drake said as he gave the flowers the plant food and the plants grew.

The head plant said, "Thank you. I will come." The flower popped up with a pot and dirt and the rest of the plants grew legs as now they could walk.

The wicked witch was worried, she did not see Drake. Drake came to the wicked witch's castle, the flower was giving life to all of the dead plants around the castle grounds.

"Hello, Miss wicked witch. I have something to give you."

"What!?"

"I give you this flower."

She could not move, the wizard got closer to her. Her pretty blue eyes closed. The wizards got even closer. The Wizard was now so close. The Wizard then gave her a kiss on the lips. The Wicked Witch Doris turned.

As she was about to speak, Drake took out the wand and ripped out her heart. Drake got even stronger and turned vicious. He took the special flower and he destroyed it. The darkness came quickly to the castle; much darker than before. The flowers felt the other flower being destroyed. They walked to the castle, and they saw Drake sleeping. The flowers took their vines and pierced Drake's heart.

Doris was giving Craig a warning to stay away from her and making him a villain like her. Craig ignored it and he proceeded to the Willing flower.

Craig entered a part of the city. Still the nightmares, Craig wondered if he was still in the nightmare or not. This place looked so real. Not a dream. Craig was in his city. Walking down a street that he had walked down at least a hundred times before, he stopped and went into the bar.

The people were dressed normally. And it was Karaoke night. Craig walked over to the DJ.

"Excuse me, sir. Can I sing a song?"

"Of course, you can. Please fill out this piece of paper."

Craig filled out the paper, name of song and group.

"Ladies and Gentlemen, we got our first singer of the night. Craig, please come up."

The song started. Craig had chosen an old song by an awesome heavy metal group called KISS.

"You got to Rock all night".

As Craig sang this song he stuck out his tongue. The Nations Gabbers run over to Craig.

"Please excuse me. I noticed your tongue. Are you related to Gene Simons?"

"No. But I love his music."

The Nations Gabber needed a story. So, they made up a story.

"Yesterday June 12th A group of reporters went to the club for some beer, and they were having Karaoke night. A man started to sing. It was Gene Simons lost child.

After the child's birth. The child ran away never to be seen again. The child stepped into a time vortex. Thousands of years later the child is seen again."

Craig left the club and walked outside. Craig reached the end of the Night Mare's land and walked down the green path road.

"Damn it. Damn it. He is almost at the Willing Flower. I must stop him. But how? Flying monkeys, attack him, bring him back to me."

The captain monkey started to fly and then stopped. The rest of the flying monkeys could not fly.

"What the hell? What is wrong?" "Ooh ooh, ha ha ha."

"Stop talking in monkey and talk to me in my language."

"We can't fly. Something is preventing us from flying."

"Damn those shoes are getting stronger on him by the minute. Brrrrrooom, come now and we are off."

Doris took her broom and flew off. She saw Craig and she landed in front of him.

"Well, it looks like we meet again and now I have to destroy you myself."

"Go ahead, if you must, but before you do, I want to give you something."

Craig took his hand and was about to blow Doris a kiss. Doris took off on her broom and flew away so fast. She didn't know she could go that fast. She went supersonic. The first time Doris every flew that fast.

Craig entered a field with beautiful Willing Flowers. They were all sleeping. All around were men, lying with the flowers, all sleeping.

In a soft voice Craig spoke. "Hello, Willing Flower, may I speak to you?" A flower spoke and awoke.

"Who are you? and why do you awake me?"

"My name is Craig and I need your help."

"And why do I have to help you?"

"Because a person needs your help. She ended up on the wrong path and I want to save her. And I was told that you have very powerful powers."

"So. And why should I help you? Give me a reason. Look all around you. These men tried to take us and destroy us, but we make them sleep."

"I can give you something in return if one of you was to come with me."

"What can you give me? We are powerful as you said."

Craig thought and he clicked his shoes once. A watering can appeared. Inside it was 5-10-5 plant food for flowers.

Craig poured this on the flowers and they all bloomed bigger and much healthier.

"Wow, that was very good. Thank you. For that I will be happy to come with you," said the Willing Flower

With a pot in hand the Willing Flower appeared in Craig's hand and he was instantly going to Doris's castle.

Doris knew Craig was coming. She had an hour glass ready for Craig. Craig enters the witch'es castle. Craig saw a magic ball and looked in it.

"Craiggee, where are you? Craiggee, where are you?"

"I am right here, aunty Elm. Right here."

"Craiggee, I hear you but I can't see you."

"I am right here you stupid Bitch." At that spit second Freddy Krueger popped up.

"Oh, here I am."

"Now, why the F are you here? You're in the wrong story dude."

"Well, everywhere has an Elm Street."

"No shit. But I am in a land where there are no streets, so get lost."

Doris popped up, through the magic ball.

"Oh, aunty Elm, Oh aunty Elm. Well, that old goat is not going to be seeing you anymore. Once the hourglass stops, you will die."

"Oh, really and what happens if the hou glass happens to disappears?"

Craig clicked his shoes twice and the hourglass is gone.

"Damn you! Damn you!"

Doris came running into the room and slammed the door open.

"I am going to choke you to death."

Craig took the Willing Flower from his back and gave it to Doris.

She took the flower and she changed instantly. As she changes, Craig gave her a kiss on the lips.

Doris looked like a person that Craig once new, but older. He can't figure out who.

Doris looked at Craig and said, "You are nice, and my heart was ice. Your kiss melted my heart and now I have changed."

"Xmose, the girls are not out yet?"

"No, they better not be. Calling truck two are the girls there?"

"Yes, sir, all the girls are here and counted for."

"Great, let us see what happens now."

The dark forest became light, and all the dead trees came back to life. Doris and Craig, together on a carriage driven by six Clydesdales horses.

The two entered the Munchkin land and they got married and lived happily ever after. The area became red, and the area changed.

"Hey, Xmose, what's with the color red? It does not look right."

"It is my new advancement. The illusion machine is reading his brain; all of his fantasy's and his life. Making them real. this part is his life will react to his inner thoughts and get a pain he will become soft, and we can kill him."

Craig, at the age of five, is up in his room playing with his GI –Joe doll. Craig's mother called him down as they have company.

"Hi, dear."

"Hi, Agnes. I see you brought your daughter Jackie here, too."

"Craig! Come down. You got company."

Craig saw Jackie and was very happy to see her. They went down into the cellar. Craig turned on the light before he walked downstairs.

"Hey, Jackie, do you want to see me swing on the strings?"

"You can't swing on the strings."

"Yes, I can, watch."

Xmose shuts off the illusion machine and they are all in the pitch black as it was night time.

"Why did you do that?"

"I don't want to see him trying to kill himself, ok. I want the pleasure of doing it myself. I am turning on the machine now."

Ninth grade. Craig was taking Biology and studied very hard. Being bullied, Craig always thought the brain had special powers if found. Craig does research on the brain and cloning.

Craig got a paper route and started to make money. Every week, Craig would put money away, getting a big savings account and he studied on biology, the human anatomy.

Learning about the sciences, Craig made a glass cage. One being airtight and the other with air holes.

Tenth Grade was the same usual stuff, eleventh grade nothing changed. Craig kept on studying one thing, cloning and Bio technology. Craig never studied chemistry in High school. Was not too smart. Maybe they were right, during Craig's free time he was learning on his own. It is amazing what one can do when self-taught. If they teach themselves, they would have learned everything they needed to learn.

Senior year. Time to take the yearbook pictures. Well, knowing Craig's grades were pretty bad. Craig really was not going to be bothered to be serious in writing a little insert. "Let me see, what bazar thing can I say? Who knows? It just might be the truth."

End of school year, Craig needed to retake English as he failed it again. Another Summer, Craig goes to Summer school and failed his wonderful course again, English.

During Summer School there was a girl; cute but smelled bad. She smelled like an ash tray. Craig did not know at that time he had an allergy to people who smoked. Craig started to sneeze and huge boogers started coming down his noise. He has no choice in using his sleeve.

During the break time, the two bullies came for Craig, inside the building. Craig was minding his own business when the two bullies kicked Craig's face in.

Craig did not block the kicks. Craig did not feel pain he was actual orbedthe pain. As the two were getting the free kicks, Craig's eye got big and black and blue.

In Craig's head, he has only one thing on his mind. That was revenge. Craig entered the cellar and started his experiments.

"Five ounces of Excropis, three eighths of Biofruitcuk."

Craig started making something, and Craig took a needle and he sticks it in himself. Drawing his own blood and his DNA. Craig poured the blood into the glass tube and closed it.

Craig covered the glass cage and he uses a camera that can see in the dark to see his progress.

Craig took more chemicals and made a DNA pattern cell on himself. With a lot of care and a very fine tube, Craig put this tube with a blood sample cell inside him.

A month later, man was formed. Xcromast – Man –Of- Same-Extrosketon.

"Hey Xmose. It looks like Craig made you. Did you expect this to happen when you used the illusion machine?"

"No. I took his facts as he was a kid. This is all before this. I had changed the illusions on him earlier. He did not married Alice. It was another woman, Aberrance Swats. But most of what we saw was true. In his past life. I must kill him, only one will survive."

"Golly Xmose, I don't think you have the heart to do it. He is you and you are he."

"That is why I must destroy him. If I can't, the women will. They do not have any DNA of Craig or me."

The phone rang it was MIT.

"Hello?"

"Hello. May I speak to Craig please."

"Speaking."

"Mr. Galuta. Your experiment is brilliant. May we have the formula so we can make it ourselves?"

"Sorry, sir. I destroyed all my notes."

"That is a shame. We don't know how you did it, but we want to copy the DNA."

"Sorry, sir."

"You have a great weapon here; the United States would pay you a great deal of money for this."

"A weapon! Are you crazy? I made a life to help this planet with the food population not to destroy mankind."

Time went by. It is the year twenty-six ten and the MIT people look at Craig's computer.

"Hello, this is Craig. I have put a virus on my computer. If you try to excess any of my files before the year two thousand nine hundred and seventy-five, the virus will wipe out all information on the hard drive. You got thirty seconds to shut off my computer."

"Those bastards probed me every hundred years trying to get the answers. They tried to copy me, but they died in a matter of days. The doctor thought I was their experiment as I was the original. Maybe I knew what Craig did, that is why you guys are still here."

The sky changed colors. The color was a blue green color and changed to blue, but the color is slightly off as Craig was in an illusion once more. This time he was in a game that he had played many years ago. A game he never completed and now he was playing it for real.

Craig got knock out. Some person hit him over the head. Craig is in the carriage and three men sat on stools; all four men were tied up and one man had his month covered.

"Well, well you're finally up. The Imperials did a number on you."

"I guess, where are we?"

"Hey, would you shut up back there!"

"What is the matter with him? Said a man from Rorikstead"

"He is King Good Doer, and he is Dragon Born and you better shut up or he is going to blast you with his voice.."

"Well, if he is Dragon Born, how did he get caught?"

"I don't know?"

Craig goes over to the King. And Craig whispered, "Sir. I have a knife hidden right here. If I can set you free, will you do the same for me?"

"Yes, I would."

Craig took the knife and cuts the King's hands free. The King shouts out and the man on the horse falls off. And the King frees Craig and Craig frees the other two men. The four ran off into the woods and Craig ended up a small town called Oceans Call.

"Ah, Craig. Welcome to Ocean Call. Here we have everything you might need. Oh no, look at that. A Dragon."

"Dragon. Run for your life!" yelled and old hag.

"Craig, follow me. Our house in in the middle of the stream; it is safe there."

"Ok. By the way, I did not get your name and how did you know mine?"

"My name is Officer Sackcloth, and you were talking in your sleep in the carriage. You got clocked pretty good."

"Oh ok. So how do we kill the dragon?"

"You need to speak to the old fart Jarl. He lives in White Fun. Trust me, it's fun over there. They have hot women over there and they make you feel really good; you know what I mean."

Craig walked over a bridge and noticed that he had a bow and arrow and a sword. The sword was made of silver, and it was lightweight and razor sharp.

Two wolves came and started to attack Craig and Craig swung the sword and killed the wolves dead.

A beautiful countryside. The trees were very green and the sky blue, like a baby's ass if the asses of a baby was blue. It was a good walk to the city of White Fun and Craig had reached a dirt path leading to the city of White Fun.

"Halt! You can't enter to the city. We are in lockdown."

"Lockdown? Why?"

"There is a damn dragon on the loose, and nobody is permitted to enter or leave White Fun."

"I saw that dragon. It was at Ocean Call. The people wanted me to talk to the old man Jarl."

"Oh. I see. You better talk to the old fart, boy. Let me open the doors. Ok, now you can enter."

The place looked beautiful. Small shops, a place to by weapons and armor, and they had an Inn. Just up on a hill was the Club. It is where all the hot ladies of Winter Fun hung out."

Craig looked to has left and saw a stairway leading up a steep hill. There, on top of the hill, was a castle. The people called it Dragon Reach.

Craig reached the door and opened it, and a hot fox elf came running over.

"Who are you? Why do you want to bother the Jarl?"

"I'm sorry, who are you?"

"I am the Jarl's, Thane. You got that?"

"What the hell is a Thane? Is it like a pain?"

"I help the Jarl and I fight for him. Why do you come?"

"It is about the dragon that I saw at Ocean Call."

"Come with me now!"

"Can I bang you first?"

"Jarl there was a dragon sighting at Ocean Call. We need to give them help!"

"Yes, go to the tower and see if the dragon shows up there. And you, how did you enter my castle?"

"I saw the bad ass dragon at Ocean Call, old man."

"Very good. Help my men and I shall reward you with brand new armor. This armor was made just a few minutes ago by a wizard name Ick Face."

"Thank you, sir. I won't fail you."

Craig ran out of the castle and went to the tower. Craig reached the tower and a solider was yelling.

"Get back, hide the dragon, he is coming back."

"How do you know that the dragon is a male? You see his balls?"

"No, I did not. All the ladies are in bed with babies in their tummies after screwing any male that they can find. The dragon seems to be doing all the work so damn it he is."

"Not all women are in bed having babies and screwing men. I kind of wish I was doing that. Ha, ha, ha. Dude. Hey, here comes the dragon." said Craig.

The dragon was fierce, shouting out his fire breath. Craig took out his mighty bow and shoots the dragon.

With the help of White Fun soldiers, the dragon is defeated. Craig walked over to the dragon and saw how mighty and big the thing was.

"Hey, what is going on? Look at this dragon. What is happening to me? I can't believe it myself. No. I can't fly but I feel very powerful."

"You, my friend, are Dragon born," said the soldier.

"Dragon what?"

"You are Dragon born. You are very special. Now try to shout and see."

"Well. I am always shouting; this is not going to be any different. Ok."

Craig reached down and shouted and what a loud noise that was.

"Wow! I shouted. What do I do now?"

"See the Jarl. He might have an idea."

Craig started to walk over to the castle and he heard something.

"Car shit your face!"

Craig looked all around and looks at his feet. He step in dragon crap and he looks around and saw nobody. He wonders who was talking. Craig entered the castle.

"Hey old man. I just killed the dragon."

"Yes, you have and here is your new suit of armor. Anything else that you might like to talk to me about?"

"Yes. I absorbed the dragon's soul, now I am Dragon Born!"

"Yes, you are. That is what I heard the Grey Hair men call you."

"Jarl, you can't believe this little weakling is a Dragon Born, can you?" said the Jarls right hand man.

"Hey, Jackass. Do you want me to shout at you and see?" said Craig.

"Now, now, gentlemen. Boor, you must be level-headed to serve me. The Grey Hairs was calling him. Now go, but before you do, I give you Silea, your House Carl."

"Thank you."

Craig walked down the stairs to the lobby of the castle and there she was. Silea. Craig's House Carl.

"I am Silda your House Carl. I can carry and fight for you."

"How about sex. Can you have sex with me? I am a man with needs."

"Yes. I can perform many deeds. You need to get a special amulet and we can get married."

"Yahoo! And I am not the Yahoo, lady. Where can I get this amulet?"

"You can get this amulet at Riften. It is where all the thieves hang out."

"Great. Let's go, but before I go to Riften, I must see the Grey Hairs."

"Ok, let's go. I'm right behind you."

Before Craig opened the door to leave the castle, he gave Silea a very long kiss with his tongue in her mouth. The girl never had such a huge smile on her face as she did right there.

Craig walked down a road and a very mean wizard was attacking a peddler. Craig took out his bow and shoots the wizard dead.

"Oh, thank you, sir. I thought I was done for."

"No problem. Who are you?"

"My name is Joe. I live in Blitts. Town. I have a farm there. You are welcome to anything you like."

"Well, thank you, Joe. If I have a chance, I will visit you."

Craig continued down the road and he came across a tower.

"Stop and pay me a toll and so you can pass," said the woman bandit.

"What? A toll, are you nuts?"

"Ok, so you die then."

Just a split second later, Craig's House Carl, Silea, jumped in front of him and cuts her head off.

"Well, Silea. We better be careful."

"Yes."

"I am going to see what's inside this tower."

Craig entered the tower and saw a chest. Craig opened the chest and finds gold, four pieces and a bottle of health. Craig walked upstairs and he saw an opening. There was a bridge, and the men were shooting arrows at Craig.

With a mighty shout, Craig blasted the men right off the bridge, and they fell to their deaths. Craig started to walk up a ramp and a man with an ax ran towards him.

"I am the chief, and I am going to kill you!"

Craig took out his bow and shoots him right between the eyes and Craig killed him instantly.

Craig walked over the bridge and he saw another bandit. Craig got out his bow and shoots him dead, too.

"Wow, Silea, there are a lot of bandits here."

"Yes. This is there hideout. The Chief bandit was wanted, and you killed him. Good going."

Craig started to walk up a path and came across a sleeping dragon. Craig heard someone talking to him in a voice that he had never heard before. Craig took out his bow and started to shoot the dragon. The dragon started to fly; attacking with a freezing shout. Craig managed to dodge out of the way. Silea took out her bow and both of them were shooting the dragon. The dragon was now on the surface, still moving and he was fierce. Shouting his freezing shout, Craig dodged the shout and Craig gave a shout right back. Craig felt his hands getting hot. Craig put away the bow and started shooting fire from his hands. And the dragon was dead.

"Hey, Silea, come here. Look at this. Oooh. I feel good. I just got another shout."

"Yes, and you can stop yelling too. I am right here."

"Let's go find the Grey Hairs."

Craig and Silea started the journey to "Irvants".

"Craig. Look out!"

Out of nowhere, an assassin tried to kill Craig. Craig took out his mighty sword and sliced off the head of the assassin.

Craig went to see who is this pitiful fool was. There was a letter saying, "We are the dark brotherhood, we want this fool Craig dead."

"Well, the Dark brotherhood can kiss my ass. I will go and kill their ass before they kill mine."

Craig walked more and saw a fort of some kind.

"Halt. That is close enough."

"Who are you?"

"Never mind who we are. If you get closer, we will show you who we are."

"Well, if you are going to be that way."

Craig took out his mighty bow and started shooting the evil wizards of Frog Fort. Shooting the wizards right between the eyes and killing them instantly. Craig sneaked inside the building to see if there was any food there.

There were two wizards sitting down and Craig shot the two wizards dead. And he called for the House Carl.

"Here you go, Silea. An apple for you."

"Oh, thank you, Craig."

Craig left the fort and he headed to the town Irvants.

"Welcome to Irvants. Remember. If you disrespect the law, you disrespect me."

"Yes, you are right, sir."

"Hey, Jack, are you heading up to the mountain to see the Grey Hair's."

"Oh, hell no. I am too frigging old now. Shit, I got bad knees too. I don't know the F I am going to do. The Grey Hairs need my food."

"Yo, you need some food to be delivered to the Grey Hairs? I am on my way to see them myself. I can do it for you."

"No shit. You will do that for me? Thank you, boy. After you deliver it. Come back and see me. I will pay you. Just put the sack in the chest there. You can't miss it."

"Ok, thank you."

"Oh, by the way, watch your step. The steps are frozen, and there are wolves up there too."

"Ok, thank you. I will watch out for them."

Craig started his climb and he came across a man, a loafer.

"Hey, dude, what's up?"

"Oh nothing. I am just shooting the breeze. If you think you are going to see the Grey Hairs, you better watch out for the big ass bear. He nearly killed my ass."

"Ok, thank you."

Craig walked slowly up the mountainside and he saw the bear sleeping. Craig took out the bow and he shoots the bear in the head twice and, with a shout, killed the bear.

"Wow. That was easy. Now if I only had the Staples button every time I did that."

"Craig be careful. I see another person sitting on the ice. That is not normal."

"Ok. I will get my sword out just in case."

"Hello."

"Hi, who are you?"

"I am just a nobody. Just leave it at that. If you ask me again, I will have to cut out your tongue."

"What the F?"

Craig without any hesitation, took out his sword and cuts off the girl's head.

"You can kiss my ass. Cut off my tongue. Who the F are you? Dead shit. That's who."

Craig entered an ice valley and up on the side was a troll.

"Craig be careful. The trolls here can regenerate health. You must be fast in killing it."

Craig took out the bow and the troll jumped off and lands on the ground. Craig was rapid fire shooting the arrows at the troll and kills it instantly.

"Wow, this is a good work out."

Craig walked on the path for about ten minutes, and he saw a chest and he put the sack of food inside.

Craig and Silea walked inside to see the Grey Hairs.

"Who are you? and why are you two here?"

"Well old F, you summoned me here and I don't go nowhere without my House Carl. Ok."

"Am I hear you. I once had a House Carl too. She got old and died. I screwed her like a screw, pal."

"Ok. What do you want?"

"Oh, let me see if you are truly dragon born? I see you got dragon shit on your shoes. Thank you, you should have wipe your feet first."

"How in the hell did I know I was going to step in dragon shit. I would have smelt it, wouldn't I?"

"I guess you would have, ok let me see."

Craig shouted. The two men go back ten steps.

"Damn, you are truly dragon born. Good. I need you to prove yourself. So, get me the Claw of Dragon Master. But before I give you the direction, I give a shout and another. The three shouts make one powerful shout. I give you another shout for quickness, whirlwind, you are going to need it."

The Grey Hairs, gave Craig the two shouts and the direction and they were off to get the claw of the master.

Walking down the icy path, two ice dragons were attacking. Craig quickly put away his sword and fired from his hands with blazing force, destroying the two ice dragons.

"Where did these come from?"

"Those are ice dragons. They live in these parts of the land. They can withstand heat and you might see them on the lower lands."

"Ok. Are you ready to get the Master's claw lady?"

"Estoy listo!"

"And we are off!"

Just below the mountain were two men that were serving Marvin.

"Hey, are you the one called Dragon born?"

"Who me? No, they call me Michael Jackson."

Craig turned around like the late King of soul.

"He, he, heee. If I am dragon born, why do you care?"

These were Marvin's cult somewhere far away.

"There is only one dragon born and that is Marvin."

With a little song, "Marvin, Marvin. You are the one. The king dragon born we do swear to be at your side."

With speed of the shout and a sword in hand, so fast that the Marvin worshipers did not see Craig coming, Craig cut off the heads of the two men.

"I can't wait to see more of this land, it is so beautiful," said Craig.

"Yes, it is, but very dangerous never-the-less. We shall reach the hall of the dead in an hour or so. And there should be bandits waiting for us."

"Why you say that?"

"There is said to be very powerful magic that lies in there."

The days seemed very short here. The hours went so quickly. Just a few minutes ago it was noon time, and now it was pitch black, at the time it looked like it was ten o' clock. With the light of the full moon, it gave enough light for Craig to see a raised wall, but it was slanted for people to walk up on. Craig started to walk. A man with a hoarse voice said,

"You shouldn't be here. Are you lost? To damn bad. Now you are going to die."

Craig took out his sword and Silea took out her sword and both of them attacked the bandits that were guarding the entrance to the Master's Claw.

"Wow. How many do you think are going to be in there?"

"Well, I don't know. There are going to be druggies in there too."

"Oh swell. That is what I need. More druggies to spoil my plans."

"Yes, theses druggies used to be Nords. They were Nords to served Aldrin. He was a bad ass dragon. His brother, however, is a pretty nice dragon, if you think dragons can be nice."

"I would like to see him some time."

"Craig, stop. Look just up ahead. It looks like mages and bandits are going at it. Let us wait a few minutes."

"Ok, sounds good to me. It looks like the mages wins. Now for my blast of fire power."

The mage burned up, just like a bunch of matches and, with a scream of pain, the mage is dead.

The building was very weird indeed. Walking down a set of stairs into what appeared to be a cave. Doors and plenty of light. Even with the candles that were burning, it was pretty much light in the room. Just beside the dead bandit was a chest. A very nice chest. Not a woman's chest. A chest that might have some goodies inside. Craig opened the chest. There was a blazing new sword. The sword was super light and made of gold. You would think that the gold sword would be heavy. Craig looked at the blade. Craig says to himself,

"Shit. Imitation gold."   Craig with his mighty strength broke the sword in half. And he, of course, grabbed the hundred pieces of gold.

Craig entered the doorway and walked down a ramp. The floor seemed to be going down. Craig heard fighting.

"Craig. Stop. I think I hear Druggies."

"Druggies, damn it. We got druggies down here."

"Yes, we got druggies down here. The druggies were servants that were cursed by Adrin the dragon. They are like zombies. Be careful. Some of them might be dragon born and they have shouts like you."

"Very good. I will shout them down. Better than that, I will take out my bow."

Craig took out his bow and sneaked very carefully to the druggies and Craig saw that the druggies were facing in the opposite direction. Craig pulled back the bow and the arrow went speeding into the Druggie's head and killed it.

"Hey, Sliea, this druggie has gold. He does not need it, seems that he is dead and dead again."

Craig looted the druggie and walked ahead. Towards Craig's right and left there were upright caskets. Who in this world would have caskets standing up? Craig gently pulled back the bow and shoots the caskets, as Craig saw a druggie inside, waiting to pounce. Quickly Craig shot another. One more popped in front. The Druggie was looking in the other direction. Craig shot him before he turned around.

The Druggie had gold. They won't be needing it, Craig was saying to himself again. This Druggie has an ancient sword. It seemed a little stronger, but light enough to do some great killing, so Craig took the sword.

At this time, Craig's suit with its special functions gave Craig his food. An apple appeared and Craig ate it. A green Granny Smith apple. "MMMM, good," Craig said out loud.

The two entered a room and this room was even stranger. The room was even larger than the others and it also has a bridge like walkway, and a druggie was up there, waiting.

Craig saw the druggie and as the druggie walked across, Craig shot the druggie dead. There was an opening and Craig walked through it. There was a stairway leading up. Craig and Silea walked up and walked across the footbridge and Craig loots the druggie. This Druggie was richer than the others. It had fifty pieces of gold.

"Craig, be careful. I sense that there are going to be "Restless Druggies" over here."

"Wow. "Restless Druggies." I wonder what "Restless Druggies" are."

As soon as Craig said that five restless druggies ran around like their head were cut off. One by one, Craig took the arrow and shoots the druggies dead.

Now every time Craig shot the druggies, Craig felt stronger and more powerful. Feeling a little hot, Craig turned around and kisses Silea on the lips. She was feeling a little hot now too.

"Oh, Craig, please. We need to go to Riften."

"Oh, yes. Riften. Ok."

Down a narrow hallway.

"Stop!"

"What is the matter, Craig?"

"A booby trap. And it is no "Booby"."

Craig jumped over what was a presser point disk on the floor. And came to another room.

This room was a little smaller and a restless druggie came running out and Craig took out the sword and started one on one fighting the druggie. Craig stabbed him dead.

"Wow. The restless druggies have all the loot. This one has two hundred pieces of gold."

Craig started to walk down a ramp. Very deep underground now. Craig heard a funny sound and not funny ha ha. There were skeletons. Some with swords and others with bows and arrows.

Craig started shooting the skeletons with his arrows. One by one the skeletons were no more. Each skeleton had some arrows and a few pieces of gold.

"Wow, Sliea. You hear that? I hear a voice in my head. Sounds like someone is calling me."

Craig walked over to a wall. The wall was slightly curved, and a shout Craig absorbed. Craig walked up another ramp and he heard more skeletons and Craig quickly shoots them dead.

Craig jumped down from where he was and looked at a funny gate. That was shut and towards the left was three small stones that would light up when walk by and the gate would open .

Craig used his speed shout and the gates open as Craig entered the little area, Craig escaped the room with his speed shout.

Surrounded by heat traps on the floor and frost spiders, Craig killed the spiders and Silea escaped the tomb. Craig opened the door. There was a small pedestal in the middle of the room.

"Someone took the Master's Claw. Who in the hell took the claw? Another dragon born. Wait did I fail? There is a letter.

"Dear dragon born. If you are truly dragon born. Come to the Sleepy Giant and ask for the Jolly Green Giant room and pay big bucks too. I know you got the dough pal. I will be waiting for you. And don't you dare make me wait! Signed Friend J

"Well, Silea. Do you know where the Sleepy Giant is?"

"Oh, yes. It is in Ocean Call. You can't miss it." Craig and Silea were on their way to Ocean Call.

"I am going to kill you," said an Assassin.

"Who are you?" screamed Craig.

"I am an Ass. I was told to kill you," replied the Assassin.

"Well, you're right about that. You are an Ass."

"I mean assassin. The Dark Brotherhood gave me an order."

"Well, too damn bad. You're not going to collect."

Craig took out two of his swords and shouted at the assassin and cut him up and killed him quicker than a red fox can jump. Craig reached the Ocean Call town. There was a lot of sand in the area. There must have been water here a long time ago.

Craig walked past a trader's shop. A place where you can buy some odds and ends. Must have a lot of odds here. The people here were wearing clothes that were dated over thirty thousand years. But the ladies looked just fine.

Craig saw the Sleeping Giant and walked in. A young blond-haired woman met them. She must have been in her late teens. She was a knockout, and she knew Silea.

"Hi, Silea. Who is your friend?"

"Please excuse me, I need to sleep in the Jolly Green Giant room, Hoe, Hoe, Hoe."

"Ok, Ok, We, don't have a Jolly Green Giant room. But you and Silea can use my room free of charge."

"Wow, that is super."

"Craig said to, Sinea, wants a threesome."

"What? A threesome woo! "

Craig walked down the stairs to the special room.

"Sinea says Yes, keep on dreaming young man. I had to make sure you're not Thamshits."

"Who are the Thamshits?" Craig replies

"The Thamshits are a group of dragon worshipers. They want the dragons to exist. Once they saw the dragons were alive again, they wanted the dragons for themselves so they could use the dragons to take over our Skyrim."

"Damn those Thamshits. How can we stop them?" said Craig.

"Not so fast there, slick. I need to make sure you are truly dragon born."

"Fine. I will shout at you then," said Craig.

"No. I want to see you kill a stinking dragon and I want to see you take the soul."

"Sounds like I am on the "Crazy Train"," said Craig.

"Sinea, can I please come along. I am Craig's Thane?"

"Oh sure. I know you know he is dragon born. But I need to see it for myself. "

"Fine. Where do we go? and when?"

"We are heading to Recker Island. There we can find our first dragon. But before we go. I need to slip into something more fitting. My uniform. I hope you don't get too excited."

Sinea, with no shame, Took off all her clothes and put on her battle gear. This crazy town, they do not wear any under garments, they are totally naked underneath their clothes.

"Damn, how can I fight a dragon now? I think I am "Tom Brady" my balls are inflated oh wait I think his balls were deflated."

"Let's go. Follow me and don't follow behind. We don't have any time for nonsense."

"Huggene, watch the bar for me. I am heading out."

"Ya Ya, Ya. Go right ahead and kill a bad ass dragon. Have all the fun, while I bust my ass here."

"Hey, tell her Huggene. Tell your boss off!"

"See Ya, gentlemen. Have a bottle of wine on me."

"Thank you. You're such a wonderful woman!"

Craig started to run, right behind Sinea.

"We are coming across the bandits hideout. We don't have time to confront them, so let us run fast."

"Don't worry. I killed the ass. Wait, maybe I didn't."

"Holy shit, what is that?" Craig yelled.

"It is a tiger. I will kill it. Stand back," screamed Sinea.

"Damn, that thing is huge. All the animals here are huge. What are they on? Steroids?"

Moments later, Craig, Sinea and Silea reached Recker Island. About ten miles down the road was the ocean and another fifty miles more ocean.

"Craig. The dragon site is just up ahead. Be ready."

"Damn it. I thought I killed this dragon already."

"Wait, you saw this dragon already?" yelled Sinea.

"Yup."

"Yup? What the hell is Yup?" yelled Sinea.

"Yes," said Craig.

"Over here we all speak a common language. That is called English. I believe it's the favorite language of Donald."

"Yes. If I ever saw Donald, you know what I would say to him?"

"What?"

"You're Fired! HA, ha, ha."

"Here, look at this dragon. He is making the dead dragons come back to life."

"Damn it. That dragon took off. And this dragon speaks."

"Yes, I speak. And you are going to die, as the dragons will take over."

"Yes. I heard that before, dragon. I am dragon born. Killer of dragon's ha, ha, ha. now watch my mighty bow," laughed Craig.

Craig started to shoot at the dragon. One arrow does not kill him. Craig shot another and another arrow. Craig's last arrow killed the dragon. The dragon lies like a huge pile of cucka. The soul transferred to Craig.

"Well, well, I guess you are dragon born. I guess I owe you some kind of explanation."

"No. Not really. Since I must kill the head dragon before he kills any more people. So now what?"

"I don't know. I might have an idea. Meet me back at Ocean Call at the Sleepy Giant. I just might have an idea."

"Oh goody. I tell you, I got a lot of ideas too. Before I head back, I need to do something that is very important."

Sinea takes off, going in the opposite direction. Craig goes back to the Grey Hairs and gives them back the Master's Claw. As Craig entered the city, a dragon appeared.

"Run for your life. A dragon is here."

"Soldiers get ready, shoot your arrows, let us kill a dragon."

Soldiers, and some towns people, took out their arrows and Craig was right there with them. Craig shoots the dragon right in the head and killed it almost instantly.

The soul of the dragon went into Craig and he was running up the mountain to the Grey Hairs. The old fart was sitting on the cold ass floor mumbling who knows what.

"Hey dude. I got your claw. Now what?" said Craig.

"Now we give you your shout. Now you have the words for shouting. Use them wisely. And try not to shout in public," said The Grey Hairs.

"Maybe now I can twist and shout," said Craig.

"You are always welcome here, my friend."

"Thank you. Running up the five thousand steps, you won't be seeing me any time soon."

Silea and Craig went off to Ocean Call.

"I am glad you made it. I well be getting you an invention for a party. You're going to sneak in. Look for any information about the dragons. And I don't think your Thane should go. She might get killed."

"Ok. Sorry Sinea. You must stay."

"And one more thing, I will meet you in Slawitstude. There will be an wood elf. See him and give him any weapons that you might need and meet me at the stables," said Sinea.

"Great, going to a party and I am going to crash it."

Craig was off to Slawitude. On his way there he stopped over at Riften. There were two guards standing at the entrance.

"Halt. You need to pay to get in. It is called an entrance fee."

"What are you nuts? I am not going to pay you a tax to go in here."

"Sh, sh, I will let you in. We don't want people to know what we do."

"You really sound crooked to me. Is this place all run by the Thieves Guild?"

"No, not really. There are some honest people here. We are sort off."

"Ya, you're telling me."

Craig entered the town and there is a local bar call the Bee, She Bar. Craig opened the door and saw all kind of people, they seemed to be people. Walking talking lizards and tigers and human-like people.

"Hello, sir. I overheard you talking, you are a member of the Love Temple?" said Craig.

"Yes, our temple is the only one around in Skyrim. If you have the girl, we can get you hitched. More houses you buy, more women you can have."

"How much is the amulet?"

"It's free. It won't cost you a dime. Here you go then. I hope you find the lucky chicken."

Craig walked out of the bar. Craig turned his head and saw the ocean. Beautiful. Craig walked towards it.

Craig came to a boat yard and he saw a strange looking boat. A boat that he saw somewhere before.

"Hello there chap. Come, Come and take a ride on my ship."

"Your ship is pretty funny, different. It does not look anything like the others."

"And you're absolute right. I made this ship, and it does more than any other boat can do. This ship can sail right to the sun."

"No way."

"Come on board. on my "Yellow Submarine" I have a small crew. They mostly like to play."

"Like to play?"

"Yes, they like to play and sing. We have a great time on this yellow submarine."

"Hello there, young fella. Let me introduce ourselves. Right there is John."

"Hello."

"We have Ringo."

"Whaaad's up?"

"We have George, Pete, and Stuart."

"Helloooo," all three said together.

"And me, Paul, and you already met the captain."

"Yes."

"Ok then. Let us get a seat now," said John.

"This is your captain speaking. Buckle up and we are off."

"Where to?" Craig said excitedly.

"Right to the sun," said Paul.

The men got out their instruments and they started to play. Paul started to sing.

"In the town where I was born. Lived a man, who sailed to sea. He told us about his life, in a land of submarines."

Craig listened to the song as if he had heard it before. Craig put on a smile.

"This is your captain speaking. Something just happened. We just hit a small time warp. It should last only a few minutes."

"What's a time warp?" said Ringo.

"Yes, a time warp? Look you're getting older," said Paul.

"And you, too. We all are," said John.

The grouped start to play and sing again.

"When I get older, losing my hair, many years from now."

Craig jumped in as if he knew the song.

"Would you send me a greeting or a bottle of wine. When I'm sixty-four."

The submarine left the time warp and the people on board went back to normal.

The ship landed somewhere outside Slutsatude . A town where it uses to be called Solitude.

Craig opened the gate and there was an innocent man getting hanged. Craig stopped the mistake and the guards starts to attack him; shooting their arrows at him. Craig used his shout to not to be harmed and Craig ran off.

Up on the hillside was a building, a fort. A bunch of bandits were just there waiting. Craig took out his bow and, one by one, Craig knocked off the bandits.

Later that night, when the guards were settling down, Craig entered the town and meets the elf. He was going to smuggle his weapons into the Thamshits Embassy.

"Hi there. Sinea told me you can help me."

"Is she nuts?"

Now with a whisper,

"She is having you go in. She better know what she is doing. Even I can kick your sorry ass."

"Oh, really pal. If I did not need your help, I could put you away for a long time. I am dragon born."

"Oh damn. I am sorry. I did not know. Please excuse me. I really hate the Thamshits. They killed my family. And ate them. They told me that they did not taste good, so I became a sort of a slave."

"Damn. I am walking into a cannibalism party, how sick."

"Do you have the weapons that you need? Give me what you can live without, and I will get the weapons in."

"Here you go. I am off to a party. See you there."

"Ya, try not to get yourself killed in the meantime."

Craig opened the door to the bar where he just met the elf and started to walk to the farm to meet up with Sinea.

"Stop, wait. I think I know you," said the guard.

Craig kept on walking, and finally saw the farm.

"Hi Sinea. I am here."

"Good. I need to take the rest of your things. If you bring anything in there, you are screwed, and they won't let you in. I will keep your stuff safe. Put on these party clothes and hop on the carriage."

"No dressing room."

Craig started to take off his clothes and the hot Sinea watched. Craig noticed he was not wearing underwear. And when he dropped his pants, Sinea had a huge smile on her face.

"Damn, that thing is huge, I never saw one as big."

"Someday, maybe you can try this baby out. Yes?"

Craig rushed and put on the clothes and set off to the party. Thinking about deflate gate, deflate gate. The carriage stopped and Craig jumped off. Walked up to the gate.

"Please excuse me. I got an invitation to come to this party."

"Let me see. Yes, please go right in."

The Thamshits ambassador was at the door. Craig's stomach dropped. I am going to get caught, he said to himself.

"Hello, and who might you be? I don't recognize you."

"My name is Craig."

"Oh yes. Craig, a new member. Welcome. We got new flesh cooking on the fire."

Craig said to himself, "I should kill all these freaking fools now." But Craig knew he needed to get the information for Sinea.

"Hi there. Sir may I get you something?"

"Yes," said Craig.

"Take this drink, come back when you're ready. Here you go my friend. Come back soon," said the elf.

Craig walks over to a man sitting on a chair doing nothing and talks to him.

"Hi there, sir. It looks like you need a drink," said Craig

"Well, thank you, kind sir. If I can do anything for you just say it," said the drunk.

"Yes. I need you to make a ruckus. Please."

"Yes, I can. Just leave it to me.

Hello, Hello people. I need your attention please."

Craig ran over to the elf.

"Let's go, let's go," said Craig.

"I will open the door. You need to escape as fast as you can. So, I won't be missed. Your stuff is right over there in the chest. Now go," said the elf.

"Who is that in my kitchen?" said the woman cook.

"He is the man is going to fix your stinking mesa," said the elf.

"Oh, the F I am. Odio mesa!!!"

Craig slipped on his battle gear and the bow is out ready. Craig walked slowly and saw the Thamshits mages and guards.

"I can't wait for the dragons to kill all the Nords, so we can take over," said one of the guards.

"Yes, you're right. Let's get back on duty," said one of the mages.

Craig slowly walked into the room and saw one the guards with their back turned and with a mighty pull the arrow went through the guard, and he drops.

"Who is there?" said the mage.

The mages came running down the stairs, Craig was lucky, he ran into a room that was close by.

"Wow. I thought I heard something. Must have been my imagination. Wait. Who killed Agnes? She was a good guard. I will find you and rip out your heart," said the Mage.

Craig sneaked into the room again and saw the Mage walking up the stairs. Craig pulled the arrow back so tightly and off it went; Right through the Mage's body.

"Sorry there, Mage. I need my heart."

Craig looked all around. Saw all kinds of good stuff and took it. There were cheeses and pies. And gold. Lots and lots of gold.

There was a door leading outside and Craig opened the door. The place was surrounded by the Thamshits and Craig was knocking each and every one off. One by one the died. Craig felt a little stronger every time he killed someone.

There was a building outside in the back. A separate building. And it looked very important. Craig opened the door. Three men started to attack Craig. Craig shouted them with the freeze shout, and they were frozen solid. A few of soldiers died instantly and Craig took out his bow and shoots the others dead.

Craig walked through the house and saw a stairway going into the cellar. Craig shoots the mage and the guard dead and walked over to the chest. Craig pulled out a journal and read it.

"The Imperial leader Esbarno is still alive. We must find him and kill him. He must be in his nineties or hundreds. Sinea is also wanted. We find her, we kill her. For the dragons we need more information, where we can find them."

"Hello, there."

"Please. I don't know any more. Please," said the prisoner.

"Don't worry. I am not going to hurt you. Let me free you and tell me why you are here?"

"My name is not important. They, the Thamshits, want to kill Esbarno. And I won't tell them where he is hiding. But it looks like I can trust you. He is hiding in a dungeon in Riften."

"I know you are down there, spy. Come on out or we will kill your friend here," said Thamshits guard.

"We should get out of here now. The guards will kill you," said the prisoner.

"No. We are going to help my friend."

Craig took out his mighty swords In both hands, Craig had two very sharp swords made of a special metal call Dwarf gold.

Craig started to swing the swords faster and faster, the guards dropped like flies.

Craig took all the clothes off the guards and loots them. Luckily for these guards, they had underwear on.

"Watch out. There is a Frost Troll down here!" said the prisoner.

Craig took his hands and used the flames that came from his body. And his super fire shout that he just got made Craig even more powerful.

Craig returned to Ocean Call and sees Sinea. There she has all of Craig's weapons and gear. And boy Sinea is a nagger.

"What did you find? What did you find? Did you get anything useful!" screamed Sinea.

"Yes and no. The Thamshits don't know why the dragons are appearing. They wish they were the ones doing it. The Old fart Esbarnno is still alive. Barely, he is about ninety years old."

"I can't believe my best friend Esbarnno is still alive. We go way back. Where is he?"

"He is at Riften."

"Yes. A great place to hide. He must be in the Rat Hole. You must find him and bring him to me or else."

"Or else what?"

"Or else we all are going to die. Esbarnno knows about the dragons and the dragon born. He is our only hope."

"Ok. I am off to Riften."

Craig took out a map that was in his pocket. The picture of Riften was glowing. Craig touched the picture and 'poof' he is at Riften.

Craig entered the town of Riften and found the Rat Hole. Craig sneaked up and shot some bandits that were about to attack him, as Craig was an outsider.

A building that looked so small but was huge in size. The building went down about eight stories.

Craig walked through a bunch of men and ladies that did not notice him and he went into the dungeons of the Rat Hole.

There, hiding, were Thamshits, waiting for Craig to find Esbarnno. Craig took out his bow and shoots dead a Thamshits wizard.

"Who is there!" yelled a Thamshits guard

Craig loaded up the bow and slowly found the guard and shoots him dead.

The rooms were dark but there was enough light to see in some areas. The main rooms were well lit and some of the hallways were so black you could not see in front of you. Craig reached a door, which was locked. Craig knocked.

"Hey, anyone home?" whispered Craig.

"No. Go away!"

"Hey Esbarnno. Sinea sent me for you."

"Sinea sent you to find me. She is still alive. No, No. This is a trick. Leave me."

"Hey dude. I am dragon born and Sinea needs your help."

"Ok, Ok, let me open the door. This lock here gives me a hard time. Hold on."

The old man started to unlock the ten locks and it takes him five hours to unlock the doors.

"Wow. I could have watched two or three movies while waiting," Craig said to himself.

"Ok let me get a few things and we are off."

"And how long do I have to wait? What are you looking for? Let me help you. I don't have all year to be here."

"Please, just one moment I think I got it. Yes, I do. Let's go."

Esbarnno and Craig were off. More Thamshits were hiding and Esbarnno and Craig, as a team, killed the Thamshits.

When Craig reached outside he looked at the map again and Ocean Call was lit up. Craig touched the picture and 'poof' again he is in Ocean Call.

"So where is Sinea?" whispered Esbarnno.

"She is at the Jolly Giant."

"Oh, she finally bought herself a bar. An inn to be precise."

"Yes, it is an inn."

"Be careful. Loose women go there. When you're sleeping. You can become a father to many women."

"What? Damn, it is like the "Little Whore House in Texas"."

Both men entered the Inn at Ocean Call and Esbarnno greeted Sinea.

"Hi Sinea. We got a lot to talk about."

"Yes, but not here. Let's go, follow me, now, Craig, close the door behind you."

"YES, mam!"

"Well Sinea. it is true; the dragons are coming back again. Augrin is doing it. We need to fine the temple of Lost Dragons."

"Craig. We need to go to the Lost Dragons Temple. You can follow Esbarnno and me, or we can split up. It is up to you."

"Oh goody. I will meet you there."

"Good we will be less noticeable.

Hey, Huggene, you are the new owner of my Inn. I don't think I will ever be coming back."

"Great. I always wanted your Inn. Now I can be a pimp that I always wanted to be."

Esbarnno, Sinea, Craig's House Carl, and Craig were off. Craig went the opposite direction, yet the roads led to the same place. A longer route. Craig had a feeling that he can do more shouts and more magic by taking this longer route.

Sileastarted to shake.

"What is wrong, Silea a?"

"I feel like there is another presence here. They could be Vampires."

"Ok, my armor is pretty strong, go back home and I will see you there."

"Oh, please be careful, Craig."

"I will."

Silea ran back to the castle and Craig started to walk towards an old fort. The map lit up again. This time, Fort Knuckle Brains. Craig slowly took out his bow and arrow. Five Vampires came crawling out of trap doors on top of the fort.

"Holy crap, that arrow almost hit me. Oh, shit this other did and cut my suit. I am in trouble."

"Xmose. I wondered when you are going to get our guys in there."

"It was a matter of time, Xzeem, only a matter of time. He does not know it is one of us yet and my last surprise will be the last."

"Ok Vampires take this shout," Craig yelled out so they could hear.

With a very loud shout, Craig managed to have found all three fire shouts and the Vampires were burned to death. The screams that they were in pain sounded real.

"Xmose. Our guys are dying here."

"Well, I know the illusions are real. If Craig dies in here, he dies for real, if our guys die in here, it's for real too. Anything goes."

Craig walked for hours and reached the temple of Lost Dragons. The temple was surrounded by Farmerheads. A group of watch up farmers now called Farmerheads that lost their land from a war that happen over a hundred years ago . Learned to fight and make heavy armor and killed anyone that intrudes onto their property.

Craig bent down in sneak mode and started killing each Farmerheads. Esbarnno and Sinea arrived at the same time and was helping Craig kill off the Farmerheads.

"Craig, Sinea, we are here. Let's find out what we need."

The three walked inside a cave and there were three Farmerheads waiting for them. They started to shoot Craig with their arrows. Craig Shouted again with the Fire breath and the three Farmers got burnt up like toast.

"Hey, Xmose, this is not really working man. This guy must have nine lives and we can't even kill one."

"Don't worry, Xzeem, my plan is working. We are going to lose a few men When the time comes, Craig will be dead. Now, get our secret weapon out now."

Xmose walked over to the phone that was near the front of his truck and talked to the other truck.

"Listen up. Get the girl ready."

The new girl that Xmose created, the girl Sakra clone. The girl looks very pretty, just as Sakra was, now created to be a killer.

The Illusions still on, the girl went to the night club. In White Fun, she waited for Craig to enter. She must have stayed in there for days, even months, because he was still exploring the beautiful land of Skyrim.

Craig reached the city of White Fun and went right to the castle. Looking for his House Carl. Craig found her and they were off to the city to get hitched.

"Stop!" screamed the Jarl.

"What, sir?"

"You need to buy a house, before you can get hitched, my young friend."

"You are right."

"Here. I got you a house for twenty thousand gold. Right here, in White Fun. My colleague will write up the sale."

"Well, thank you." Craig and Silea were off.

They both hopped in a carriage and the carriage took them to the place to get married.

The two got off the carriage and the band began to play. The song was "Woman" and there was John playing the piano.

"Good day. Welcome town folk to this wonderful of holy shit, I mean holy matcha mourning.

As we all know, our marriage sermon is very short. Ok you two, you're married. Have kids now go."

"Damn. Talk about being fast," laughed Craig.

Silea and Craig went to their new home. As they both kissed, Craig felt funny and three seconds later, Silea was pregnant. She was about to be due in any moment. Damn, this place is fast, Craig thought.

Craig walked out of his house and traveled, using his map, to a bridge called Dragon bridge. A shaped dragon head was on the bridge. It was a head of Aguin. This was where this dragon was born. People forgot about it, but the legions were still there. Aguin was killed on High Tower Mountain where his younger brother guards the porthole where his brother has vanished.

Craig left dragon bridge and went to where Two Barks the dragon, Aguin's brother, was.

"Hello. It is my pleasure to see a young Two Barks."

"My name is not Two Barks old dragon. I thought you are Two Barks?"

"No, ha, ha, ha. No. They call me Two Barks, yes this is true. All who are dragons and dragon born are Two Barks, just call me Fred. I like that human name. Fred."

"Ok Fred, I need to kill your brother. He is creating a disturbance and I don't want my child to be killed by your stinking ass brother."

"Yes, you are right, Young Two Barks. Get me an Elder Scroll. You will learn "Dren". It is the only shout that can kill my brother."

"You can't teach me the shout?"

"No. I can't. This shout was made by Nords. They learn how to make the shouts by my stupid brother and the Nords, they turned on him. Good but bad."

"I will find this scroll and I will BE Back!" Craig with a huge smile on face.

Craig ended up way across the other side of Skyrim and finds the Elder scroll. What a task that was. Craig stopped and sat on a rock for a while to catch his breath. Craig just thinks what just happen?

"What are these creatures? They are metal robots of some kind. Metal spiders?"

"Xmose. Let's use the metal spiders and kill him now!" screamed Xzeem.

"Don't worry, my plan is working out as I planned. Craig will get weak and when he goes to that night club, as I predict, he will be killed."

"But this Illusion is getting him closer to Ireland. We are helping him."

"He will never reach Ireland!"

Craig battles Aguin. The battle took five hours to complete. Craig entered the town of White Fun and the town was mostly destroyed.

"What happened?" cried Craig.

"Two dragons, just came out of nowhere, destroyed our town. Only place left is the night club and the castle on Dragon Reach."

"My wife, is she ok?"

"Sorry the Dragon ate her, and he spat her out and he was pissed."

"He was pissed?"

"Ya, she was having a child and the child came out at the same time as the dragon ate her. Your child, he is safe. Running around somewhere. A real pain in the tuchus."

"Yes, sounds like he would be my son. Did he get a name yet?"

"No, that will be up to you. What are you going to call him?"

"No idea, maybe Meat Head, Bone Head, Fat Head. No, he needs a strong name. Master. Yes I will call him the Master."

A strange light papered over the city. Craig yelled out the word Master!

The boy came running over and gave his dad a hug. "I am here, Pa."

The night came quickly and the two went to Ocean Call to the Jolly Giant Inn and slept. Time went very quickly. The young boy became a young adult, and he was off to join the Stormcoats .

Craig like the Stormcoats easy to remember and they never tried to kill him. Craig walked to White Fun and entered the club.

The club looked very modern. It did not belong in this time. Craig found a seat. A man on the microphone spoke.

"Ladies and gentlemen, before we start our karaoke, the group that you have all been waiting for!!!From the other side of Skyrim. Odio Mesaaaaaa!!!!!!!!"

The group started to sing and they were wiggling their rear ends.

"Odio! Odio! Mesa, No ma's mesa, No ma's de mesa." The band wiggled their rear ends and they kept on saying,

"No ma's de mesa!"

Craig loved the song and he stood up and shouted, "Odio Mesa!"

The whole crowd stood up and together they yelled out, "No ma's de mesa!"

"Ladies and gentleman. The first person to start the karaoke tonight is Craig. Craig, please come up."

"Wow. I don't know how I can top that."

"Don't worry, they are professionals. Please put this on. This will give you the music you need to sing your song."

"Ok, cool"

Craig put on a crown-like thing on his head. He heard the band begin to play.

"I got the world on that string I can make a rainbow. I got that string around my finger. What a world I am so in love. Life could be a string I'm sitting on a rainbow, I got the string around my finger, what a world what a life I am in love."

Just as Craig ended the song, a beautiful woman walked over to Craig. Craig does not see she has a knife in her hand.

"You are a very good singer," said Zee.

"No. I am not. What is your name?"

"My name is Zee; please may I give you a kiss?"

"Ok."

Craig gave Zee a kiss, and the knife dropped from her hands. She had never had a kiss like that before. Her body started to tingle. The other girls were there for back up. They saw the kiss. The kiss that she could not resist. The girls wanted the kiss too. Craig did not mind. One by one, the girls of Xmose's army were changing sides.

"Craig. I was here to kill you and I cannot."

"Thank you," said Craig.

"Us girls were supposed to be backup, and we were supposed to kill you and we cannot."

"Well, thank you, ladies, for not killing me."

When that was said, the illusion disappeared and the only thing that was around were the three trucks and Ireland could be seen twenty miles away. The girls went back to their truck. Xmose was watching.

"Damn it. How did he do it? Craig is a sore that you can't get rid of."

"Face it, Xmose, you can't stop him. He will reach it."

"Not if I have anything to say about it."

Xmose was having a problem with the truck and Craig was off.

Craig reached the force field. Kit hitched the connector and Craig entered.

"Good day. My friend tells me I been traveling for a very long time. Could you please tell me what day it is and year?"

"Yes, I can. It is October the twenty eighth, three thousand nine hundred and ten."

The boy ran off. Craig heard a voice. He never heard that voice before. The voice, soft sweet.

"Can you see me?" said the girl.

"Can you hear me?" said Craig.

"CAN you SEE ME!!!" a little louder from the girl.

"Can you hear me; my heart is in pain."

Craig looked at the girl. It was Alice. The special girl that he hurt many years ago.

Xmose still has the illusion machine. But this illusion was very much real. Craig touched the girl. In a split second, like a nuclear bomb, everything got destroyed, even the places that were protected by force fields. Ireland's force field was not connected well. It had a small leak, the poison from the bombs slowly seeped in.

Craig, fully awake, entered a bright room. Craig only saw white, and then he appeared.

"Well, Craig, you are here."

"Yes, I am. Now what? I am a bad person; I don't belong here."

"No, you're not. Good and bad, you have learned from your mistakes."

"The rumors say if anyone sees you they die. I must be dead."

"Yes, you are, But I am going to give you one wish. What will it be?"

"I can't just make one wish. It's a very long wish. Could I ask you a silly question?"

"Go right ahead."

"Did it really take you six days to create this planet? And it only took me a half a second to destroy it?"

"HA, Ha, ha, no it took me five days to create it. The sixth day I realized I made a mistake. I could not fix it so the seven day I rested."

"What was the mistake?"

"I created humans."

"Ah ha, And the mistake haunts the oh mighty one."

"But not all humans were mistakes and you have proven to me that you are the best creation that I had made."

"You are kind, and I don't even deserve it."

Craig just stood in one place. Craig found himself in front of a window. A very large window. Just on the balcony were two trees. Small. One was a plum tree and other an orange. Craig took out a book and started to read it. It was a book of poetry, all in Yiddish.

"I can read Yiddish. I can't believe it. My reading was not that good." Craig looked up and smiled.

The doorbell rang, Craig opened the door. It was a young woman. Very sad.

"Excuse me, sir, I was told a holy man lived here and he can say a prayer for healing."

"Who? Me? Ha. I am not that holy, my dear. But nevertheless, I can say a prayer for you."

Craig looked all around for a prayer book and could not find one. He took out his book of poetry and said something sweet.

"Oh, thank your, sir. Here. I only got twenty dollars."

"No please, I can't except your money. Please, right down the street, a block or two, is a place, you will know it when you see it. Give the person the twenty dollars. They need it more than me."

Craig knew he does not need any money. He has everything; food and shelter.

The girl walked down the street and saw an old shop. A sign on the door that said,

"Please buy something to save a life."

The girl walked in.

"Oh, hi dear, what will you buy? I have everything."

"I'm sorry, mam. I don't need anything, but I have twenty dollars I can give you."

"Oh, thank you, thank you."

The old lady ran so fast to the phone. She dialed very fast.

"Hello, Doctor. I have the twenty dollars, please give the young boy the shot. Young girl you just saved a life. A young baby needed a shot to get better. Without this shot, in ten minutes, he would have died. Thank you."

"Wow. I am happy at what I did," said the young woman.

The young woman went to the hospital. She took a few minutes to get herself together. She opened the door. She walked over to her father.

"Hi, Dad. I saved a life today. Just moments ago. I gave an old woman, who has the help shop in need store, twenty dollars. I have done a great thing. I just wish that the twenty dollars would help you."

The life support machine started to make a sound. Not a normal sound. A sound that seemed to be strong. The doctors ran over to the old man. They started to cry in joy. The young girl did not know what was going on.

"What is the matter? Why are you crying?"

"By some miracle, your father is better. The disease is gone."

The eyes of the father opened. He smiled.

"If I am dead, I hope I never awake. If I am alive, may I never sleep again."

"You're alive Dad!" cried the young girl.

Craig got his wish. To live forever, to help cure the people who deserved it.

Craig sat down on his chair. Every day he would read his book of poetry and cry. People would walk by his room every day and hear this man cry. They were afraid to knock. When the man came out of his room, his eyes where red. He would have a smile on his face as if nothing was wrong. He used a cane and never really used it. People might think he would fall over as he was over a hundred years old, with a long white beard.

Craig found a bench outside of his apartment and sat. He saw in his mind a girl he once knew. Years have passed and he is remembering a beautiful kind girl. She was having a tough time with bills and, a miracle, she played the lottery and won nine hundred million dollars. Craig stopped and started to cry inside, thanking for the kind thing that a Shem had done.

"Hello, sir," said a young boy in his twenties.

"Well, good afternoon, young man."

"Sir, this is a little funny, but people say you are a holy man and you can help me."

"HA, Ha, ha. My fellow, I am old, but holy, no I am not. I have done things in my life. I cry each and every day. Not one holy man would ever do that."

"Yes, true. A holy man is not perfect. I am not perfect. I have a small amount of money, fifty dollars, can you please say a prayer for my mother. She is ill."

"Of course, I can. But you promise me that you will give your fifty to the person down the street who needs it more than I do. You will know when you see it."

Craig took out his poetry book again. He looked for something about a woman. Page after page, Craig found that perfect poem. In English it went like this.

"A life is about a tree.

A tree of life is strong you see.

Kindness in your heart will never be forgotten,

If you are true your wishes will come true,

The girl's heart you broke in two,

Will forgive you too."

The young man did not understand the poem, it was done in Yiddish, and he had a tear because it sounded like a prayer.

The boy's mother was indeed very sick as she had an incurable disease. Craig went to the hospital and saw an older woman, about seventies years old. Craig looked up to his lord and said,.

"If I am blessed with the power to heal, please give this woman the good parts of my life, if I have any, and make her live a little bit longer."

Craig walked out of the room. Craig walked down the stairway as the young boy exited the elevator.

Craig could hear the rain fall. It was very loud. Craig felt something, it was a good feeling. Craig somehow knew. Not taking, but to give is more important.

"Hi, Ma. How are you feeling? I know you can't."

"Yes, I can. I am feeling much better."

The doctors came running over.

"Wow. I can't believe this?"

"What doctor?" screamed the young boy.

"Your mother, she somehow is cured, she is not sick anymore."

The boy just cried, and the mother smiled and said, "Its ok. I am fine."

On the day, May 1st 1971, No light, no sound a door way that opens, on this day Craig Galuta made a wish. Not preparing for the consequences. It was only a matter of time before he entered the Twilight Zone.

The End.

Synopsis

This science fiction book took me over 20 years to do. This book never had a beginning, and it really had no purpose. It was a dream that I had, and I just wrote it down. It was years I went on Facebook and I am being a very outspoken person. I said a few things that were on my mind, and I should have kept my big mouth shut. And for that, I hurt a girl who I believed I kissed in first grade. When I went to my class reunion, I saw a person and she said she was nobody and she looked straight in my face. Maybe she wasn't or maybe she was the one. It was the next class reunion, I asked a classmate if this person was there, I only gave the first name because I did not know the last name. She gave the name, and I was in tears. I did my research I found the one, I made an apology to her, and she might have said it was worth two cents and a crinkled piece a paper. So, I made my story Science Fiction, documentary, romance, fantasy, and humor. I included all when I talked about this girl in the beginning. I made a promise to her that I will not say or make any words to reflect her name on my Facebook page nor will I do it here. But it seems I wrote this before I had finished my book, and this is a new version updated. I guess I lied. It is so hard when a person does not say anything as I still cry when I think of her. I don't want to put a strain on her marriage, I won't mention her name. The second book, it might not talk about the girl, but the third or the last book I don't know yet will be about her. I hope I can change the ending. Either way, the ending won't be what you expect. But I gave a little clue in the end of this book. The second book does not say. My two final books, the second one now completed it talks a little bit of Alice, so the story sounds good, the third book, well it has a twist.

BIOGRAPHY

Craig Glatky was born in a small town in Massachusetts. In his school days he got bullied and being strong he had overcome the pain that was cause by the bullies. Using self-technique, he is alive and kicking and Craig's imagination got him to write his book. It was some time in the early grade when Craig wrote a two-page story, never a book, and English being one of the worst subjects. Craig loves to write. Craig is a bowler bowled candle pins some duck pins and a ten pin. Playing with the hall famers and beating some of the best bowlers. Craig also learns the fundamentals of critical thinking and chess playing, at New England Institute of Technology. When he finally won his chess match.

Craig Glatky has two Associates degrees, one in the science of electronics and the second the science of plumbing and heating.

www.ingramcontent.com/pod-product-compliance
Lightning Source LLC
Chambersburg PA
CBHW061250310726
48971CB00007B/2297